I0772152

For the older sisters who carry everything
who've been told their love feels like judgment
who wish they could be gentle
who make themselves needed,
because that's close enough to cared for:
You are enough.

Contents

Before we begin...

Dear reader,

This book is an explicit paranormal romance novel. There's a good balance (imo) of spice and plot, but there is a notable amount of the former, and I just want to take a moment to make sure these pages are a safe space for you. In *Bergamot & Bygones*, you'll find:

- Dirty talk

- Overstimulation

- Unprotected sex

- Rough sex (incl. light choking)

- Free use

- Knotting/Ruts/general omegaverse cliches

For a full list of trigger warnings and tropes, please visit my website www.sanakielauthor.com for more information. Take care of yourselves out there, friends!

Prologue

Maggie had never heard her father scream.

Not the time he'd tried to hold off his turn so she wouldn't be so intimidated the first time *she* turned, not the time he'd been hurt while fighting off alphas who had scented her before she'd started on suppressants, not ever.

But this weekend, she was home from university, and her father had gone outside to break down a tree that'd fallen over their driveway. She heard the revving of the chainsaw, and then she heard him scream.

There was so much blood.

Maggie managed to guide her father and his shredded shoulder into the cab of his pickup, and had floored it to Port Cadie Medical Center. As doctors and nurses swarmed to help her dad, Maggie wrapped her arms around herself in the too-bright lobby, telling herself to stop shaking.

Her wolf was scared.

Maggie felt her vision blurring as adrenaline faded; she couldn't get enough air, couldn't think clearly—

A nurse bumped into her, apologizing in a soft voice.

Maggie's human saw his scrubs, met his gentle eyes, registered the wheelchair he pushed, and understood that he was coming to help.

But Maggie's wolf saw a tall man barreling towards her weakened father, and her wolf had always been stronger.

She felt when some of her magic left her.

She tasted it bleeding into the nurse as her teeth sank into his shoulder, while her claws held him still.

There was still so much blood– from her father, from the nurse, and Maggie realized too late what she'd done. The lights of the PCMC Emergency Room blurred overhead and the nurse, her first turn, caught Maggie as she fainted.

One

The wave curled in, a wall of saltwater pushed her underwater, and Reyna opened her eyes to admire the sunrise filtering through the Atlantic. Pinks and oranges glistened through the blue gray waves, and, past where the waves were breaking, Reyna could see tails and wetsuits dangling off the sides of surfboards.

Above water, surfers were calling out, claiming waves and ragging on each other, but under the surface, it was still.

Underwater, she could be still.

Underwater, it was just tides and light, silence and cold. Underwater, Chesa's business loan coming due wasn't something Reyna had to worry about, nor Mom's medical bills, nor the fact that her lease was up in a couple months and the housing market in midcoastal Maine was abysmal for everyone who wasn't a millionaire.

Underwater, it was her and any number of spirits of the sea, depending on the deity a soul believed in. She wasn't alone, and the ocean wanted her just as much as she wanted it.

Reyna blew out a slow stream of bubbles, watching the air wriggle towards the surface. Some bubbles dissolved, some merged, some burst on the surface together, and Reyna's lungs constricted.

She closed her eyes, let out the last of her air, and kicked herself back to the surface. Her board crested and she pulled herself on top of it, welcoming the crisp sting of autumn air, the way it burned down her throat. The cold stung her cheeks, making the water feel almost warm, and Reyna smiled in spite of herself.

There was nothing like a freezing surf to get her out of her head.

October was far from the coldest month to surf at Bar Harbor, but Reyna took time on the water whenever she could. A couple of surfers cheered for her run, and Reyna waved them away, paddling through the lineup to the back, where a pair of surfers were waiting past the breaks.

"Leave it to a human," Daphne called as Reyna got closer, tucking a strand of pale green hair behind her ear, "to drop in on the most perfect set wave, and just absolutely eat it."

As a siren, Daphne needed no protection from the cold temperatures, and looked just as at ease in her one piece swimsuit in October as she would have in July. Meanwhile, Reyna wore a hooded wetsuit, with five unflattering millimeters of neoprene to ensure she could stay out on the water for as long as possible.

"Leave it to a siren," Reyna pulled herself up to straddle her board, "to get beaten to a wave and then complain about my form."

She dodged the wave of water Daphne shoved her way, and Niamh chuckled beside them. Niamh was in her human skin at the moment, but the selkie could handle colder temperatures than Reyna and Daphne put together.

Other surfers were dropping in, so their trio hung back, lapsing into a comfortable silence as the morning stretched. Golden rays caught crested waves, and the water turned from purple to blue to gray as light spread. All around Reyna the sounds of the sea hummed— crashing waves, cawing birds, fizzing spray.

Port Cadie was a special place.

In the heart of Acadia National Park, Port Cadie was older than New England, older than the States, older than really anyone liked to think. The rest of the country was having a hard enough time with their differences but in Port Cadie, denizens were human and super-natural, every shade and species between. They had their challenges, to be sure, and no American city could be a utopia, but Port Cadie was for people who loved the wilderness so much that their peers were incidental.

The town was isolated and isolating, and it suited everyone just fine.

Reyna wiggled her toes in her wetsuit, and sighed internally; she needed to head in. The girls understood, they always did, and let her back to shore with plans for another predawn surfing session in a couple of days.

Reyna jogged across the packed sand of the beach, the wind like ice against into her skin. It always felt much colder on land than it did in the water, and she started her car with shivering hands as she jammed the surfboard on top of it. She cranked the heat up inside her 4x4, grabbed her towel and executed the world's least graceful deck change into oversized gray sweats.

Chucking the dripping wet suit into her backseat with a flop, Reyna held her hands up to the heating vents, and realized her glove box was vibrating.

Well, her phone, in the glove box.

She couldn't imagine who would be calling her at this hour– Chesa was at the shop, Mom slept late most mornings these days, and even though Reyna's job was soulless, no one at corporate wanted to work on a weekend enough to bother her today.

Reyna got to her phone just as the call went to voicemail and the screen faded to her screensaver: a digital scan of a film photograph of two kids darting out of the coastal Maine high tide.

That picture always made Reyna smile.

She and Lee had probably been eight or nine years old that summer, chasing fireflies out on Great Cranberry Island, while his grandmother baked tarts with fresh blueberries, picked too-early in their enthusiasm. The gritty picture couldn't capture the way Lee's fair skin mottled despite the gallons of sunscreen he smeared over it, nor the deep olive the same sun had turned Reyna's skin.

First schoolmate, then best friends, she and Lee had spent many summers at his family's cottage out on the island, until they'd gone away to college. Both in Massachusetts— him for nursing and her for supply chain management—and then they'd both found their way back to Port Cadie.

The phone started ringing again, startling Reyna out of her nostalgia. She didn't recognize the number, and hadn't gotten a chance to listen to the voicemail yet, but the fact that they'd called back so quickly let her know they weren't giving up.

"Hello?" she accepted the call before it rang out.

"Oh, thank God, finally," a woman said, relieved. "Is this Reyna?"

"Yeah," Reyna said, putting the call on speaker as she looked over her shoulder to back out of the lot. "Who is this?"

"This is Alex; I think we've met–" the woman cut off, clearing her throat, and her voice took on a more strictly professional tone as she recited how she'd been trained. "I'm calling as the surgeon on duty at Port Cadie Medical Center; I have you as the emergency contact for Leander Després."

Reyna had met her before, bringing coffee for Lee after a graveyard shift or at various holiday parties over the years. An anesthesiologist, Alejandra Benedict was the kind of unearthly beautiful that so few humans were, which Reyna remembered before she registered Alejandra's formal reason for calling.

"Emergency contact?" Reyna echoed, braking suddenly. "What's going on; is Lee okay?"

A car honked at her, and Reyna flipped them off in her rearview mirror, throwing her car into gear and pulling out of the lot.

"There's been an accident; I understand you're local," Alex said, professionalism and urgency warring in her voice, "is it possible for you to come in?"

Reyna had just been in a near-arctic sea, and this was the first time today she felt truly cold.

"How bad is it?" she asked, her voice sounding distant, already planning her drive to the hospital.

"It would be really great if you could come in, Reyna," Alex said meaningfully.

Reyna knew doctors couldn't disclose context over the phone, for liability's sake, but the lack of information made her want to scream. Details were how she functioned; she was a senior logistics coordinator for the most famous coffee chain in the country, and she got there by turning dredges of information into solutions.

But Alex was giving her nothing but a soft suggestion, and Reyna felt sick with helplessness.

"You'd tell me if he was dead," Reyna said, suddenly, cutting off a car as she merged onto the access road. "You have to, right? Otherwise it's false hope and there's libel?"

"He's not dead, Christ, but it's–" Alex broke off. "You know how it is, Reyna, and I'm sorry, but you have to be here when I tell you, okay? I'll meet you at reception, or I'll send Mateo if I can't. Just get here."

Reyna hung up shortly, trusting that her car was big enough and bright blue enough for other cars to respect her turn signals as she followed through without checking them. She pushed the speed limit as she raced across the island, running through scenarios.

Maybe a new virus? No, they wouldn't have told her to come. Maybe an allergic reaction to something, and he couldn't drive himself home? No, the hospital would have an antidote.

There were at least seven ways that the entrance at Point Cadie Hospital could've been more efficient. Reyna checked them off in her mind, trying to focus on anything other than what was waiting for her inside reception, as she careened into the parking lot, gritting her teeth and spinning her car into the first open spot she saw.

The nurse at the reception desk was a pretty minotaur, and her enormous eyes were sympathetic as she escorted Reyna to the elevator to where they were holding Lee. Reyna tried not to think about how insane she looked, wincing as she caught a glimpse of her reflection in the elevator doors.

She was nearly as tall as the minotaur, all broad shoulders and long build, looking every bit like someone who got her aggression out by swimming laps. Despite a lifetime of admonishment to stay out of the sun, Reyna's skin stayed a firm tan, a combination of her Filipino heritage and mornings watching the sun reflect off the sea on her board. Her dark curls – a gift she and her sister both shared from their German father – were sun damaged at the ends, and tended more towards frizzy than curly these days. Now they lay tangled where the curls had knotted towards the ends, below her shoulders, and Reyna was aware she was leaving salt water drips on the floor.

The elevator dinged on the fourth floor, and when the doors opened, Reyna was relieved to see a familiar face waiting for her.

Mateo Degas was a physical therapist at PCMC; he and Lee had been roommates back at university and he gave Reyna a quick hug as she stepped out of the elevator. Reyna appreciated how he started walking right away, explaining as he went.

"Alex got called into an OR; that's why she didn't meet you," Mateo started off, "but Leander's stable. He...shit, do you want to sit down or something?"

Reyna gave him a look, and Mateo winced, walking faster.

"Yeah, I figured," he mumbled, turning them down a less crowded hallway. "The short of it is: he got bit."

Reyna waited for Mateo to say more, but he didn't. It was technically a full sentence, but it didn't explain the worry on his face, or the way she'd rushed here. Before she could demand he explain, Mateo stopped them in front of a closed door to a small room. He tipped his head towards the door and Reyna steadied herself and looked through the window.

And there he was.

Leander Després, her best friend since they were five, all 6'3" of him crammed onto a hospital bed. His thick glasses were folded on the small table beside the bed, and several scary tubes were running in and out of his arms. A heavy bandage was taped to his neck, and there were restraints around his upper arms, waist, and ankles. Lee's dirty blond hair was splayed over the pillow, his blue eyes were closed, and as she watched his chest rise and fall under the hospital gown he wore, Reyna took the first full breath she'd drawn in forty minutes.

"What happened?" she asked quietly, not daring to look away.

"There was an accident," Mateo said, his voice also gentle. "An undergrad brought in her dad, who'd nearly cut his whole arm off with a power tool. She managed to drag him into the ER, but when Leander came rushing in with a wheelchair, she only saw him in her periphery vision. She panicked, and before any of us could realize what was happening..."

He paused, and Reyna pulled her focus from Lee's sleeping figure to look at Mateo. His brown eyes were kind when they met hers.

"She's a young werewolf," Mateo explained. "It's kind of like a rattlesnake—when they're afraid, they have no idea how much venom they're capable of dispensing. Leander had nearly passed out before she pulled off of him."

Reyna could almost hear Lee making the same rationalization.

It wasn't on purpose, he would say, it's honestly my fault for not considering how she would react to someone like me rushing towards her wounded father. Her wolf would take over; it's not something she could help.

Reyna shook her head, looking back at Leander's sleeping form.

"So now what?" she asked. "He's a wolf too?"

Mateo hesitated.

"We're...we're not sure yet. That's up to him, and how he responds to the magic. He might push it out, he might turn, but for now it's a high fever."

Inside the room, Leander's brow furrowed, and Reyna jolted out of her inaction.

"Do you get in trouble if I let myself in there?" she asked.

Mateo's mouth quirked up in a smile. Reyna could guess the correct answer, but she also knew Mateo knew she was the closest thing to family that Lee had.

"I have to go check in on a couple patients," he said, patting her shoulder in an approximation of a hug. "If anyone asks, I told you to go back to reception."

Reyna smiled at him, glancing down the hallway before letting herself into the room.

There was a chair beside Lee's bed, and she pulled it over as quietly as she could manage. She looked up at the various machines around his bed, wishing she'd paid more attention during any of the medical dramas Chesa loved. The machines held steady; that had to be good, right?

Lee stirred, just slightly.

His frown increased, and his hands were twitching, and Reyna's heart constricted as she looked at them. Those hands had taught her how to tie her shoes, had helped her get her timing right when she learned to drive stick shift, had haunted her before she'd learned her infatuation was one-sided in high school, and let it go. Before she could think better of it, Reyna reached for Lee's hand that was closest to her, slipping her fingers between his.

He couldn't know it was her, but his hand tightened around hers, and Reyna lowered herself into the chair.

It didn't mean anything.

He was her best friend, and friends...friends were each other's emergency contact. Friends dropped everything to sit by friends' bedsides while they fought a fever. Friends knew the number of freckles on friends' faces, friends watched friends' faces fondly while they slept. Friends counted their breaths, friends hummed old favorite comfort songs, friends jumped every time a machine beeped.

Friends definitely fell asleep in uncomfortable hospital chairs, pushing every ounce of goodwill they could into joined hands, praying to anyone listening that their friend would wake up.

Two

When Leander was five, his family had moved from Wyoming to coastal Maine.

His first day at school, a kid knocked him to the woodchips and stole his glasses; through blurry eyes, he watched a curly-haired girl snatch his bully's hat and rub it inside a trash can until his glasses were returned.

When Leander was six, he couldn't remember not being friends with Reyna. They took swimming lessons together at the Y, crab walked around the pool and held their breath underwater until their eyes burned from the chlorine, and Reyna was always the fastest kid in the pool.

When Leander was eight, his parents were fighting again, and he biked over to Reyna's house. They sat at the table rolling lumpia until Mrs. Mendler called his parents to say they'd lost track of time, was it alright if he spent the night? Reyna snuck out of bed to bring her stuffed rabbit to him on the couch, so Leander wouldn't feel alone in the living room.

When Leander was nine, his parents separated, and his grandmother took him for the summer. Chesa had girl scout camp, so Reyna came with him; they spent the summer on Great Cranberry Island finding shells on the rocky beach, trying to catch fireflies at dusk, fighting over how burnt marshmallows should be for the perfect s'more.

When Leander was sixteen, Reyna fell asleep in the passenger seat on a drive back from a concert in Montreal. Her hair tickled his ear when she slumped to rest her head on his shoulder, and Leander made the rest of the drive in silence to keep from waking her up. He told himself it was just a feeling, it would pass—after all, his parents had been in love, once. It would be better to not name it, better to be around her and be her friend, than to try to flame it into more and watch it burn out.

When Leander was seventeen, Reyna had asked, with uncharacteristic nervousness, who he was taking to prom. Leander panicked, said he'd never really thought about prom, and couldn't picture anyone he'd wanted to take. He'd watched Reyna's face fall, then a smile take its place as she announced that that was perfect, because they could go as friends, and not have to worry about any of the pressure of finding dates.

When Leander was eighteen, he had his first day of school without Reyna Mendler, and he thought that maybe this distance was what he needed, a chance to put it all behind them. He did everything he was meant to do — got drunk with the guys in the dorms, lost his virginity to someone a little older, made memories with people that didn't know his home address — but two years later, when his mom's car crashed, Reyna was the one he called.

She came right away.

Leander had felt the hospital walls closing in on him, but then she'd been there. Back at college, people sent flowers, told him they were sorry for his loss, asked what they could do, but Reyna had simply done it. Even though Leander was the nursing student, Reyna talked to every doctor so he didn't have to, inventoried every receipt and parking slip, found information for funeral homes and pocketed it before he could look at them and feel sick. He remembered staring at the hospital ceiling, thinking that he didn't know what he'd do without her, and how he'd better not fuck it up because now she was all he had.

It was a wild rush of memories that rampaged through his brain as Leander stared at the same hospital ceiling, now, almost a decade later. This time, he was the one they'd be calling for, and a part of him wondered if he should've done something differently, all those years ago, but he couldn't decide what, not when his body felt like it was burning.

Leander's skin was rending.

Heat rioted through him, and he felt his scrubs go damp as sweat poured off of him. He couldn't move, and the part of him that was still sane wondered who'd restrained him. He felt straps above his elbows, cotton between his teeth, restraints around his ankles.

He knew it was protocol, knew how strong the bindings were, but as magic coursed through him, Leander thought maybe he was stronger.

He dislocated his shoulder before he felt a sedative curdling in his veins.

And Leander was an emergency room nurse; he knew what happened when magic entered a body against its will.

Some hearts couldn't handle the invasion, seized and stopped. Some minds tried to fight, lost and stopped. Some souls rejected it like an organ transfer, refused and stopped.

But sometimes, magic was met.

He was in a dark room.

In the same breath that he realized he wasn't quite awake, Leander realized he was not alone. The shadows around him quivered, as though divine creation was separating light from darkness, and then a figure manifested.

A wolf.

Materializing from the light that made shadows of the rest of the room, the wolf stood across from Leander. He shook his fur as though growing accustomed to a corporeal form, and darkness flew like water off of his coat.

The massive animal stood still, steam curling from his nostrils as he watched Leander. His paws shifted, but he made no move forward. His head tilted slowly to the side, cocking curiously, and Leander realized he'd instigated the movement, and the wolf was mirroring him.

The wolf's tail swished behind him, and his head turned abruptly as his snout pointed upward, scenting. Leander inhaled too, and a familiar smell enveloped him.

Bergamot and eucalyptus.

Leander hadn't realized his skin was still burning until it was eased. The wolf's tail flicked lazily back and forth, his eyes closing as he settled. His long snout rested on his crossed paws, and the wolf grumbled something like a sigh.

Leander knew that smell, but it seemed new to the wolf, so he quieted the part of him that wondered where Reyna was. If she was worried about him, if she was already at the hospital, if someone had reassured her he was okay.

They stayed there, Leander and his wolf, until oranges faded from the air.

Eventually, the wolf rose.

He looked in Leander's direction for a long moment, and then he turned. His steps were soundless as he walked away, until his steady gait was absorbed into the shadows again.

When Leander awoke, the hospital lights were bright behind his closed eyes, and his skin felt raw again.

He could tell he was still bound to the hospital bed, and his shoulder twinged in protest. Bergamot and eucalyptus lingered on the air and Leander turned towards the scent, knowing who he would find, and there she was.

Reyna.

She was asleep, her tall frame folded stubbornly into a chair beside the hospital bed. It made sense that she was here; she'd been his emergency contact since his mom passed, but the sight of her settled something in Leader, like a reassurance.

Her shoulder was wedged against the wall to stay upright, and her arm was extended across the gap between the chair and the bed, holding his fingers in her sleep-loosened grasp.

Leander tightened his hand around hers, appreciating the coolness of her touch against the sandpaper of his skin. He doubted she'd be holding him if she knew he was awake. Physical affection had always been easy between them, but something had shifted after college, and she'd pulled back. Leander hoped it was just a shift, and not that she sensed his feelings for her ran deeper than friendship and reacted accordingly.

He couldn't remember the last time he'd seen her sleep.

It was a creepy thing to try to remember, and Leander was grateful this monologue was internal as he watched her. He wished his glasses were on, so he could see her more clearly, but the slightly blurred edges of her were still familiar.

She must've come straight from the beach; the sweats she always wore after a surf were wrinkled. Seawater had dried in her hair, the salt making her curls sharper.

He wondered how long she'd been in the room, and felt a twinge of guilt when he noticed the purse in her eyebrows, like even in her sleep, she was worried about him.

If she were awake, he'd tell her that was his job.

Of the two of them, Reyna had always been the problem solver, the one to stare down a challenge until it flinched, moving with a fullness of confidence that baffled Leander. Reyna's fortitude was a combination of factors—being the eldest daughter of a particularly high-achieving mother, being one of a few women in a male-dominated field, learning from a very young age that protecting her mother and sister wasn't something anyone else would take on. It made Reyna a person of aggressive action, and Leander knew it must've killed her to simply watch while magic burned through him.

As if she could hear him thinking, Reyna drew in a sharp breath, wincing as she woke. She blinked slowly, long lashes fluttering before her brown eyes focused, and Leander was sure he looked like shit, but she smiled at him like she didn't care.

"You're awake," she whispered, then she blinked, yanking her hand from his and pushing herself upright. "Oh my god, you're awake; are you okay?? We should call a nurse, right, okay, everything's fine, we need to–"

"Wait," Leander protested, but Reyna had already leapt out of the chair and darted into the hallway, waving her arms like she was hailing a taxi. A moment later she was back beside the bed, looking down at him nervously. Her hands were fluttering, and Leander stifled a smile, knowing she hated inaction, but that caretaking had always been his skillset more than hers—she had no idea what to do in this situation.

"Can I have my glasses?" he suggested, and she shot him a look like she knew he was placating her, but appreciated it too much to chastise him for pandering to her.

She grabbed them off the side table, fitting them onto his face, and Leander's ears burned slightly as she bent to make sure they fit correctly. Satisfied, she fumbled to find the switch to change the cot from reclining to seated, and Leander winced as the bed pulled the hospital gown over his sensitive skin.

"You're okay," Reyna told him, more decisive than comforting, like she could will him to wellness, and Leander smiled in spite of himself.

"You'd better not be laughing at me," Reyna grumbled.

"Wouldn't dare," Leander said, and Reyna glared at him, since they could both hear the amusement in his voice.

Leander lifted his wrists, and Reyna's eyes lit up, relieved for another task, and set about unbinding his arms. She pulled the straps free of the latches, and Leander watched her hesitate when she saw the red marks left by his straining against them.

"Lee..." she whispered, her fingers ghosting over the raw skin. Leander looked up, surprised to find Reyna so close to him. She was frowning at his arm, her jaw tight, and he hated that that furrow was back on her brow, hated that it was because of him. Before he could address it, Leander heard the door open, and when he looked up, a blond doctor with gleaming white teeth and broad shoulders filled the doorway.

"Well, well, well," Whit drawled, in a voice that, despite knowing it was a genuine accent, still sounded like a Matthew McConaughey impression to Leander. "Looks like sleeping beauty's finally awake."

Reyna turned sharply, her eyes unimpressed as they flicked over the doctor in the doorway.

"You're not Alex," she said, managing to sound both disappointed and dismissive, and Leander almost laughed at the look on Whit's face. Unfortunately, in addition to being as vain as the day was long, Whit was one of the best surgeons on the eastern seaboard.

"Whitman Pace," Whit said, flashing a feline smile and tucking a clipboard under his arm as he extended a hand to Reyna. "I don't believe we've had the pleasure."

Reyna's eyes narrowed. "I know you're not introducing yourself to me instead of checking on your patient."

If Whit was ruffled by her rebuttal, he didn't show it. His smile remained in place as he shifted back on his heels, shrugging easily.

"Després's fine," he said calmly, lifting his chin at Leander, "aren't ya, big guy?"

Leander normally endured Whit's southern charmer routine from a distance, but it felt different to see it directed at his best friend. Reyna hardly needed his protection, but it grated nonetheless.

Unfortunately, Whit was right.

Leander had witnessed turns before, knew that new wolves metabolized quickly to adjust to housing magic.

He felt warmer than usual, like something was buzzing under his skin, but when he looked down to where the welts had formed under the bindings, there was only clean, newly-healed skin. Also, it did seem like the hair on his forearms was thicker, but surely that couldn't have happened already? Surely he wasn't unconscious for a few hours and he had sprouted a pelt...

"I'm fine," he agreed, realizing Whit was waiting for an answer.

"See, he's fine," Whit said cheerily, tapping Leander's leg with the clipboard and leaning against the foot of the bed before returning his attention to Reyna. "I'm guessing you're Reyna."

"And you're still not Alex," Reyna said, stubborn to a fault, and Leander had to admit he enjoyed watching Whit get rebuffed twice.

The Texan rolled his shoulders so his white coat stretched across his broad chest.

"Doctor Benedict," he said, his voice taking on an uncharacteristically serious tone, "has been on call for thirty-two hours. I know I'm a sorry substitute, but I wanted to relieve her while she could still keep her eyes open to drive home."

Reyna shifted on her feet, her arms crossing in front of her as she tipped her head, which Leander knew was as close as she got to admitting that maybe she was being too harsh.

"So are you gonna check on Lee, or just announce that he's fine?" she asked.

Whit's eyebrows raised for a moment, before he finally looked at Leander's chart.

"Vital's are good, blood rate is high but that's expected..." he flipped back a couple pages, then smiled disarmingly up at Reyna. "Not bad for a pup."

Something in how he said it, like it was only a relative standard, had Leander's eyes flicking to Reyna, wondering if she'd heard it too. She was already watching him, and her hand lifted to rest on his shoulder, defensively.

"You're a wolf, then," she said to Whit, not a question, and Leander wondered how she'd noticed something in two minutes that he'd missed in years of working with the surgeon, but Whit only grinned lazily.

"I'm not a wolf," he said, which felt like less of an answer than it was.

Reyna waited.

Whit sighed.

"I'm a jaguar, darlin'," he said, the pet name sounding entirely platonic in a way only a man from Dallas could pull off.

Leander was grateful for Reyna's hand on his shoulder, like a tether; how had he not known that about his coworker? Granted, they were hardly friends, but it did surprise him.

Reyna's eyes narrowed. "American jaguars are extinct."

Whit tilted his head back, his expression going smug. "Not in Texas, they aren't."

Reyna's thumb pressed into a pressure point in the side of Leander's neck, and he hummed, in spite of himself.

He appreciated what she was doing, reassuring him in spite of this revelation, but her touch was eliciting a stronger reaction than he was used to. It must be the new wolf, young and over-reactive. Leander's eyes fluttered closed, and he fought the urge to nuzzle into her hand. He swallowed, pushing the impulse down.

It was bad enough that his heart was already gone for his best friend, who'd never looked at him in any way other than absolutely platonic, but now his new wolf had to pick up a crush too?

When Leander forced his eyes open, Whit was staring at him, an expression of unabashed amusement on his face.

"Your boyfriend's fine, Reyna," Whit said, not breaking eye contact with Leander, a blatant taunt.

Leander felt his cheeks flame, and thought about how useless it was to have a wolf under his skin, if it couldn't stop him from blushing.

"He's not my–" Reyna started, before she caught herself. "Whatever."

"Oh, he isn't?" Whit asked innocently, but he looked at Reyna a little too intently for Leander's comfort.

"Whitman," Leander said, an unfamiliar tone of warning on his voice, and he felt Reyna turning to look at him in surprise.

Not that Whit noticed.

Instead, his lips thinned in a smile, and as it widened, fangs clipped out from the corners of his mouth.

Leander didn't know how it happened.

One moment, Whit was goading him, baring his teeth at Reyna, and the next, the surgeon's head hit the back wall of the room. Leander heard an infusion pump clatter to the ground, and machines started chiming alarms as tubes yanked out of his body.

Whit's neck flexed under Leander's elbow and Leander shook his head, trying to clear it. His temples were throbbing, his hands were trembling, and when Leander ran his tongue across his teeth, he felt his tongue snag on sharp canines of his own.

What the hell?

Leander felt a stinging in his palms, and he didn't want to know, but he had to check—he unclenched his fist. Sharp claws extended from his fingers, an unnatural dark brown where his normally clipped nails were. As he flexed his fingers, the cuts in his palm closed, but blood still dripped down to the floor.

"Easy," Whit muttered, and Leander looked back to him. The surgeon's voice was calm but his eyes were rimmed with a glowing gold. Leander tried to quiet the roaring in his blood, forcing his arms down and releasing Whit.

"Are my eyes doing that?" he asked, his voice more ragged than he had heard it. He looked back over at Whit, to see the golden glow fading into a familiar hazel.

"They are," Whit said, "it's just harder to see on lighter eyes. And it's not as intense; cat night vision is a little better."

Leander realized Whit had let it happen, let himself he thrown against a wall.

"You're gonna be fine, kid," Whit said, and Leander wasn't sure what to do with something close to empathy. Whit was only a couple of years older than him, but in that moment, he felt every day of the difference. Whit's voice was almost sympathetic, like he was talking to a spooked animal. Maybe he was.

"Lee?" Reyna asked, her voice sounding small.

She didn't sound afraid, just uncertain, and Leander had to cling to that. Her voice came from behind him, and Leander knew he was irrational, knew he'd already overreacted, but he actually didn't think he could keep a handle on the situation if Whit looked at her again.

He stepped sideways, reaching behind him to hold Reyna in place, and keeping his eyes on Whit. He felt Reyna go still, tried not to think of what that meant, and he watched Whit's slow smile return.

"Interesting," Whit said.

He'd produced a toothpick from nowhere, and he fitted it between his teeth. Leander was aggravated beyond belief, but a part of him registered how steadily Whit was holding eye contact, letting him know he was with him, not looking at Reyna.

"I'm sorry about that, darlin'," Whit said easily, addressing Reyna but not looking away from Leander. "Just wanted to push him a bit, so he'd understand why they're gonna make him take a few days off."

"Alright, you've made your point," Reyna snapped, and a part of Leander relaxed, hearing the steel in her voice. "Are we done?"

Whit chuckled.

"I'm gonna go," Whit said, the toothpick switching sides in his mouth. "You get her out of here, get discharged yourself, then cool off for a couple days. If you need to talk before they schedule a psych eval, let me know."

Leander recognized it was more grace than he deserved, but he couldn't respond beyond a gruff nod.

Whit shook his head, reaching out to clap Leander's shoulder.

"Ah, I remember those days," he said breezily. "The claws'll go away when you calm down, the fangs too; you can ice 'em both. Good to meet you, Reyna."

"Doctor Pace," Reyna said, which Leander figured was her giving him the deference she'd reserved for Alex, as an apology for how this had ended.

Whit winked at Leander, rolling his neck as he stepped away from the wall, before letting himself out into the hall.

The room was silent.

After a moment, Reyna's hand closed over the fingers Leander still had clenched around her elbow.

"He wasn't going to hurt me," she said, gently.

Leander almost laughed; that hadn't been what he was afraid of. His pulse was still pounding, and though his body felt mostly healed from the turn, his mind was exhausted. It was too much, too strong, and he couldn't believe he'd reacted how he had.

Reyna must've misconstrued his silence for something else, because a moment later, she pulled his hand from her arm, and tugged on it slightly.

"Come lie down, yeah?" she asked, and Leander turned to look at her. He never let himself stare at her these days, not how he wanted to. But his wolf was stronger than his will, and he indulged, drinking in the sight of her.

Golden skin, even in the garish hospital lights. Round features, gentle smile, sharp eyes. Beautiful.

Another word whispered around in his mind, but he hushed it, too tired to fight it. He let her lead him back to the bed, crawled back into it, showed her how to hook the IV back up. The word echoed as she settled back into the chair beside his bed, repeated as he closed his eyes, resounded as he let sleep claim him again.

Surrounded by bergamot and eucalyptus, Leander let the lullaby lull him to sleep: mine, mine, mine.

Three

It was Reyna's seventh consecutive call of the day, and the fourth in which she hadn't said a word past opening pleasantries. Her mic was already muted, but she switched her video off before tipping her head back, fanning her fingers out to massage her scalp through her curls as she looked up at the ceiling.

She wished she were on the water.

Reyna pulled in a deep breath, inhaling the amber and sandlewood scent of the candle under the lamp at the corner of her desk, imagining she could hear the sea, instead of her coworkers droning on.

The wax warmer lamp had been a gift from Leander, a consolation prize when her penchant for wood burning wicks had set off her building's hyper-sensitive smoke detectors too many times. Reyna blinked at the ceiling, her hands slowing.

She hadn't heard from Leander since she left the hospital.

To be fair, he was recovering from an attack and what she understood to be a pretty aggressive lifestyle change. The hospital had a policy for things like this, and he'd been mandated to take a few days leave. Leander wasn't great with inactivity, so he was probably driving himself crazy but refusing to reach out to anyone.

"Anything else, folks, or are we good here?" someone asked on the call.

Reyna sat up, watching everyone on camera shake their heads, and the ones who weren't on camera send in obligatory reactions. She sent a thumbs up emoji and dropped of the call, checking her calendar and sighing as she joined the next call.

Her boss, an air elemental with a penchant for his team being on video as well as audio, was on the call, so Reyna flipped her camera on, smiling inanely at the screen.

As she crossed her legs, her knee bumped the desk, scattering the small bit of order she maintained. Reyna winced, rubbing her knee as she started reorganizing, hesitating as she moved her notepad back to where it'd been.

A manila folder peaked out from underneath the notepad.

It held three packets, three black-and-white printed listings for homes around Port Cadie, and Reyna had been alternating between rereading the pages and pretending they didn't exist.

She hadn't drunken the capitalism kool-aid enough to convince her that home ownership was the ultimate nirvana, but she would like a place of her own. Somewhere where if something broke, she didn't have to call a landlord and wait until he was convenienced to get it fixed. Somewhere she could burn candles without fire alarms shrieking at her. A place where she could bump folktronica records and not worry about someone banging on her door to tell her to turn it down.

Maybe even a garage.

Reyna pushed the envelope back under the notebook, wishing she could push it out of her mind just as easily.

Unfortunately, real estate anywhere around Acadia was prime pickings for people looking for vacation homes, second homes, and not much else. Reyna had been dutifully saving for a couple years now, but it wouldn't be worth anything if she couldn't find a place that some Boston businessman didn't swoop in to outbid her.

She had till the end of November before her lease was up; she would find a place. It would be fine.

Her phone started vibrating against her desk, the Facetime from her sister overriding focus mode. Reyna worried her bottom lip between her teeth, wondering if she could get away with answering it while still on the work call.

"Something more interesting on your phone, Reyna?"

The wispy voice unintentionally answered her question, and Reyna remembered she was on video just as she registered it was her boss who had asked her the question.

"Sorry," she said, declining Chesa's call and hoping everything was okay.

"As I was saying," her boss continued, "We are going to need an updated estimate for the vendors by next week. Can you get us something to look at before the weekend?"

"Sure thing," Reyna said, checking her text messages. Chesa hadn't texted, no heads up or explanation…"I can have it back to you by end of day Thursday."

"Make it Friday morning," her boss accepted. "I'll review it before they wake up out West."

"You got it," Reyna said.

Chesa called again.

Reyna pursed her lips, smiling apologetically at the camera.

"Sorry," she said, holding up her phone, "family emergency. I'll rejoin if I can."

Her boss waved a hand, pacified by her agreement to get revisions on his desk in the next day.

Reyna hung up on the call, pulled off her headset, and answered the Facetime.

"Hey, Ches," Reyna said to the empty stock room.

"I'm here!!" her sister called from off camera, and a moment later, she appeared on camera, balancing a number of unfolded takeout boxes.

"Sorry," Chesa said brightly. "I wasn't sure if you were at work, so I ran to grab these after dialing."

Reyna smiled at her sister, as her worry abated.

She and Chesa were the kind of sisters where they looked definitely related, but nothing alike. Where Reyna was tall and broad-shouldered, Chesa was petite and curvy. Reyna had received their father's size and their mother's coloring, and Chesa their received her mother's curves and their father's skin tone. Chesa was what their mother had called a classic beauty ("if she could just lose a little weight"), whereas Reyna was striking ("if only she were less intimidating").

Chesa looked like she gave the best hugs and smelled like cinnamon sugar, so when she'd turned down a plethora of full ride scholarships to start a bookstore/bakery in Port Cadie, it'd almost made sense.

Almost.

"So, what's up?" Reyna asked, pulling herself back to the conversation.

"Oh, you know," Chesa shrugged, dropping the takeout boxes on the counter where her phone was propped, and starting to fold them. "Nothing, really."

Reyna felt her relief ebbing into frustration, and willed it away.

"It's the middle of the workday and you didn't text," Reyna said, trying to keep her voice light, "is everything okay?"

Chesa snorted, setting a folded box to the side. "Of course everything's fine; I'm just saying hi. Not everything's an emergency, you know."

Reyna pressed her hands together under the desk, feeling a pressure building behind her temples but knowing she couldn't rub at them.

She didn't want to be this way.

She wanted to be the kind of sister who'd be delighted by a midday call, who'd effortlessly support her baby sister, cheer for her myopic dreams.

Instead, she was the kind of sister who had automatic payments sent to most of her college friends and all of her surfing cohort to pay for coffee subscriptions in their names. She was the kind who ordered coffee and pastries from The Jade Vine for every in-person meeting they had over in Bar Harbor, and put a stack of business cards on the table by the coffee carafe, in case any of her coworkers saw. She was the one who paid mom's medical bills and told Chesa her half was actually a quarter of what it was, because she didn't know how to tell her that she should keep chasing her dreams, when her dreams weren't staying afloat on their own.

She was the impatient one who heard too often that she took things too seriously and didn't have to, and she was about to prove everyone's point if she said it out loud.

"Working on anything fun?" Reyna asked, instead.

Chesa wrinkled her nose. "I can't get the proofing right on the leche flan croissants."

"I'm happy to be a taste tester, if you have any botched batches to spare," Reyna offered.

"Noted," Chesa sighed, stacking the boxes she'd folded and reaching for another, "once I figure out how to keep them from being soggy."

"You'll get it," Reyna said, unhelpfully.

Chesa smiled at the encouragement, and Reyna watched her sister as she worked. Chesa really was in her element in the shop, baking delicious treats, sneaking familiar flavors into lattes and suggesting independent books to customers based on their coffee order. Chesa was an incredibly intuitive person, creative, and Reyna was glad she had a job that fostered that side of her.

"So how's paying down the mortgage going?" Reyna asked, curious, and realized her mistake a moment too late.

To Reyna, challenges were problems were meant to be resolved, and they could always be resolved out loud. To Chesa, challenges were confirmations of her insecurities, and sure enough, and Reyna watched the hurt look flash over Chesa's face.

Her sister's shoulders went back and her chin lifted, and Reyna felt a flash of guilt.

"You had to ask, didn't you," Chesa muttered.

"I'm just–" Reyna started, but Chesa huffed.

"I'm making my monthly payments, okay, Ate?" Chesa said, archly. "It's not paying down the principle or whatever, but I'm doing my best."

"I know," Reyna said quickly, and that was what made it hard. Chesa was trying her best, and the shop was pulling even, but Reyna had to ask. It was an inability to leave well enough alone, a compulsion to fix things, to tidily resolve.

"Do you?" Chesa asked, cardboard scraping as she folded boxes quickly. "Because not all of us can work at soulless corporations that let us actually have savings accounts instead of living paycheck to paycheck, and then somehow have extra cash to hand out pity money to our siblings."

Reyna's jaw tightened. "It's not pity money, Ches."

Chesa shook her head. "Sure. Sorry I interrupted your super-busy corporate work day, okay? I'm sure you've got lots going on."

Reyna closed her eyes.

"Chesa–" she started, but Chesa reached for her phone, and a moment later, the call disconnected.

Reyna stared at her phone as the call minimized, at the picture of two kids playing in the sun.

A week ago, she would've called him without thought.

Lee would listen to her, affirm that Chesa shouldn't have called in the middle of the work day, then gently suggest that maybe the reason Chesa took every inquiry as judgment was because maybe Reyna was judging.

Reyna turned her phone face down.

It wasn't last week, and she hadn't heard from Leander since he'd hulked out and rammed Doctor Pace into the wall, then not talked to her in since.

Reyna couldn't think about that right now.

She reached for her notebook, needing to write out her thoughts, if she couldn't voice them. Her fingers snagged on the manila envelope and Reyna paused, Chesa's words floating through her mind unbidden.

Not all of us can work at soulless corporations that let us actually have savings accounts instead of living paycheck to paycheck...

This was a bad idea.

It was overbearing to the max, so deep down the path of micromanaging that Reyna doubted even Leander could justify it.

Reyna grabbed a pen and flipped open her notebook, trapping the manila envelope underneath it as she wrote a number: the amount in her savings account, courtesy of one (1) soulless corporation. Beneath the total, she marked two columns and two rows, a pros and cons list that her mind was filling in faster than she could write. She paused before she started filling them in, then wrote the first things she thought, the most honest.

Pros for a house

- Not having to shovel snow off car in winter

- Something to show for workaholic tendencies

- Have something that's mine

Cons for a house
- Shovel a driveway

- While no rent, still have mortgage payments

- Can't afford Acadia, so live farther away from Ches/Lee/Mom

- Also likely far from the ocean

Reyna paused in that cons column, wondering how to condense "how much am I gonna enjoy a house if my sister's business is going broke" into a few pithy words. She tapped her pen against the desk, then shook her head; she didn't have to write it down to know that it was scratched in bold over the other points. She moved to the next column.

Pros for paying off Chesa's loan
- Chesa's autonomy

- No more guilt-inducing calls about money

- Less overhead responsibility for The Jade Vine

Cons for paying off Chesa's loan
- Continue renting

- Chesa will be hurt before she realizes this'll be good for her

- Never beating the Control Issues allegations

Reyna read over the page.

Then read it again, trying to think of ways to stretch that number at the top of it, and coming up blank. She could add a dozen things to each column, but the crux of it was that her savings could cover one or the other, but not both.

Her phone buzzed again, an Outlook reminder that her next meeting started in 15 minutes. Reyna spun the pen over her hand before setting it down, getting up from her desk and walking into the kitchen. She grabbed a glass and set it on the counter, mind racing now that she was no longer writing it out.

This was too much.

Or maybe it was perfect, or maybe it was both, but still not her job. Her bluetooth headphone case was on the counter and she shoved one in her ear before ducking back into the living room, calling Lee before she could get in her head about it, and leaving the phone in the living room so she couldn't hang up.

Back in the kitchen, she opened the utensil drawer, rooting around for a stainless steel straw as the phone rang.

"Reyna?" Leander answered on the third ring; it sounded like he was in a store, with a low murmur of conversation in the background.

"Hey," Reyna said, and she found the straw. "Got a sec?"

"Yeah, um...yeah," Leander said and she could hear him moving, a door opening and then gentle wind against the phone as Leander stepped outside. "Just at the library; you're good?"

"I'm good," Reyna bumped the drawer closed with her hip. "You?"

"Oh, you know," Leander said, and a gust of wind blew against the phone; Reyna could envision Leander sitting on one of the benches against the library. "Other than the obvious."

Reyna pressed her lips together; it'd been a stupid question to ask.

Of course what Leander was going through was bigger than her sibling stress. Reyna had a fair amount of non-mortal friends and coworkers, but nearly everyone had come by it naturally, and she truthfully didn't know if there was a stigma around the fact that Leander was turned.

"Can I ask about that?" she asked hesitantly, not sure what the rules were here.

"Honestly, that's what I'm doing," Leander said. "They have me on leave from work, and online forums seemed like echo chambers, so that's why I'm at the library. I found a couple books, but it's weird, since it's something you're meant to be born into."

"That's good that you're finding resources," Reyna said lamely, hating that it sounded like she was staffing a project. "Is there...I don't know, are there like groups at work or something? A hospital's got to know how to connect you to something like that."

"Yeah, I got the contact for a peer support group; the first meeting is later in the week. Just trying to read up before then, you know?"

Reyna smiled softly, dropping the straw into the glass. "Hey, if you could handle AP Econ, you can handle a support group."

Leander huffed a laugh, and she knew he was thinking of the farce of a class their junior year of high school, when the school had had an Economics course for long enough for half of them to fail, and then promptly dropped the curriculum.

"I don't know if I could say I *handled* that class," Leander said, then he cleared his throat. "So...I can't really remember if I owe you an apology or not."

Reyna had been pouring cold brew into her glass, and the pour got heavier as she registered his words, before she pulled it back. Chesa had made her a batch over the weekend, and she wouldn't appreciate it if she spilled half of it on the counter, so Reyna carefully capped the cold brew as she tried to make sure her voice sounded casual.

"No worries," Reyna said, definitely not thinking about Leander putting his body between her and a threat, and fangs he'd tried to hide. "You were probably hyped up on painkillers or something, and everything I've read since then says it's a really intense/reactive time, post turn."

"I'm waiting for it to get less intense/reactive," Leander muttered. "Wait, you're doing research?"

"Having answers is pretty much my MO," Reyna said, trying to decipher his tone.

Leander let out a long breath.

"I...that means a lot, Rey. I know you like to be like that, but you have a lot going on, so I didn't expect you'd take this, too."

Reyna stirred the coldbrew with the straw, wondering if Leander could hear the ice and metal and glass clanging together.

"I don't know if I'd call it research," she deferred. "It's certainly not a stack of books at the library, but some, yeah."

The line was quiet for a moment.

"Well, anyways," Leander said, after a minute, "I wasn't that out of it, after the turn. I just felt a lot, and thinking back over it, it's like half my mind is convinced it's perfectly natural to be overprotective like that, and the other half of me is just picturing you calling me and Whit *Neanderthals*."

"Two things can be true at once," Reyna said, and she looked down at the ice cubes spinning in her glass. "I should've called you earlier, to check in."

Leander made a dismissive sound, and Reyna could tell he'd waved a hand in the air in front of him.

"I should've called *you* earlier," he parroted, but he did mean it from his perspective, "to check in."

She couldn't decide why it mattered so much that he'd felt the distance as much as she had. It wasn't like they were always texting or on the phone, but theirs was a kind of comfortable communication that seemed pretty unceasing, regardless of frequency. The last few days had felt like an interruption, and she hoped this meant they were back.

"I'm good, if you're good," she said.

"I'm good," Leander said, and Reyna nodded to her empty kitchen.

She put the cold brew in the fridge, and grabbed a mason jar of sweetened condensed milk, needing a sharp conversational pivot. "Okay, so I need you to tell me if my control issues are at play."

Leander laughed, and Reyna smiled at the soft sound.

"Alright," he said, "what's going on?"

Reyna spooned a dollop of the sweetened condensed milk into her cold brew. "Am I a bad sister if I don't think Chesa's business loan is going to solve itself?"

Leander paused, and Reyna appreciated that he was thinking it over before answering. "So you're worried she's going to go under?"

Reyna snorted. "Not if I can help it."

Leander was quiet, and she braced herself.

And that was the heart of it, wasn't it? Reyna knew that she could fix it, but didn't know if that made her a meddler, an enabler, or an encourager.

"Alright, say it," Reyna muttered as the silence stretched.

"You can't have it both ways," he said, and she could tell he was trying to put it gently. "She's either an adult whom you trust to handle it, or your kid sister whom you have to bankroll."

Reyna dropped the dirty spoon in the sink. "Historically, Option B."

Leander hummed. "Sounds like you've already made up your mind."

She had, but that wasn't the point.

"It's not that I don't believe in her," Reyna said.

"Okay," Leander agreed, and Reyna frowned. When he was agreeable like that, it was just so she could talk herself through it.

"She's broke," Reyna said, bluntly. "It's...I've never run a business, Lee, so I know I don't know what it's like. But I don't understand how she trusts it'll work out, without changing anything."

"And the uncertainty's hard for you," Leander said, not quite a question, but Reyna nodded.

"It's killing me how overwhelmed she is," Reyna admitted, knowing it sounded selfish to lament how Chesa's stress was affecting Reyna's life. "I can't tell if I'm impatient or empathetic."

"Yes," Leader supplied, and Reyna huffed. She stirred the cold brew with the straw, watching the color lighten as the milk melted into the coffee.

"Okay," Leander spoke after a long moment, "I have to say it."

"Please do."

Leander took a deep breath. "You're trying to solve problems for her because you think it's your responsibility, but I'm nearly certain that she hasn't asked you to."

"Oh, is that all?" Reyna asked, meaning to joke, but it fell flat.

Leander hummed, like he heard it, but let it go. He started to say something, stopped, then cleared his throat.

"I know it's different for us," Leander said, and Reyna pursed her lips.

Responsibility meant something different to Reyna's immigrant mother than it had to either of Leander's parents, and he didn't have any siblings to pull focus. Chesa was bright, and creative, and incredible, but it was never going to be on her shoulders to worry if Reyna could make ends meet.

"I know you'll do what you think is best for her," Leander said, after a moment.

Reyna wrinkled her nose. She didn't know if that was true, since she felt pretty torn up about it, and was making her friend hold her hand through it.

"Thanks for talking it out with me," she said.

"Anytime," Leander said, his voice soft, and it settled somewhere in Reyna's heart. That was one of her favorite things about Lee, how he meant it. He wanted to listen, wanted to hear her rationalize her way around her problems, and would let her make her own decisions at the end of it.

The line was quiet for a moment, and Reyna hoped it was okay.

They were okay; they had to be, they'd been through a lot. A weird moment at the hospital where Leander acted like they were more than they were, that wasn't anything friendship-threatening. It would be fine, like everything else.

"So," she said brightly, "what're the next steps to getting you back to work?"

Leander sighed, and she could hear him shifting, probably running his hand through his hair. "I have to have an evaluation, and they're still trying to fit that in."

Reyna carried her coffee back to her desk, rooting around for a coaster before giving up and setting the glass on top of her pros and cons list. "I get why they have to do that, but it sucks."

"Sure does," Leander said quietly, almost dejected. "The board meeting is next week, too, so I really need to be back to work in time for that."

Reyna grimaced to herself; she should've remembered that was happening.

Leander hadn't set out to be involved in leadership of the nursing union, but the union director—Esther Jacinto, who was church friends with Reyna's mom—had insisted Leander put his cis, straight, white male privilege to work and stand up with them in board meetings. They'd been rallying for better staffing support for over a year, Reyna knew this, and she should've asked about it in addition to the bite thing, instead of browbeating Chesa about her loan, and asking Leander to make her feel better about it.

"Glad that's finally on the calendar," Reyna said aloud. "Sorry, I should've asked about that sooner."

"Oh, that's fine," Leander said immediately, and from the way he said it, Reyna knew he wasn't bothered by it. It was just like Lee to have very real, very dire, things going on, and yet treat Reyna's struggles like they were the important ones.

"I actually..." Leander trailed off. "I might have some questions for you, with that? I know how much of your day is corporate legalese with unimpressed Boomers, so it'd probably be wise to run some of our approach by you."

"Of course," Reyna said immediately, hoping he would. The two most important people in her life were the kind that always new how to help—a nurse and someone who made a career out of baking, they were exactly the types of people folks wanted around in a crisis. There were few situations in which Reyna's ability to discuss carnets and agility and HS ad nauseam was beneficial, so she'd take any chance to put her soulless corporation job to use.

Her computer pinged, and Reyna pushed down a sigh. "Speaking of unimpressed Boomers, I've got to go; I have another call starting soon."

"Yeah, no worries," Leander said, and she heard him pause for a moment. "Hey, Rey?"

"Yeah," Reyna paused on her way to hang up, waiting for him. Leander took a moment, and she wondered if he hadn't meant anything, before he spoke again.

"You're a good sister," he said.

It was how he said it, simple, full of conviction, that made Reyna's breath catch.

If she was a good sister, she'd believe in Chesa, trust her enough to claw her way out of this, and not need to swoop in and make it better.

If she was a good sister, Leander telling her wouldn't make her want to cry.

"Call me if you need help with the union/board meeting prep, yeah?" she said instead, and she knew Lee could hear it in her voice how it'd affected her.

"Sounds good," he said softly, and Reyna hung up before he'd heard anything else she hadn't said.

Four

Golden skin and heavy curves, her thighs flexing as she moved over him. The dark tangle of her hair, the soft sweep of her jaw, the dark shadow her lashes cast down her cheeks, tears glistening in the brown of her eyes. The arch of her back, the fullness of her breasts in his hands, the catch in her breath as he stroked his thumbs over her nipples. The dent in her lip from her teeth biting down, the whimper she made despite trying to stay quiet, the way she sobbed his name, the way she felt around him, tight and hot and perfect, like a dream...

Shit.

Leander woke up with a jolt, rubbing a hand over his face, glaring at the clock that told him it was later in the morning than he normally slept. Dragging himself into the shower, he stepped under the stream without waiting for it to heat. The cold water made him shiver, but did a good enough job of pushing the hazy temptation of his dreams farther away.

Before this week, Leander couldn't remember the last time he'd had a wet dream.

But every morning since the turn, he woke to his alarm blaring, come soaking his pajama pants, and a physical ache in his chest because Reyna wasn't in his arms.

Leander raked a washcloth over his skin, wondering how long it was going to take his wolf to realize Reyna was his friend. His longest friend, the closest thing he had to family, and then some, but he'd been hormonal and in love with her before, so he could get through it again.

His wolf just had to get the memo.

In the five days since he'd woken up with something else under his skin, Leander had been hoping everything would metabolize on its own, but it wasn't looking promising. The obligatory psych evaluation wasn't scheduled till Monday, and hospital wasn't staffing him without it, so he was running out of options.

Leander was glad the mirror was foggy as he got out of the shower; he didn't want to look at his reflection just yet.

He still wasn't used to the changes in his body, no matter how subtle.

The stack of library books on his kitchen table told him that, as someone who was turned, he would never transition to a full wolf. He could adopt some of the traits when agitated—the fangs at the hospital, for example. Or, and he was less proud of this one, the fact that he'd awoken to a face full of feathers after a particularly intense dream when he'd apparently extended claws and shredded a pillow before he woke.

Leander hadn't even tried to force that concoction of come and feathers into his apartment's washing machine, and had just thrown out the tattered pillowcase. Leander grabbed his glasses off the bedside table, and the motion knocked a notebook to the ground. Leander grimaced at the crumpled pages on the floor, his notes for the upcoming union meeting.

The nursing union had been trying to shift the board's stance on mandated minimum RN-to-patient staffing ratios, something that affected nurses and patients and the general well-being of the hospital, and he should be prepping for that confrontation, rather than losing himself in hot dreams about his best friend.

And not just hot dreams.

Leander had always been vaguely protective of Reyna; she wasn't someone who needed, or even wanted, a savior, but Leander had always taken a quiet pride in being there for her, in whatever capacity she'd let him. He was fairly certain there was a lot more going on with Chesa, plus Reyna's housing plans, than she was letting on, and normally he'd let it go, but with a new intensity, Leander was having a hard time drawing lines.

It was like the protectiveness, along with the attraction and the pining, had been ratcheted up, and without the distraction of work, Leander was pretty sure he was going to go mad before he ever got to a psych eval.

Leander was drying his hair with a towel when his phone started to ring.

Now, Leander had Whit's number saved, the same way he had every surgeon's number saved, but the man had never texted him, much less called.

"Després," Whit boomed as soon as Leander accepted the call, like this was a normal and frequent occurrence. "How're you doing?"

"I'm fine," Leander answered, suspiciously. "What...did you need something?"

"Just checking in on my team," Whit said congenially, and Leander could hear the sounds of the hospital around him, as he walked through halls. "Can't a man do that?"

Leander didn't buy that for a moment, but the only thing he had on the docket for the week was the Shifter Peer Support group, and that was tomorrow. Knowing for a fact he was more comfortable with silence than Whit, Leander made his way into the kitchen.

Whit cleared his throat as the silence stretched, and Leander smirked to himself as he rooted through the fridge. He wondered if he could conjure something other than English muffins and eggs, by the powers of wishful thinking.

He could not.

"You know, I'm just," Whit said, eventually, "practicing leadership skills. Taking initiative, showing awareness of people that aren't necessarily directly on my team."

Something in his voice sounded like he was reading a performance review, and it suddenly made much, much, more sense.

Leander wedged his phone between his ear, grabbing the carton of eggs and not bothering to hide the amusement in his voice. "Dr. Simon told you the only shot you have at replacing him as Chief once he retires is if you start interacting with staffers who aren't also surgeons, didn't he?"

The line was silent as Leander cracked an egg.

"Maybe," Whit muttered, "in so many words."

Leander grinned, enjoying this more than he should. "What words, Whit?"

Whit sighed. "Something to the tune of 'get your head out of your ass and treat support staff like they're medical professionals instead of your backup dancers'."

A week ago, Leander would've counted Whit foremost among the class of egomaniac doctors who saw surgery as a way to prove their own genius, and he still wasn't sure that that wasn't accurate. But the fact that he was willing to eat crow and admit that he had a bit of a complex wasn't nothing, and Leander could appreciate that Whit was at least trying to take Simon's counsel to heart, and value people for more than the white coat they did (or didn't) wear.

God knew plenty of other surgeons couldn't bring themselves that far.

"If you want to do a solid for a lowly nurse," Leander said, dumping the eggs into a skillet and summoning an olive branch, "can you get my psych eval moved up?"

"Unfortunately," and to his credit, Whit did sound genuinely contrite, "I have even less goodwill with Psych than with nurses."

Retrospectively, that didn't surprise Leander. Still, it'd been worth a shot.

"Damn, Pace," Leander couldn't help but rib him, "the whole department?"

"Yeah, get your licks in," Whit grumbled, but Leander could tell he was trying not to laugh.

Leander cracked some pepper into his eggs as they cooked, and acknowledged that the current Chief knew what he was doing: once Whit deigned to interact with other people, they'd see he wasn't half as unpleasant as he seemed content to be seen.

"Well, no worries," Leander said, despite the fact that he was likely worrying his way into a hernia. "I feel very supported by PCMC's lead neurosurgeon, and will tell Doctor Simon as much, should he randomly ask me."

Whit hummed, processing through Leander spelling it out that it'd probably been a little selfish to reach out how he had.

"We should get coffee," Whit said, suddenly.

Leander was scraping a spatula around the pan, and he paused. "Come again?"

"Yeah," Whit said, and Leander could practically hear him nodding, "yeah, no, let's do that. I can talk you through some of this were-stuff, since you don't have a prowl."

"A what now?" Leander asked, though he recognized the determination in Whit's voice as he latched onto a new idea. Being Reyna's friend came with the territory of knowing exactly how it sounded when a person of action had an idea that they thought solved everyone's problems.

"I guess a prowl's just jaguars," Whit mused. "What is it, a pack, for you? Either way, you don't have one, so yeah, let's do it."

"Hold on," Leander protested. "I have a support group, they're meeting tomorrow, they—"

"Yeah, but 1:1's gonna be better, trust me. You know Aster's?"

If Whit kept leaping between conversation points this quickly, Leander was going to burn something. "Yeah, the pub near—"

"Great, meet you there after my shift. Good talk, Després."

Whit hung up before Leander could process that this was now a plan, or even double check when Whit's shift was done.

Leander ate his breakfast standing in the kitchen, replaying the call in his mind. He hadn't really thought through what it'd mean to have a pack—if that was something he was supposed to want, if he even needed it—but there wasn't anything he could do about it now.

Everything in his apartment was reminding him that he'd been stuck in said apartment for three days, and, with the knowledge he'd have to leave eventually, Leander threw everything he could think into a tote he'd gotten for subscribing to a magazine back in college. It was a quick walk to old town, which was ideal, since Aster's was by the hospital and he'd need to walk back to his place before driving there, and Leander turned towards the Jade Vine.

Through the front window, he could see Chesa bustling around, tending to customers and laughing with the barista. The bell above the door chimed pleasantly as he let himself in, the smells of espresso and jasmine cookies mingling with books. There was an excited squeal, and that was the warning Leander got before Chesa was flying around the counter, launching herself at him.

Leander chuckled as he caught her, endlessly amused by Chesa's compulsion for physical affection where Reyna shunned it. Chesa was only about chest high on him, and she did give great hugs, even if today she squeezed him a little too tight.

"I'm glad you're okay," Chesa mumbled into his chest, reminding Leander that it hadn't been a full week since he'd been turned. "Next time, call Reyna sooner, yeah? She's been weirdly mopey about it."

She had? What did that mean?

"I'm hoping there isn't a next time," Leander said, and Chesa snorted as she stepped back.

"Chamomile?" she asked, going back to the counter, and Leander nodded, adjusting the bag on his shoulder, as he looked around. There were a couple of tables open, and he wasn't sure if that was because they were between the morning rush and lunch, or if Reyna's worries were rubbing off on him. Regardless, it wasn't too crowded, so he wandered over to the book section while Chesa started brewing his tea.

"Anything good?" he asked, as he browsed through the shorter shelves.

"It's all good," Chesa said wryly, "otherwise I wouldn't stock it."

He saw a lot of Reyna in her, though neither sister believed him when he said it. They were both creative in their own ways, stubborn to a fault, self-sufficient and proud, and deeply loyal. Physically, they were pretty distinct, but they'd been raised together, and it was obvious.

Leander bought a notebook that he didn't need, and pretended not to notice when Chesa saw through it to, and pulled a pen from the jar beside the cash register for him. He took his notebook and new pen to a counter seat at the window, not wanting to take up table space if it was needed.

He pulled a folder from his bag, the file he'd made to help himself keep all of the union talking points organized. There was a google drive somewhere, but he needed the paper, needed to be able to hold it. He was that way with books too; even though an E-Reader would be infinitely more economical, he just couldn't focus unless he had something tangible.

Leander flipped through the pages in the folder—the board decision from their sister hospital down in Portland, statistics on employee satisfaction and retention, and correlation to patient care, testimonies from former union leaders. It was compelling stuff, and he knew they had a case here, it was just complicated to see it all laid out, and try to figure out the single best way to present it all.

A mug and saucer clinked as Chesa set them down beside him, squeezing his shoulder encouragingly before flitting back to the counter.

He was just short of having it memorized, but he read through it again, just in case he was missing something. He wasn't sure what he was looking for—a through-line, an epiphany, something —but Leander knew he was a better reviser than creator.

Leander sighed, rubbing his eyes under his glasses after his fourth fruitless reread.

He knew who could help him, and she'd said he could call her about it, but he couldn't bring himself to do it.

This sort of thing really was up Reyna's alley, but Leander just...couldn't.

He didn't know how he was supposed to interact with her like everything was normal, when he had a wolf in his subconscious that made it damn near impossible to ignore feelings he'd been ignoring for years.

How would that even go—"Hey can you help me put together an agenda for this meeting with the board? By the way, this whole wolf thing is fighting against years of repression because the last thing I want to do is ruin our friendship with the fact that I have feelings for you, but the wolf doesn't know that, and I had to hide outside the library the other day when you called because the way you said my name made me embarrassingly hard in the middle of a random afternoon"? Yeah, there was no way.

He refused to be "The Nice Guy", the lovesick friend who wasn't actually a friend, just lurking until feelings were reciprocated. He wasn't waiting for her to realize what was in front of her, he was just someone who wanted to be in her life, in whatever capacity she had room. And since she didn't see him in a romantic light, then there was no romance.

Which was fine, or had been fine, until this stupid wolf decided it wanted more.

He mulled over his notes until twilight fell, then made his way over to to Aster's; even from the outside, the pub looked full. Leander hoped absently that Whit had grabbed a booth, or at least wasn't planning on having this conversation in full hearing distance of the rest of the hospital at the bartop, but he couldn't be certain.

As he pushed open the door, the smell of cheap drinks and bitters met him on a rush of warm air. At this hour, the bar was filled with hospital staff, fresh off their shift change, disguised in layman's clothes. But the discerning eye could notice the starchy posture of surgeons, the comfortable stillness of nurses, the dazed exhaustion of interns. Through the dim lighting, Leander found Whit sitting at a booth near the back of the pub, lifting a tankard in acknowledgment. Leander made his way through the crowd to Whit's booth, his step faltering slightly when he saw the pink drink on the table in front of Whit.

"Took a wild guess," Whit said on a chuckle, nodding at the Shirley Temple he'd ordered for Leander.

"Jokes on you," Leander muttered, shrugging out of his jacket as he sat, "Shirley Temples are great, and I won't have a hangover in the morning."

Whit's eyebrows raised amusedly as he took a sip of his own drink. From the color and glass, Leander guessed a whiskey ginger, which did somewhat surprise him, as Whit gave off the impression that he was a "whiskey should only be neat, and coffee should only be black" sort of man.

"You won't have a hangover anyways," Whit said lightly, setting his glass back down, "newer metabolism and all."

Leander had read that in one of the library books, but it was a hell of a jump from knowing it was true about someone, to knowing it was true about him.

"Yeah, so let's talk about it," Leander said, pulling the Shirley Temple towards him.

"Okay," Whit said, shifting like he was crossing his legs under the table, "so have you done your exemption paperwork?"

"I have," Leander answered, wondering what Whit would suggest if he'd said he hadn't filled out the paperwork. Said paperwork was what granted him extended medical leave, what covered the current absence he was taking, and if he needed to take supplements or suppressants for some reason or another.

"Good," Whit said, taking a long sip of his whiskey ginger, "that's the biggest thing, work wise. And you have a group meeting later this week?"

"Yeah," Leander said, "tomorrow."

Whit nodded curtly. "They'll cover most of what you need, in terms of support and lifestyle changes. The good news is that since you're turned, you're not going to have to worry about typing."

"You're born with a secondary sex?" Leander asked, thinking through the sections of the books he'd read, wondering how much applied to jaguar shifters as well.

"What," Whit smirked, "you trying to guess mine?"

Leander didn't have to guess; Whit put off alpha energy strong enough that even someone without pheromones could tell.

"It's an indefinite you," Leander mumbled. "And I was just reiterating."

"Hmm," Whit seemed amused, taking another sip. "Well, you're right, you don't have to worry about finding your way as a beta, or omega, or anything, since you're still more mortal than monster."

Leander tried not to wince at the use of *monster*; it felt dehumanizing. He supposed he wasn't fully human, even if he didn't identify as monster, but either way, he didn't feel comfortable ascribing the noun to Whit, or even Maggie.

"So, all you'll have to worry about is ruts," Whit said easily, "which I assume you know about from undergrad, and porn."

Whit said it so matter-of-factly that Leander hadn't been expecting it, and he choked on his Shirley Temple. He wasn't much of a porn guy—not on principle, he just found the lack of intimacy in most shoots to be discomforting—and certainly hadn't been prepared to discuss his preferences with his coworker on a weekday afternoon.

"From the former," Leander rasped, once he managed to draw in a breath of air.

Whit lifted an arm to the back of the booth, his chest opening to the room around him, and his expression turned intent. "So what's the deal with Reyna?"

Leander was glad he hadn't tried for another sip of his drink, as he would've choked again.

"She's my friend," he said, a massive understatement, but he was wary of Whit's motives.

"Just that?" Whit asked, his expression unreadable.

Part of Leander wanted to keep up the front of nonchalance—protect the thing that he had with Reyna, that she didn't know about, play it lowkey so Whit would leave it alone — but another part of him thought of how Whit's fangs had extended in the hospital room.

"Best friend," Leander amended, hardly recognizing the steel in his own voice. "Why?"

Whit grinned. "Sounds like maybe a little more than that."

Leander felt his cheeks heating, a mortifying trait he'd never been able to shake, even as his hackles continued to raise at the tone of Whit's voice. Whit pushed off the back of the booth, leaning forward in a swift motion and templing his fingers on the table.

"I'm gonna be honest with you, Després," he said, the amusement in his voice giving way to something more serious, "this isn't puberty again. It's not being horny, and not understanding your big feelings—it's a biological imperative. Every atom in your body is needing to breed, mate, claim. There's apps you can use, be partnered with someone during their heat and your rut; everyone wins. But it...it's better with someone you care about."

The bar was loud, but it seemed to fade on Whit's last words.

For a moment, Leander let himself think about it.

Just for a moment, an indulgence in the idea his subconscious had already been insisting on: the girl he'd wanted before he knew what wanting was. The woman she'd grown into, the way their closeness had never wavered, and what it could mean to be even closer...but he couldn't do it. Reyna hadn't been interested before all of this, and there was no way he could just drop it all on her. He knew she would help him out, would agree if he needed her without a thought for what it could mean, what it might do to them.

Without knowing that once Leander had gotten to love her out loud, under the pretense of a rut, that he wasn't going to be able to go back to just friends.

Ice clinked in a glass and Leander was jolted out of his reverie and back to the bar. Whit had leaned back, his arm over the ledge of the booth again, and he shook his head in Leander's direction.

"You know you have to tell her," Whit said.

Leander traced his thumb absently over the condensation beading down the side of his glass. "I can't."

"Won't," Whit corrected, and Leander glared at him.

"She wouldn't–"

"I get the feeling she would," Whit interrupted, cocking an eyebrow, and Leander glowered at him.

"She would," he admitted. "And that's the problem."

Whit drained the rest of his glass. "And you think the best way to straighten out the problem is deciding for her?"

Leander certainly knew better, but no way was he admitting that. "It'd complicate things."

Whit shifted to pull out his phone, swiping through the open apps before he turned his phone around, and slid it across the table to Leander.

It was the weather app, opened to a view of the next couple of weeks.

"Normally," Whit said, "I'd say take your time, figure out where your head's at, and act accordingly. But next weekend is the full moon, and it's probably going to trigger a rut. So you have to decide now: are you going to tell your best friend you're in love with her, or are you okay with fucking someone else while you're feeling the most out of control you've felt in your life, and wishing it was her?"

Leander knew Whit was being incendiary.

But his words still rattled him, and Leander didn't like any of their ramifications. That he'd been dishonest with Reyna, that he would have to ask her for help in this thing that would probably destroy their friendship, that the alternative was an impersonal salve of someone else's body.

He ran a hand through his hair, coming to the slow and unfortunate realization that Whit was right.

He didn't want to do this but he owed her the truth. If she rejected it, if she rejected *him*, then he'd figure it out with the apps Whit'd mentioned. But at least at first, she deserved to hear from him—an explanation of the hospital, and what the next week would bring.

Five

"If this cold brew isn't labeled in any kind of way," Reyna called as she leaned out of the industrial fridge in the back of the Jade Vine, "does that mean I can have it?"

"All of it might kill even you," Chesa called back from the front of the shop, where she was rewriting the chalkboards, "but help yourself to a glass."

"Sounds like a challenge," Reyna said, shutting the fridge and lugging the gallon jug over to the counter.

It was restocking day at the Jade Vine, and Chesa had a million projects going at once. She was redoing the menu boards, testing a new type of coffee cake, restocking shelves and stamping paper cups.

Well, Reyna was stamping cups; Chesa was doing all the other things.

Where Chesa was creative, Reyna was methodical, and their relationship could only survive so many "what happened?? it was fine before it went in the oven!!" baking fiascoes. Give Reyna a deep blue ink pad, a rubber stamp, and a mountain of paper cups, and she could make herself useful.

Reyna poured herself a cup of the cold brew, and Chesa came back into the kitchen, sliding chalk markers into a jar by the door and heading to the fridge. Reyna slid the cold brew gallon down to the end of the metal counter she was working on, Chesa put it back in the fridge and pulled out a crumb coated cake, bringing it back to the counter as well.

"That's a pretty color," Reyna said, lifting her chin at the light purple color of the cake, visible under the thin coat of icing.

"Right?" Chesa agreed, spinning the cake lightly on the platter. "I thought ube was a nice spin on the typical Thanksgiving/autumnal sweet potato."

They worked in silence for a few minutes, some pop album playing faintly from where Chesa had left her phone in the front of house.

Chesa was arranging edible flowers on top of the cake, pressing red pansies into the pale purple icing. When she finished the cake, she carried it over to the fridge and swapped it for white one, which Reyna assumed was coconut.

"Stetson came by the shop the other day," Chesa said casually. It was her old childhood nickname for Leander, that he'd never been able to shake, since she used to think he looked like a young Bruce Boxleitner in their favorite 80s tv show. Reyna held the stamp for a beat longer than normal against the cup, to make sure she didn't smear it.

"Did he?" Reyna asked calmly, when what she wanted to say was *interesting, he's barely talked to me except to say that he wants to run his union presentation by me, and given me a sweet pep talk when I asked, but that was me calling him, so it doesn't count.*

"He did," Chesa said, switching to yellow pansies for the white cake. "He seemed okay."

Reyna nodded, stamping the next few cups in rapid succession.

Chesa cleared her throat. "So are you gonna tell me what happened? Or do I need to ask him?"

Reyna pursed her lips. "Nothing happened."

It was mostly true.

Except he'd woken up in a hospital bed and looked at her like he hadn't ever, and she didn't know what to do with that. He threw a surgeon into a wall, and then he had barely spoken to her since.

"Very believable," Chesa said.

"He had a very big medical situation," Reyna appeased her.

"But you're helping him with the union thing, right?" Chesa persisted. "So maybe things are normal, and he just needed a few days."

"Yeah," Reyna said, distractedly.

Chesa sighed, and it was a loud sigh.

"What is it?" Reyna asked to the next cup she was stamping.

Another sigh from Chesa.

"You worry too much," Chesa said, walking the coconut cake back to the fridge. "About him, about me—just let it go, every now and then, you know? It might actually work out."

Reyna closed her eyes, grateful her sister's back was to her as she rooted around in the fridge.

Reyna didn't worry because it was fun.

She didn't *like* that this was who she was, that she was controlling and decisive and sometimes too harsh with both. But, damn it, someone had to be. Someone had to hold everything together so that everyone else could let it go. That'd been her job as long as she could remember, and she was good at it.

Even if it did make her feel like a killjoy when Chesa said things like that.

Chesa returned with a plate with a couple slices of bibingka in one hand, and a second coconut cake in her other.

"These didn't sell," she said, sliding the bibingka plate down the counter to Reyna. "People got confused that they weren't lemon bars."

It wasn't quite an apology, but it was close.

Normally Reyna would grab the small cakes with her bare hands, but being mindful of the fact that she probably shouldn't get sticky rice-and-coconut-goodness over the coffee cups, she grabbed a fork. When the tines sliced through the bibingka, the top of it crackled, and Reyna raised an eyebrow at Chesa, who was pretending not to watch.

"Did you crème brûlée a batch of bibingka?" Reyna asked, and Chesa shrugged.

"I don't think that's a verb," Chesa said casually, like she wasn't holding her breath while Reyna brought the fork to her mouth. "I just put some raw sugar on top so it would kind of caramelize in the oven."

It was delicious.

It tasted like childhood and memories, not too sweet, with the sugar on top adding an extra crunch.

"It's really good, Ches," Reyna said, around a mouthful, and Chesa lifted a shoulder bashfully, a small smile on her face as she drizzled chocolate and caramel over the top of the coconut cake.

Reyna licked her lips, setting the fork down as she continued her stamping.

As a woman in STEM, Reyna was used to kicking down doors and demanding her flowers, and she sometimes forgot that her sister was softer. For her boldness and stubbornness in starting her own business, she was also someone who deeply longed for validation, which Reyna knew she didn't provide enough.

Reyna made progress through her stack of cups, making a point to hum contentedly with every bite she took of the bibingka, and Chesa seemed quietly pleased when Reyna asked if she could wrap up the rest to take home.

Reyna watched her sister from the corner of her eye.

Chesa was focused on the cake in front of her, carefully arranging almonds on the chocolate and caramel drizzles. She was biting her lower lip in concentration, adjusting the almonds with a small pair of tweezers, and Reyna smiled to herself.

This was why she worried *too much*.

So Chesa could have her dreams, so she could be stressed about the way toasted almonds looked on top of caramel and chocolate, not her mortgage payment. So her not-so-business-savvy sister didn't have to be business savvy, and could sell the things that brought her joy, brought the neighborhood joy. So Chesa could be broke but happy, content in her creativity, knowing Reyna might worry too much, but someone was.

In her back pocket, her phone vibrated.

Shaking herself out of her malaise, Reyna fished it out, seeing Leander's name on the screen and checking the time, grimacing when she realized she was late.

"I gotta get back," Reyna said, texting Leander that she was on her way.

"Tell Stetson hi," Chesa said to the cake, sounding amused.

Reyna looked at her sharply. "How'd you know it was Leander?"

Chesa glanced up, a fond expression in her eyes.

"He's the only text you answer when you're with me, Ate," she said. "One of these days, you'll realize that's true, whether you want it to be or not."

"You're the only two that get through my *Do Not Disturb* settings," Reyna protested, and Chesa huffed.

"Whatever. There's some day-old pastries in a bag by the door, if you want to share any with him."

Reyna grabbed them, and left her stamped cups in a stack by the register. The door chimed over her head as she walked out, and Reyna paused outside. Standing on the sidewalk and turning back to look at the Jade Vine. The shop was an old house, nestled amongst the crisp fall foliage of the street, looking like a postcard.

She couldn't shake the image of her sister's quiet contentment out of her head.

Reyna sighed, reaching for her phone, and the mobile app for her bank. She paused over her accounts, and thought wryly that Chesa really didn't know the first thing about how overbearing she could be.

It was more money than she'd ever had in one place.

Sitting there in her account, just asking her if she loved her sister more than she wanted a house. And Reyna thought of unsold bibingka, of the overproofed croissants in the brown bag in her arm, of Chesa's determination to believe and create, and trust in the universe to catch her, and Reyna thought that in that moment, maybe she was the universe's pointer finger.

She initiated the transfer.

Reyna pulled in a deep breath, waiting for the notification to pop up, tell her that a banker would be in touch in a few days to confirm. She exhaled, tipped her head back to look up at the Jade Vine one more time.

This was the right thing to do.

It'd be her sister's, Chesa wouldn't have to worry, *Reyna* wouldn't have to worry...it'd be fine. She turned sharply, jogging over to her car and peeling out of the parking lot.

When she pulled up to the apartment, Leander was sitting on her stoop.

She waved as she pulled into her parking spot, and he waved back, recognizing her car. Looking in her rearview mirror as she gathered her things, Reyna watched his smile fade. He was shaking his shoulders loose; he looked nervous, she realized, which made Reyna nervous.

"Hey," she smiled widely as she got out of the car. "I know public speaking isn't your thing, but we're going to crush this, okay? Don't worry."

Leander nodded, pushing himself off the stoop.

He looked how he always did, like he never presumed anyone would notice him, an oversight that Reyna took consistent advantage of. He was wearing dark brown corduroy pants and a thin sweater that was nearly the same color, and Reyna wondered offhandedly if LL Bean knew they could run a whole ad campaign around her best friend. His fair complexion and soft eyes didn't so much give All-American quarterback, but he'd pass for bashful boy next door any day.

Reyna was proof positive that that look had its own charm.

As Reyna got closer, she tossed Chesa's brown paper bag at him. "Chesa says hi."

Leander caught it easily, a small smile pulling at his lips as he registered it.

"Hi, Chesa," he said, dutifully. "Um...so I actually want to talk about something other than the board meeting, if that's okay?"

"Sure," Reyna keyed into the apartment and ducking under Leander's arm when he held the door open for her. She tried to keep her voice casual, but between his nerves and the topic change, she was starting to get anxious too. "Everything okay? Should I make tea?"

She was much more of a coffee person herself, but Leander always calmed down with tea, so she kept some on hand.

"If you're having some," Leander said politely, setting Chesa's bag down by the table before folding himself into a chair.

Reyna kept her posture neutral as she stepped around him into the kitchen. She flipped on the kettle and grabbed two mugs from the shelf, as well as a sachet of chamomile. She got her French press out, and measured coffee grounds while she waited for Leander to explain what was going on.

"How's that going, by the way?" Leander asked from behind her, and Reyna was confused until she turned and saw him pointing to the open manila folder on her table.

"It's not really," Reyna said, trying to keep her tone light. This was the right move; she really did think that. She would figure out what she needed to do, and she could do that better, knowing Chesa was taken care of.

The kettle beeped and Reyna sloshed near-boiling water into Leander's mug and her French press. She carried his mug over to the table, pulling out a jar of honey she kept for the same reason she kept chamomile, and setting both in front of Leander.

"Thanks," he reached for both. "You're sure about that? I know a house has been—"

"Did you have something you wanted to talk about?" Reyna interrupted, not wanting to have the home discussion right now. Maybe later, once she'd figured out what she was going to do. She went back for her French press, glancing back at the table at Leander.

Leander had been tall since high school, when everyone else evened out and he kept growing. Since Reyna wasn't short herself, she often forgot, but seeing his lanky body crammed into her kitchen chairs reminded her.

Reyna turned back to the counter, frowning at the direction of her thoughts. She'd buried her crush long ago. Just because he'd acted protective *once*, and looked nervous in a way that had all her savior instincts acting up, didn't mean she had any business resurrecting it.

She spooned a dollop of sweetened condensed milk into a mug for herself while she waited for the French press to brew, carrying both mug and press over to the table. The kitchen was silent while Reyna waited for Leander to share what was on his mind, the only sounds the gentle clanging of his spoons stirring honey into his tea.

Leander crossed his ankle over his knee and then lowered his foot to the ground again. He reached for the tea, and then set it back to the table when he realized it was still too hot to drink. He rubbed his palms against the tops of his thighs and Reyna was beginning to wonder if he was going to get it out.

"So do you need a kidney?" she asked, and Leander blinked, then shook his head, a smile pulling at the corner of his mouth.

"Uh, no," he said, and he reached for the tea again. Rather than lift it, he wrapped his hand around the mug, his fingers hovering over the perimeter, accepting the warmth but not burning from the hot ceramic. He still looked distracted, like he was wading through the correct way to voice his thoughts and Reyna wished he could just get them out.

"That's good," Reyna said idly, "because I'm pretty sure you have to be the same blood type... Although do you even have a blood type anymore? Is there a secret fifth werewolf blood type? Or do you have—"

"Rey, okay," Leander laughed, leaning back in his chair and crossing his arms across his chest. "I need a favor."

"Not a kidney?" Reyna clarified, relieved he was talking.

"Not a kidney," Leander echoed. "Although, that'd probably be easier...I talked to Whit."

"That's something," she encouraged.

He smiled, barely, and then it was gone a moment later. "So the biggest news is I'm not, like, full werewolf. I can't turn anyone, and I don't have any of the alpha/beta stuff that people who're born into it do."

"That's less complicated," Reyna said, not wanting to put adjectives like *good* or *bad* on something that was so nuanced.

Leander hummed. "Yeah. Uh, yeah, for sure."

He was staring at his mug like it held the secrets of the universe rather than a sachet of chamomile tea.

Reyna could see a tenseness in his jaw, a tick where he was clenching it tightly. She thought of how when he'd first woken up in the hospital, she'd held his hand, and how he'd held her right back, and she wondered if that would help now. She poured her coffee, distracting herself with the artificial pumpkin fragrance that filled the kitchen, before she was tempted to reach for him and find out.

Leander raked a hand through his hair and he stood up. Her kitchen wasn't big enough for him to effectively pace but he gave it his best shot.

"This is the biggest favor I've ever asked of you," he said to her back wall. "And you can tell me to fuck off. I mean it, Rey; it's a weird thing to ask and the last thing I want to do is make you feel like you have to, so I need to know that if you're freaking out, you'll tell me, and I'll literally never bring it up again."

He was rambling.

And Leander wasn't a proficient public speaker, so he sometimes did seem to burst with words and energy, but he normally erred on the side of saying too little rather than too much. This was pure nerves talking.

Reyna reminded herself that they weren't the same blood type, and she wasn't a major organ donor match, and even if she was, that would've been a more formal conversation. This—in the kitchen, over honey and chamomile—felt more like a breakup than a favor.

"Okay," Reyna said, aiming for encouraging, but landing on confused.

Leander crossed the room quickly, sitting back in the chair across from her. He leaned forward and pushed his glasses up his nose; behind them, his eyes were slightly wide, but focused on her.

"You can say no," he repeated, earnestness written across his face and Reyna appreciated his candor, but it was halfway to giving her a panic attack.

"You have to ask me for me to say no," she said, and he let out a long breath, pushing back in the chair. He looked at her from his seat, expression inscrutable, and then he closed his eyes.

"I'm going to go into a rut," he said, finally, and Reyna's mind fully stalled.

Six

O ut of everything she'd expected to hear him say, that hadn't been it.

Reyna knew, in an extremely agnostic way, that this was something people who turned had to deal with. Just like any other natural cycle, only this one actually did rely on the moon. She realized that Leander had launched into a verbose explanation, another clear tell of his nerves, and she felt like she was registering his words a full minute after he'd said them.

"It's probably going to be kickstarted by the full moon next Saturday," Leander was saying. "I get time off of work, and there's apps to find people, or pills you can take...it's supposed to be really intense though."

Reyna was a horrible person.

A horrible, selfish person, because her best friend was saying he was going to have this intimidating, overwhelming experience, and all she was thinking is *that's hot*.

It wasn't even the taboo of it all—Reyna had had friends in college who'd signed up for the apps Leander was talking about, something of a kink for them— but for her, it was Leander specifically. The idea of her meek, mild-mannered friend, being so honest and overwhelmed by what he needed, being overcome by something that wasn't being helpful, having to confront his base *wants* alongside his base *needs*, that was a frankly staggering thought.

She wondered why he was telling her this.

For a moment, she considered that it might have something to do with the way he'd looked at her when he first woke up, or the way he'd kept his body between her and Whit. But then reality crashed back in, and she remembered that that was just some primal reaction he was having, and he'd gotten over it in the time since then, so he probably just wanted her to get his mail or something.

She cleared her throat. "So, what, do you want me to house sit?"

Leander reached for the mug again, his fingers curling around the outside of it. He was steadying himself, and when his eyes met hers again, there was something deeply vulnerable in them.

"I'm asking if you'd help me through it," he said.

Reyna was certain she'd misheard him.

Because if she hadn't, her best friend was sitting at her kitchen table, asking her to have borderline feral sex for a weekend.

"Logistics," Reyna managed to demand, her mouth dry, needing more details.

"Right," Leander said, and she noticed his cheeks were flushed slightly. "It should only be for a couple days, three, tops. I don't really want to be around people, so I was thinking of going out to Gran's, on Great Cranberry Island. I know it's a lot to ask, and you'd have to clear it with work."

"I have PTO," Reyna said, her mind clinging to the semantics of this rather than any of the roiling emotions she was feeling. She took a sip of her coffee, not even tasting the pumpkin spice. "What would you need from me?"

Leander's cheeks got redder, and he let go of the mug to rub at the back of his neck. "Uh. So it's gonna be an intense few days, and I need—"

"Not that part," Reyna cut him off. They were adults, and he was a healthcare professional; it shouldn't be weird to sit here and talk about something perfectly natural. Biological, even. And yet...

Leander's jaw was tight; she could see his teeth clenching every few seconds. She wondered if his canines were out, like they'd been at the hospital, and the thought made her notice the other changes in him. Between the base of his throat at the collar of the sweater was a teasing shock of hair, almost translucent blond, that Reyna knew hadn't been as prominent before. It wasn't like he'd bulked up overnight, but there was something like a hum of tension running under his skin. She could see it, an almost skittishness that kept him taut, his arms and chest filling out the thin sweater like he'd just carried in cords of firewood or something.

And now Reyna could add *lumberjack* to the list of fantasies she didn't know she was carrying, right next to *rutting frenzy*.

She licked her lips, pulling herself from that useless train of thought.

"What if I'm bad at it?" she asked, wincing at how insecure she sounded. "Not *that*, but we both know I'm not the caretaker. What if you need something that I can't—"

"No," Leander interrupted her, and his throat worked as he swallowed, shaking his head. "No, it's not about needing another nurse, or doing the right thing, it's...it just can't be someone else."

Reyna didn't know how to take that.

"But I can still say no?" she asked, curious his response.

"Absolutely," Leander said. "And if you do, it'd be great if we could conveniently forget this conversation happened, but yeah. You don't have to."

She did.

Fixing problems was who she was, the only thing she was, and his telling her she didn't have to only made her more convinced she needed to help him.

"I'll call in sick," Reyna heard herself say. "It's better than scheduling last minute PTO, and this way we'll go whenever you need."

It sounded kind.

It sounded noble and correct, and what good friends would do, and Reyna couldn't shake that it felt like a half-truth. Because as much as she found herself wanting to ensure Leander was taken care of, she found herself oddly anticipating being the one to be there to do it.

Oblivious to her conflict, Leander's lashes fluttered as he closed his eyes, relief washing across his face.

"Okay," Leander said, his face flaming but his voice steady. "We should talk about limits and stuff."

Reyna wasn't sure she agreed.

It was important, but it also felt very real, very much like something they'd do if this was just a weekend away, and something they'd prepare for. Reyna fiddled with her coffee cup, feeling Leander's eyes intent on her, but refusing to look at him.

"I trust you," she said honestly, "I don't think you'll do anything I don't...want."

The word hung suspended between them, the idea of *want* heavy in the air. Reyna frowned to herself, wondering why it felt so weighted. Did she want this? Was that wrong?

Leander cleared his throat. "I think we should—"

"Lee," Reyna interrupted, "it's a medical thing. You need what you need, and I—"

Leander shook his head, stubbornly. "Knowing you'd forgive me for anything doesn't mean I want to ignore the possibility that I could hurt you. If we're gonna do this, I need to know what I can and can't do to you, so if I get carried away, it's inside the parameters that you set."

Reyna's mouth felt dry.

The idea of Leander getting 'carried away', but still clinging to boundaries she'd made, was dizzying. It made her feel a plethora of contradictory emotions, like an epiphany that lust and respect, frenzy and care, could coexist, just because Leander willed them too.

She didn't like this feeling.

Most feelings, if she was honest, but especially the ones that she couldn't turn into productivity, into an output that matched her impression of herself. Rather than delve into that, Reyna lifted her chin, in a challenge.

"I'm not into blindfolds or bondage," she said, "but if you held me down, just hands or body weight, I'd probably be into it."

Leander looked at her for a long moment, his eyes sparkling and Reyna wondered if that was the night vision Whit had mentioned, or just that he knew exactly what she was doing—throwing her kinks at him to see if he'd back down from.

She should've known he wouldn't.

"Good to know," he said, his voice softer. "I have something of an oral fixation."

Reyna blinked at him.

"Giving or receiving?" she asked.

Leander lifted a shoulder. "Both, I guess."

Both?? He guessed?? Reyna felt a heat spread across her chest, and she tried not to spiral. Had Leander's voice always been this deep? Was she going insane?

"I'm on birth control," she said, thinking back to the nebulous cliches around ruts and heats that she knew, trying to get the upper-hand back, "so coming in me is on the table."

Leander's eyes darkened, and now there was definitely a silver glow in the blue of them, but he didn't back down.

"I have a praise kink," he returned.

Reyna was sure something had broken in her apartment, because it was quite warm in the normally drafty.

It made sense, if she thought about it. Leander was the kind of person who'd do anything to help anyone, but would feel in the back of his mind that it wasn't enough or that people didn't notice.

"I don't do degradation," she returned, "or anal."

Leander nodded, a smile quirking the corner of his lips. "In this case, I imagine anal would contradict the whole knocking up/breeding thing."

Reyna made herself take another sip of coffee.

"Dirty talk is good," she said, hoping Leander would ignore the breathlessness in her voice, the way she was ignoring the way his hands were clenched on his knees. "And, just in general, I like hearing my partner. You don't have to sound like porn, or even any type of way, but I do want to hear how you're feeling."

"Consensual non-consent isn't my favorite," Leander said, "I'd rather no mean no."

Reyna nodded. "Although, free use is kind of hot."

Leander sat back, his lips thinning as he pressed them together.

"How do you mean?" he asked, voice level.

"Like," Reyna shrugged, tucking her hair behind her ear, "if you woke me up with oral or something, I wouldn't be mad."

"Good to know," Leander rasped, as he grabbed for his tea again.

He gulped down half of his mug, and Reyna tried not to smirk. This was...fun. It was fun to talk about this stuff with Leander, learn that the things she was into weren't turnoffs for him, and see what made him squirm. She tried not to think too hard about how compatible they seemed, or if that had meaning beyond the surface.

Leander set the mug down, playing with the handle again.

"I'm nervous about knotting," he admitted.

Reyna felt some of her former confidence ebb as he mentioned it. It wasn't a general kink of hers, and wasn't a part of her cursory *my best friend is a werewolf; what does that even mean??* googling.

"I'm not sure I super understand it," she said.

"Yeah, that's fair," Leander said, and he rubbed at the back of his neck. "It's essentially a benign edema—blood flow is temporarily increased not only to the phallus, but also pools at the base of it; at orgasm, neuromuscular tension is released through ejaculation *and* the knot swelling. If inside a reproductive tract, the rigidity of the knot will stopper the exit, serving as a barrier for sperm cells and seminal plasma after copulation. I get pretty sensitive after I come, and it seems like a lot."

Reyna blinked as she transitioned from processing Leander's hyper-technical explanation to his confession. He said it so simply, so easily, and Reyna sipped her coffee rather than responding. She would see it, she realized, would be with him *after*, and it would be a whole weekend of that. He looked uncomfortable and Reyna almost reached for his hand, wanting to comfort him, but knew that would be too much. Would tip them over the edge from playful sharing into something too close to real.

The kitchen was quiet as they sat with their mugs, dozens of unspoken things hanging between them.

"I like cockwarming," Reyna said, eventually. "I'll be gentle."

Leander smiled, like an instinct, and then he pulled in a sharp breath. He pushed his glasses up his nose before he looked at her. Reyna wanted to look away, but made herself hold still, be the stable and steady thing that Leander wanted her to be.

"Thank you," he said quietly, and Reyna nodded.

"That's what friends are for, yeah?" she said.

Something crossed across Leander's face, something she didn't recognize. He started to say something and then stopped himself, his tongue darting out to wet his lips. Then he cleared his throat and lifted his mug, a sip of tea fogging his glasses, before he set his mug down, empty.

"I should probably head out," he said, and he was on his feet before Reyna could say otherwise. She followed him to the door, and they both hesitated when his hand closed on the doorknob. For an insane moment, Reyna thought he might hug her.

She wasn't sure what that would mean, or why she wanted it so badly, or how nice it would be to be held, as they both simmered with thoughts of the upcoming weekend.

It'd be a couple of days on the island that held some of her happiest childhood memories, with a friend who made her flustered from being in the same kitchen. It'd be closer than Reyna had been to another person in several months, and certainly closer than she'd been to him, ever.

But Leander didn't reach for her.

He cleared his throat, tossed a nervous smile over his shoulder and let himself out, crossing to his car quickly. He folded himself into the car, and Reyna closed the door as he started it, her teeth gnawing at her lower lip.

She'd wanted him to hold her.

She'd wanted Leander's arms around her, an assurance for something neither of them had asked for, and she didn't know what to do with that.

Reyna traced her steps through the apartment to the kitchen, where she saw Leander's folder—the union presentation points that had been the whole reason for which he'd come over—sitting unopened on her kitchen table, left behind in favor of Leander's rapid retreat.

Seven

It was evening after an exceptionally warm fall day, and the cove was crowded enough that Daphne and Reyna stopped fighting for waves.

They were out past the breaks, bobbing on their surfboards and watching seasonal surfers drop in as the sun dipped behind the skyline.

"I heard about Leander," Daphne said, without reproach.

Reyna looked over at her friend, relieved to see sympathy in her expression, rather than resentment for not being told. Daphne was a music therapist at the hospital, and Reyna was never sure what was gossip and what was a violation of HR policies when her friends were each others' coworkers.

"It's complicated with people we both know," Reyna admitted, and Daphne nodded, understanding.

"How's he taking it?"

Reyna shifted on her board, pulling her legs out of the water to sit cross-legged on the board. The wind felt chilling against the Lycra of her suit, but she didn't mind so much, when the sun was this warm.

"Good, I think," Reyna said, trying not to think too hard about the night before. The kitchen had been quiet, and then Leander had gone home, and that had been that. "The full moon is next weekend...he asked for me to be there."

Daphne's jaw dropped. "You're helping him through his rut?"

"Don't say it like that," Reyna insisted, the wind mysteriously no longer feeing so cold.

Daphne shifted from straddling the board to facing Reyna, her pale legs dangling in the water, all the more noticeable as she was the only one out of the flock to not be in a wetsuit.

"I've never pushed you for the history there," Daphne said carefully. "I know you guys are close, but that kind of feels like a lot."

"It does," Reyna sighed. "But I can't imagine telling him I can't help, or asking him to find someone else."

Daphne raised an eyebrow. "You want it to be you?"

Reyna frowned, trying to parse through her feelings. "That's a door I haven't opened since high school."

Daphne's feet spun in small circles, making gentle whirlpools with her ankles. "Because it's done, or because you don't like what's behind it?"

The sun slipped behind the treeline, and the cove turned a gentle blue.

The surfers still at the breaks looked at each other, acknowledging they all only had so much time before they'd need to head in, and Reyna wrapped the sounds of the sea around her before she started speaking.

"I never dated anybody in high school," Reyna started, haltingly. "I had an unrequited crush on my best friend, and when we went off to college without anything happening, I realized it wasn't going to happen. I had all my firsts at college, nothing too serious. I was young, I was awed by a world past Maine, and there was a lot of it to see. Then graduation hit, and it seemed like suddenly everyone else had this secret agenda to get married, pop out kids, get coupled off and shift into a different phase of life. I kept waiting to feel jealous, or wish it was me, but I was mostly just perplexed by the way my entire friend group coupled off and shifted. At that point, nothing was keeping me in Mass, so I came back to Maine."

"Where you made some cool adult friends," Daphne teased, and Reyna grinned.

"I made some *much* cooler adult friends," Reyna agreed, and Daphne seemed pleased, "once I made it back to Port Cadie. But I had a couple years in Portland, before I met you and Niamh, and there was this guy. Tyler. We hit it off so quickly; he was great. He traveled a lot for work, but I was busy climbing at my job too, and it was like I finally got why everyone had settled down so quickly after college. I fell so hard for him. We planned the most perfect life together: an apartment on the eastern prom, a handthrown flatware set from classes he was taking at a pottery shop, ocean trips for him to kayak and me to surf..."

Reyna pulled in a deep breath, the sunless air feeling chilled again. "I went out one night, when he was away at a conference, but he wasn't away at a conference. He was at dinner, with this beautiful woman with a rock the size of Rhode Island on her left ring finger."

"Reyna," Daphne said quietly, and Reyna lifted a shoulder.

"I know being cheated on fucks you up; I can't imagine. But being the one he cheated *with*...it was like he made me into a villain and I hadn't even known it was happening. Tyler managed to make me both not enough *and* less than, and—" Reyna broke off, her jaw clenching.

It was years ago, and the sting had blunted, but it still hurt.

"I never saw him again. I went home, blocked his number, and just moved on. He sent me a letter though, something I knew better than to open, and still did. He told me that he really did love me, and he hadn't known how to give me up, even when he knew it couldn't last," Reyna shook her head, looking over the calming sea. "I remember wishing he'd said it was all a lie, because saying it was real...it meant that every promise, every feeling, was real, but not enough to respect me, or respect her, of make the fantasy the reality."

Daphne hummed understandingly. "So that's why you'd been relationship shy since I've known you."

Reyna nodded. "That, plus every college relationship that fizzled, that I'd never wanted more from, but also they'd never pushed for more, made me realize that there's a certain type of man to whom I'm something he can have, that his wife doesn't have to know about."

A swell pushed their boards together, and Daphne propped a foot on the nose of Reyna's board to steady both of them.

"I know Leander's not like that," Reyna said, after a moment. "But that doesn't mean I'm ready to trust how things feel in a moment, or that what he feels to be true enough isn't something that changes in light of forever."

Daphne's body shifted as another wave rolled their boards, and she looked out over the cove. A swell carried red leaves from the shore, the wind and tide pulling autumn into the sea. Daphne's pale shoulders pressed back, and she smiled gently as she turned back to Reyna. "Sounds like you're less afraid of him wanting you, than him wanting you temporarily."

Reyna's mouth opened, but words came out of it. That was what she'd admitted, she realized, but she didn't like how it sounded out loud. With fall leaves on lapping waves, it sounded honest, it sounded like something vulnerable.

"Maybe," Reyna admitted.

A couple more surfers headed in, and the waves seemed bigger as there were less boards crowding them. The lights in the parking lot switched on, barely casting light through the lingering twilight, but a reminder that there was a timer.

Daphne released Reyna's board, her feet circling again.

"You know, my dad's human," Daphne said. "I wasn't certain I was a siren until a girl I had a crush on in high school responded to my thrall."

When Reyna looked over at her, Daphne was frowning at the whirlpools in the water.

"She was the most beautiful person I've ever met, but she was straight. I knew she was straight, and I was never going to do anything about it, but one day she was talking to a group of girls in the hallway, and I was watching her thinking *gods, I wish she would just look at me*, and she did. She stopped mid-sentence, walked over to me and told me that she actually didn't want to go to prom with her boyfriend and that we should go together."

Daphne's legs stilled, and she watched the ripples fade. "Thankfully, she said it too quietly for anyone other than me to hear, and I realized what was happening soon enough to stop it. I started training that weekend, and thankfully, by the time you and Niamh rolled around, I had enough of a handle on my thrall to trust that you guys were around because I wanted you to be, and not because I willed it. I haven't...falling in love is hard enough without wondering if someone actually wants to be there."

Reyna unfolded her legs, reaching across the space between them to rub Daphne's knee.

Daphne looked up at her, a sad smile on her face.

"I don't have a rut, or a heat, I guess, so I don't know exactly what Leander's going through," Daphne said. "But I know what it is to exist in a human world, and be terribly mindful of the fact that you possess a strength that they don't. It makes you delicate, it makes you doubt yourself, it makes you rely on the humans around you to be so clear about what they need."

Reyna nodded, thinking of the times Niamh and Daphne held themselves back while they surfed or swam with her, keeping her safe. She hadn't thought about the emotional side of it, or how that could relate to Lee.

Daphne's hand covered hers, squeezing their fingers together as the waves pulled their boards apart again.

"Come on," Daphne said, letting go of her hand and lifting her legs to straddle her board. "Let's go fight a Bostonian for a wave, yeah?"

Reyna smiled, and Daphne wrinkled her nose at her, leaning forward on the board to paddle up to the breaks. They didn't have much time left, but they were the last ones in, riding sea foam towards shore as the sea turned an inky black.

Reyna's hair soaked through the sweatshirt she'd brought to change into, and she was looking forward to a hot shower when she got home; as she turned into the lot by her apartment, she was surprised to see Lee on her stoop again.

"Hey," she called, once the car was parked, pulling the surfboard off the roof. "Everything okay?"

"Yeah, pretty much." Leander jogged over, and she felt the weight of the board lighten as he took it from her.

"Thanks," Reyna mumbled, as he shouldered the board.

"No problem," Leander said, shifting it under his arm. He gestured for her to walk ahead of him, their feet crunching on brown leaves in the walkway. Reyna let them in to the apartment and Leander hefted the board onto the hooks on the entryway wall. She could feel his eyes on her as she walked through the apartment, hanging her wetsuit in the shower so it could dry overnight, trying to remember if she'd forgotten something, or if there was a reason why he was here.

"How'd the SPS group go?" she called, back through the apartment. "That was today, right?"

"Yeah, at the Selenian congregational hall," Leander said, and Reyna figured that made sense. Port Cadie had a fair amount of churches and temples, for a pantheon of gods who predated the Puritans, but neither Leander nor Reyna spent much time in any houses of worship.

From his voice, it sounded like Leander hadn't moved from the entryway, and Reyna leaned back into the hallway to check. He was standing still, staring at her picture wall. It was cheaper than wallpaper, just hundreds of pictures printed at a local pharmacy, held in place by a weaponizable amount of push pins that would be hell to fill in whenever she did move out. There were pictures of her and Chesa at the Grand Canyon, her and the girls surfing, a Turkey Trot down in Boston, and many more memories from over the years.

Reyna walked back to the entryway, and Leander lifted a hand to point at one of the pictures.

"I don't remember this one," Leander said.

Reyna smiled at the picture of two preteens, swallowed in puffy coats, holding whoopie pies and grinning widely through a sugar high at the camera.

"Maine Maple Sunday," she supplied, pointing at the stacked barrels behind them in the picture. "I don't remember where it was, somewhere up North, and we drove for like three hours to get there, because your mom thought that being closer to Canada would be a more authentic sugar shack experience. We both had too much sugar and got horribly carsick on the drive back."

Leander laughed quietly beside her, pointing to another one. "Cumberland County Fair?"

Chesa was maybe six years old, clutching a blue ribbon she'd won for a painting, and she was proudly perched on Reyna and Leander's shoulders.

Reyna nodded. "She was devastated a couple years later, when she found out that every kid who submitted through their school got a ribbon."

"I mean, at least she got blue," Leander said loyally. "I only ever got yellow for my 'art', which was an actual consolation prize."

"She got blue every year," Reyna said, remembering when Chesa had switched from finger painting to water color, to oil pastels. Her portfolio submissions for university had been stunning, and yet Chesa always wondered if they were participation trophies.

"Remember this one?" Leander asked, pointing at a blurry indoors picture. It was a class photo of a lower school field trip to the New England Aquarium, thirty kids crammed in a tiny exhibition hall, all trying and failing to look excited about the fact that the shark's they'd been promised were under four feet long.

"They plied us back onto the bus with Cool Dogs," Reyna smiled, and Leander chuckled.

"What's this one?" he asked, and Reyna's smile dimmed as she looked at the picture he was pointing at. It was a selfie she'd taken in Times Square; the lights of New York City were bright around her, so late at night, and her face was tipped back towards the neon.

"That was after Tyler," Reyna said simply.

She hadn't told Leander everything about that relationship, but he did know that after she'd found out about his wife, she'd driven to the airport and gotten on the first direct flight she could. It got her to New York some fifty minutes later, and to Times Square another hour after that—relishing being anonymous, one of millions, someone whose mistakes and misunderstandings weren't alone.

Now, shoulder to shoulder in her hallway, Reyna looked sideways at Leander. The entryway light overhead put a glare on his glasses, and she couldn't see his eyes, but his shoulders were tight; Reyna leaned against the wall, tipping her head against it.

"What happened at the group, Lee?" she asked.

Leander's chin dipped, an acknowledgment that he'd heard, and she watched his shoulders lift as he drew in a deep breath.

"The group was good. It's actually one of the groups PCMC supports, which was cool, to get to see what happens with some of those grants. It was a lot, though. Just...I don't know, with Whit, he really was highlighting what happens in the immediate future. But at SPS, there's teenagers who're prepping for the rest of their lives as shifters, and then there's folks who've been a part of it for decades, and it really just sunk in that it's forever. It's not just the weekend."

Reyna shifted, the words paralleling her conversation with Daphne too closely for her comfort.

Now was obviously not the time to bridge that gap, but it was interesting that they were both considering the impact the next week and change would have over their lives. Leander pulled his glasses off his face, rubbing roughly at the lenses with the hem of his tshirt before shoving them back on his face. Reyna wasn't sure what to say, but she imagined Leander was here because he wanted company, not because of what she'd say.

"Come here," Reyna said, and Leander stepped into her arms. Her hands wound around his neck, and she felt his close around her back, and she turned her cheek into his shoulder as his chin notched on top of her head. She felt him settle into it, his shoulders drooping as he relaxed, and his chin growing heavier.

"You smell pretty," he mumbled, and Reyna would've rolled her eyes if he was looking at her. She smelled like the ocean, and she really should wash it off.

"Eau de Atlantic," she joked, rewarded by a halfhearted laugh from Leander. "You're gonna figure it out. All the SPS stuff, the union stuff—hell, maybe there's an overlap there—and the changes, you'll get it. You're new to it, and it's okay that it's taking a minute."

She felt Leander's chin shift again, and she wondered if he was looking back at the wall, and if he was, which pictures he saw. She knew her favorites, and she wondered if he had any. His thumb was brushing up her back, a movement small enough that she wasn't sure he was aware he was doing it. It was comforting, and Reyna knew the point of this hadn't been to comfort *her*, but it felt nice.

He felt nice.

It then occurred to her that this was a longer hug than they'd shared in recent memory, so she should probably let him go.

Reyna loosened her arms, and stepped back, looking up at Lee. He looked more grounded, less uncertain, and she liked that look on him.

"I should probably rinse off," she said, and Leander nodded, stepping back. "I'll see you next week, okay?"

"Yep," he said, and he rubbed at the back of his neck. "Thanks for…thanks."

"Anytime," Reyna said, and they both knew she meant it.

Leander let himself out, and Reyna leaned back against the picture wall, hearing his footfall echo down the steps. She wet her lips, thinking of what Daphne had said earlier: *sounds like you're less afraid of him wanting you, than him wanting you temporarily.* She heard the car start up, and she walked to the bathroom, moving her wetsuit to the sink while she ran a shower, washing the sea off her skin.

Eight

The Psych Eval had gone well enough, and Leander had made it through most of the week without incident, but a hospital was possibly the worst place to have an enhanced sense of smell.

Leander was relieved to be back, even if it was in a provisional capacity, but he could almost understand why Whit walked around looking like he was a minor inconvenience away from major aggravation.

Everything was more intense.

Leander could smell when the food in the cafeteria was just on this side of spoiling, he could smell when catheters were being changed, he could smell when someone had mopped the floor of the ER two halls over.

It was more than physical scent, and that was what was most disconcerting.

It was like people's emotions were suddenly tangible to him as well.

Not in a precognitive way, but if a child was hyperventilating, Leander could tell if they were in pain, overwhelmed, missed their parents, and so on.

Even now, he could feel how nervous Esther was, mixed with the expensive colognes the Board members wore, and the stale coffee in stainless steel carafes at the end of the table.

"We understand your position, son," said the chairman, who was neither understanding nor Leander's father, "but you have to understand ours. It's all well and good for the folks down in Portland to want to have a different RN-to-patient ratio, but it's just not in our numbers."

The board members around the tabled nodded in agreement, adjusting their cuff links, as they looked at him impassively.

"Not in your numbers," Esther repeated, and she shared a look with Leander.

Leander shrugged meekly, at a loss for how to explain this a group of people whose wristwatches cost more money than Leander made in a year.

He was in this room for moral support, to put whatever privilege he had behind leaders who were as good at voicing their thoughts as they were for thinking of it. He knew hospitals had budgets for a reason, spending plans and funds and grants that they balanced, but this wasn't spending money they were discussing. It was quality of care, job satisfaction, the integrity of the hospital itself...but Leander wasn't the one to explain it to them.

He had his statistics lined up, numbers and talking points and everything, but when moments like this came, it was like they choked in his throat. Like all he could hear was teacher's shaking their heads at him in sympathy, telling the class not to laugh.

But then he thought of the scan he'd gotten this morning, the pages he'd left in Reyna's kitchen, with sticky notes and arrows and notes scribbled in the columns of his work, and the approach she'd found in his research.

"If we're talking numbers," Leander said, his voice sounding more confident than he felt, "then we should look at job satisfaction. At the high turnover rates for RNs, highly impacted by unsafe staffing conditions and job dissatisfaction, both of which cost this hospital money."

The chairman steepled his fingers.

"Alright," he said begrudgingly, "let's hear that."

"32%," Esther rejoined, "of nurses who leave the profession altogether do so because of burnout. And that's due to the hospital setting and working more than 20 hours per week. The nurses in Portland—"

"They're in Portland," another board member interrupted. "We're not a city like that, we don't have their profit model, so we can't act like we do."

"The bill is going to state senate," Esther persisted. "This isn't just wishful thinking, it's something that's going to become state policy."

"And we'll cross that bridge when we get there—what's this?"

The chairman trailed off as another man nudged his shoulder, showing him a message on his phone. When he finished reading, he looked up, directly at Leander, whose stomach sank. He didn't know what was on the phone, but he could feel relief replacing the unease rolling off the board members.

The chairman tilted his head, indicating that the phone should be passed around, and he closed the presentation folder on the table in front of him.

"I apologize," the man drawled. "No wonder tensions have been high."

Esther frowned, looking between Leander and the chairman.

"I beg your pardon?" she asked, but it didn't deter the momentum of the group; Leander could tell they were grasping any opportunity to close this conversation that didn't bolster their profits.

"We've just been informed of your," a board member paused, trying to decide on a euphemism, "recent medical condition. And with the full moon so close—"

"Why don't we reschedule?" another board member offered, "to a time when everyone's feeling a little bit more levelheaded?"

"We've been trying to get this meeting with you for months," Leander protested. "I assure you, I am—"

"We understand, son," the chairman said again, and Leander clenched his teeth. "First heats are challenging. We'll be in touch to reschedule."

Leander could've corrected him that it was a rut.

He could've stood up and demanded they finish this conversation, hear their peace, but he saw the decision written across the board members' faces, as they filtered out of the conference room.

It wasn't fair.

This was wrong, stupidly wrong, that they were here to convince administration to see reason and change conditions, but instead they'd been dismissed based off of an inconsequential—

"Després!" Esther's voice was sharp, and Leander jolted, looking over at her. They were alone in the conference room, his claws digging into the leather arms of the chair he'd been in, and her expression as she looked at him was steely.

"They're wrong," Esther said. "I know the moon's close, but they're wrong for not listening to us anyways. But if you fly off the handle here, you prove them right. So go do something not-patient-facing, I'll get started on rescheduling this, and we'll brief the rest of the union later, yeah?"

She was right.

Leander knew she was right but it wasn't fair, and it made him mad, and made him more mad that he couldn't do a damn thing about it.

"Take a minute," Esther said, her hand squeezing his shoulder as she stood. "This doesn't end because they didn't listen."

Her sneakers were silent across the carpeted floor as she left Leander in the empty conference room.

Leander took a couple minutes to make sure his claws were rescinded, and then he started stocking.

It was normally the type of work that he had to drag himself to do at the end of a shift, but he picked an empty wing and worked through it methodically. He shuffled between carts and the supply closet and stations, working the rest of his shift in the kind of solitude that kept his indignance from boiling over.

He was midway through the shift when something changed.

Maybe it was his frustration at how the board meeting had gone, maybe it was that Thursday was closer to the full moon than he thought, but *something* changed.

It wasn't just smells that were so intense.

Hi scrubs seemed to be chafing against his skin, and he could practically feel his heartbeat in his ears. Scents somehow intensified, and Leander recoiled as he walked through the halls, trying to figure out what the hell he was supposed to do about the fact that he'd just been dismissed from a meeting for being too close to his rut, but could feel himself turning on the clock.

He needed to call Reyna. Needed to let her know it was starting early, that this was happening, needed...shit. Leander could feel his skin heating, and just the thought of Reyna morphed quickly to something much less work appropriate.

He had a good four hours left on his shift.

Leander tried to pull in a deep breath, but everything was cloying, and the smell of cafeteria food a wing away nearly turned his stomach. He couldn't fall apart on his first turn, not if he wanted the board and the union and the rest of his staff to think he could be trusted, regardless of what he was going through.

Breathing through his mouth, Leander shouldered through hallways until he reached the balcony over the surgery wing, relief coursing through him as he spotted Mateo leaning against the railing.

Mateo had an elbow on the banister, a half-eaten apple in his other hand, looking calmly at the station below him.

The nurse's station in the surgery wing was barely-tethered bedlam.

The floor was a menagerie of charts and files, phone lines and pages, white coats and scarfed granola bars, madness that allowed the O.R.s to be sterile and stationary.

Leander drew in a deep breath, relaxing into the cacophony of sensations, too loud for his mind to process what was happening to him.

"You good?" Mateo asked from beside him. His question was casual but his eyes were intent; Leander was fairly certain Mateo's perception as a friend and his attentiveness as a physiotherapist made a chicken/egg situation, but he appreciated both.

"Full moon's on Saturday," Leander said, keeping his voice down.

Mateo immediately walked the apple to a trash can, throwing it out and wiping his hands on the back of his scrubs. Leander would never have asked Mateo to throw it out, but he appreciated the way the air cleared slightly.

"Someone talked to you about PTO policy extensions, right?" Mateo asked, as he walked back over.

"Yeah," Leander rolled his neck. "I'm taking off tomorrow through Tuesday, just to have a buffer on the end of it, but I wanted to get through this shift."

"For what it's worth, nobody should think less of you if you needed to head out early, " Mateo said carefully, "but, if you say you're good, I trust that."

Leander let out a slow breath, not sure if 'good' was how he'd classify his current state, but appreciating the confidence. "Thanks. What're you doing up here?"

Mateo pointed at a cluster of students in the middle of the station. They were mostly being buffeted around by nurses and doctors who had places to be, eyes wide as they took in the chaos of the station.

"New interns?" Leander asked.

"Brand new," Mateo said, sounding amused. "Physio doesn't *need* one, per se, but I wanted to see if anyone stood out."

Leander wondered what Mateo was looking for in an intern, and if there was a not-weird way for Leander to tell Mateo he could sense what each of them were feeling, if that would help. He wasn't sure it would, but it was a fun application of a new skillset.

"Hey guys," Alex appeared beside them, speaking around a pen in her teeth as she raked her dark hair into a ponytail. "Després, do you have a—"

Leander pulled a hair tie off his wrist, and Alex flashed him a smile around her pen. It was one of the first tricks he'd learned in his women-led industry; Alex had the opposite demographic, and a hairtie was hardly a grain of sand on the scales of inequity, but it was a useful habit.

"Thanks," she said cheerfully, snatching the pen from between her teeth and tapping it against a chart that'd seemed to materialize from nowhere. "What're we hovering for?"

Leander wasn't sure there was a concise way to say *hoping the absolute chaos can overstimulate me out of being creepy about my best friend*, so he let Mateo take it.

"Seeing if any of the interns seem promising," Mateo shrugged.

Alex hummed, crossing her arms as she leaned against the railing. "Anything stand out?"

"Those two," Mateo pointed, "are trying to be subtle about only approaching surgeons. That one is alphabetizing the charts when they're placed back incorrectly, and that one hasn't stopped checking out every blond who crosses the floor."

"Should we send Leander down there?" Alex teased, but Leander was saved from answering when a quiet seemed to fall over the station.

"Després!"

Leander jumped as his name was called from below them.

Whit stood at the base of the stairs, the crowd parting around him. The surgeon crossed his arms, his white coat stretching tight across his chest, and he jerked his chin to the a conference room across the hall.

"A word," Whit said sharply, before stepping into a conference room, a clear order for Leander to follow him.

"Does it count as the principal's office if he's, like, assistant principal?" Mateo wondered aloud, and Leander chuckled.

"At best," Alex scrawled a signature on the chart, tucking it under her arm again, "more like starting quarterback, if we're sticking with the high school metaphor."

"Thanks for the pep talk, guys," Leander said without malice. Alex snorted, Mateo clapped a hand on Leander's shoulder, and Leander made his way down the stairs.

Leander wondered if he could hold his breath through the whole nurse's station.

The conference room was blessedly quieted as Whit closed the door.

"What the hell are you doing at work like this?" Whit demanded, and Leander closed his eyes, taking a moment to breathe in the closed-filtered air.

"I've only got a few hours left on my shift," he said. "And I was on an emptier wing, doing restocks—"

"The policies we have aren't a joke," Whit said. "You have to take care of yourself here."

Leander opened his eyes, frowning at Whit. "Why aren't you affected?"

"I'm on suppressants," Whit said dismissively. "Are you seriously not going to leave early?"

"I'm fine," Leander said, even as the thought of leaving early made him think of meeting up with Reyna, Reyna and Great Cranberry Island, Reyna and the cabin and—

"Yeah, okay," Whit said, pinching the bridge of his nose. "Whatever, can I see your phone?"

"It's in my locker," Leander said automatically.

Whit huffed. "Dude, I don't care; I'm not chief yet. Lemme have it."

Leander waited a second longer on principle, then fished his phone out of his pocket, unlocked it and dropped it into the outstretched palm in front of him.

Whit took the phone, tapped through a couple screens, then raised it to his ear, turning back to the room.

Reyna answered before Leander registered what Whit was doing.

"Lee?" her voice seemed to echo around the room and Leander felt it like it was a physical wave, bowling over him, too deep out in the tide.

She sounded worried, she sounded like she cared, and it hit him in the center of his chest, and his scrubs felt less grating.

"This is Doctor Pace," Whit said.

There was a pause, before Reyna offered a terse, "And why?"

Whit cleared his throat and Leander fought back a smile. It was always nice to see someone so emphatically cut through Whit's bluster.

"You need to come get Després," Whit said, like this was normal conversation for him to be having with her.

"Got it," Reyna said quickly, and Leander could hear the way she shifted into action mode. "I need 20 minutes to swing by his place and grab his bag; is that okay? Where should I meet you both?"

"Parking garage," Whit said. "Twenty's fine."

Reyna hung up before either of them said goodbye, and a part of Leander preened that she was coming to get him. He realized Whit was watching him, an amused expression on his face.

"She has a key to your place?" Whit asked, his voice dry, and Leander didn't know why he would push back on the teasing, when his wolf was muttering that of course she had a key, why shouldn't she.

"Okay, Romeo," Whit muttered. "I'll be back to get you in twenty, and we'll meet your girl at the parking garage. Do not leave without me, okay?"

The concept of leaving the sanctuary of the conference room was absurd, but Leander nodded. Whit looked like he wanted to push the point, but ended up just fixing Leander with a stare, and striding from the room.

Leander had no idea how he was supposed to make it through twenty minutes, but he *was* grateful to be in the conference room.

It was insulated, both from sound and scent, with the AC on full blast, Leander's head cleared enough to handle some logistics. He called the grocer on the island, and one of the people working the small shop agreed to have her teenager drop off nonperishable items in a couple hours. He went ahead and texted Esther as well, to let her know why he'd vanished and thank her for setting him straight earlier. He found the ferry schedule and bought tickets for himself and Reyna, and paid for parking for her car through Tuesday.

That took a full five minutes and Leander glared at the clock on the conference room wall.

He couldn't believe it was happening.

The changes teeming under his skin made him nervous, and there were dozens of things that could go wrong—namely, the most important relationship of Leander's life was at stake. But, maybe this wild reality was a chance. Maybe they could figure out what it would be like to cross the lines they'd so carefully avoided, see what it could be like, what they could be. Maybe Reyna could see Leander in a different light, see how well he could care for her. He'd just have to take advantage of the time when he wasn't mindless with his rut.

So he watched the second hand tick around the clock, paced a hole in the carpet of the conference room, and waited for the weekend that he was pretty sure he'd been waiting for his whole life.

Nine

The sunset was hidden behind the mountains, and the air was clean and cool as Leander and Whit stepped out of the hospital. Leander had changed into a sweatshirt and jeans, but the cotton felt too much on his skin, like it was noon on a full summer day rather than late afternoon in the fall. He recognized the bright blue 4x4 idling at the entrance to the parking lot, and when he saw the driver's door open, and he started jogging over. He hoped that Reyna wouldn't get out, and that Whit would accept a wave over his shoulder in the direction of the receiving bay as a transfer of responsibility.

The passenger door opened with a squawk, and Reyna was turned around in her seat, looking through the rear window. "Is he waiting for you? That's unexpectedly sweet."

"It's a part of his penchant for Chief," Leander explained, knowing Whit would hate if his callous reputation was besmirched. "Thanks for getting me."

"Oh, yeah," Reyna waved a hand like it was nothing. "Your stuff's in the back; you good?"

Leander bit back the urge to say he was infinitely better now that she was here.

Reyna was in jeans and a blue button down, the outfit she always wore a variation of during the week, in case someone asked her to hop on a video call at a moment's notice. The sight of her settled something in Leander, like this was typical, like picking him up from work was as normal as her work uniform.

"Yeah," Leander cleared his throat. "We've got like ten minutes till the ferry's here."

Reyna nodded, throwing the car into gear and whipping them out of the lot. Leander gripped his knees, knowing any grabbing at the door or armrests would only earn him comments about being a backseat driver. He could feel Reyna watching him out of the corner of her eyes, but kept his eyes on the road, not certain what would happen if he looked back. In his periphery vision, he could see her hair was spilling around her shoulders, blowing in front of her face as she shoved her sunglasses up into it, an ineffective attempt at taming the curls.

"You look more lucid than I was expecting," she said, as they merged onto the highway.

Leander was glad that it wasn't showing, because he didn't feel lucid.

He wanted to close his hand over hers on the gearshift, he wanted to hold back her hair so it wasn't in her eyes, and when her eyes were unimpeded, he wanted to just stare into them. He felt like he wanted to cross the center console and bury his head in the crook of her neck, see if she smelled that good up close.

"Can we roll down a window?" Leander asked, abruptly, and Reyna frowned.

"You can just say you're carsick," she muttered, but she cracked his window and hers from the driver-side controls.

"It's not that," Leander protested, and Reyna fixed him with a look that said he might as well have clung to the armrests as they left the lot, if he was going to be this way. Leander sighed, closing his eyes as he leaned his head back against the headrest, and focusing on the wind rather than the way the car still smelled like orange blossoms.

"I'm not carsick," Leander mumbled, "and I'm not being passive aggressive. You...with everything, you smell really good, okay? I'm trying to not be weird about it."

Reyna didn't respond to that, which Leander figured was probably a mercy. He cracked open an eye to peak over at her, but her profile was unreadable to him as she stared straight ahead as she drove.

It wasn't a long drive, and when they got to the parking lot, Reyna went to the ticket stand to print out the parking slip for the car while Leander wrestled with their bags. Almost as soon as they boarded, the horn sounded the last call warning. Leander walked into the small cabin of the boat, and as soon as the door closed behind Reyna, the cabin seemed steeped in oranges. He moved through the cabin as gracefully as he could manage, and Reyna made no comment as she followed him onto the upper deck of the ferry.

Leander tossed his duffel onto one of the cold metal benches, and he sat beside it. A moment later, Reyna sat too, slouching in the seat so she could prop her feet up on the lower rung of the railing. The wind whipped around them, and the spray of the ocean chased away the scent of oranges.

The sun was starting to set, casting a golden glow over the ocean as the engine churned beneath them.

Reyna wasn't touching him, but Leander still could feel her. He was aware of the heat of her, through the wind and space on the upper deck, just the same as if she'd pressed her arm against his, and leaned into him. He half wished she would.

The wind picked up as the ferry navigated out of the small dock.

Reyna crossed her arms across her chest, and when Leander looked over, he saw goosebumps prickling over her forearms. He didn't think twice before pulling his sweatshirt over his head and handing it to her.

Reyna looked at his crumbled sweatshirt for a moment, then took it. It was a familiar exchange—Leander ran warm, even when his blood wasn't racing beneath his skin—but it felt different this time. He watched closely, but Reyna didn't notice as she tugged it over her head, pulling the collar of her shirt through the neck of the sweatshirt.

The horn echoed as they cleared the harbor, and there were a couple small splashes as the nereids leapt from the deck into the sea. The boats in Port Cadie all moved with motors, but most ferries had nymph escorts to ensure they didn't disturb anything under the surface. The ferry started towards the islands, and Reyna hesitated for a moment before leaning over to be heard over the noise of the heavy wind.

"I'm gonna go see if the galley is open," she said, her mouth inches from his ear, and it was Leander's turn to shiver, but it had nothing to do with the cold. "Do you want anything?"

Food, Leander reminded himself, she was asking about food.

He was breathing through his mouth again, as he felt her breath ghost over his ear, and tried to convince his wolf that the open-ended offer was actually quite closed. The thought of food made his stomach flip, so he shook his head, and a moment later, Reyna was gone. Leander pulled in deep breaths as the air cleared, grateful for the fresh air, but his wolf struggling with the fact that he couldn't smell her.

It didn't bode well for the weekend.

To be fair, little boded well for the weekend. But Leander had to imagine that they'd be separated throughout it, at least far enough away that they wouldn't always share the same air.

The sound of the cabin door opening made Leander look up, and Reyna ducked through the door, balancing with the rolling of the ferry. Something lodged in Leander's chest at the sight of her in his sweatshirt. He wasn't that much taller than her, so it wasn't that she was swimming in fabric, or that his clothes made her seem small. Nothing about Reyna was small, and he hadn't ever wished for her to be less than she was. But the sight of her, exactly as she was but draped in his clothes, like she'd let him keep her warm, it felt right.

Leander knew his wolf wanted more, wanted to claim her as his, wanted possession and entirety. But if he could have this—Reyna, as she was, smiling sheepishly as she wove across the uneven deck, making her way to him—that was more than enough.

"Here," she said as she sat, stumbling slightly as the boat lurched. The motion sent her off balance, and her shoulder brushed Leander's chest before she could push herself up. She cleared her throat, holding out a ginger ale to him.

"It's okay if you don't feel like eating," she settled in her seat, "but you should probably have some sugar, and maybe it'll help with whatever sensory overload you've got going on."

Leander accepted the bottle.

The lights on the dock twinkled as the ferry pulled into the terminal at Great Cranberry Island.

The island was quiet, it always was, but the walk from the ferry up to the cottage seemed especially still. It was a small building, a tidy square with a thatched roof that overlooked the sea. The moonlight revealed maple trees with multicolored leaves, floating down over the walkway, settling around a paper grocery bag on the stoop.

The screendoor had no latch, and the actual door behind it had one bolt, undone with a key that never came off Leander's keychain, and the cabin was exactly as he remembered it. A sunken sofa faced a woodburning stove, and stacks of Steven King novels were braced against a wall. Through a narrow doorway at one end, the small kitchen; through a doorway at the other end, the bedroom.

Reyna followed behind him, and as she stepped into the cottage, Leander locked his knees to keep them from buckling.

She'd smelled good in her car, she'd mixed with the wind on the ferry, but in his cottage, something clicked. Oranges mixed with ocean air and the smell of books and fresh bread, and Leander's wolf whispered, *home*.

"Oh my god," Reyna breathed, dropping her bag from her shoulder as soon as she cleared the threshold. She switched on a small lamp and the softest smile was on her face as she walked around the room; Leander's chest swelled at the sight. She paused at a window, turning back to look at him.

"Does it seem smaller?" she asked. "Did we grow that much?"

Leander had nothing intelligent to say to that, so he shrugged, pulling off his bag.

He couldn't stop looking at her. She looked so at ease here, the earliest place he'd thought of as home. Under normal circumstances, it would be overwhelming, and under his present state, it was tenfold.

Reyna went to the sink in the kitchen, turning the faucet to wash her hands. Leander followed her, and carrying the grocery bags to the kitchen, hefting them onto the wooden table in the middle of it. A moment later she yelped, pulling her hands out from under the tap, the stream of water steaming.

"Forgot about that," she mumbled, somewhat amused, adjusting the faucet to allow tepid water to come out, as opposed to the default of scalding. "Want any help?"

Leander shook his head, unloading groceries was hardly a momentous task.

As he unloaded a sack of clementines, a box of pancake mix, bagged bread, and a tin of espresso, he heard her shuffling around in the other room. They would need to venture to the store for produce, but the things he'd ordered already were a start. He wasn't entirely sure he was going to be able to do grocery runs like normal, but he certainly hoped he could.

"I didn't know if they'd have it at the grocer's," Reyna said from the doorway, and when Leander turned, she tossed a small box at him.

He caught it on reflex, turning it in his hands to see the brand of chamomile tea he liked, the kind Reyna always had at her place. The island grocer tended to stock local-to-the-island produce and shelf-stable staples, and wouldn't have the loose leaf tea that Chesa stocked.

Reyna was already back in the main room, rifling through her bag, and Leander finished the groceries before walking back into the room. She'd pulled a jacket out of her bag and was hanging it on the coat rack in the doorway; like she could sense him, she looked back at him. She smiled, something nervous, meant to be comforting, and Leander's heart pounded.

He wanted to kiss her.

The realization surprised him, not because he hadn't had the same thought a million times over the last week, over the last years, but because he was finally in a place to do something about it. The thought soured as he realized that the next few days were meant to be intense, and that he didn't know how much of himself he would be. What he knew now, what he needed now, was for this to be theirs, when he was still mostly himself.

Reyna stilled as she realized he wasn't moving.

"Are you...I don't know, good?" she asked. "Do you want to lie down or something?"

Her innocent question prompted a carousel of insinuations that Leander forced himself to ignore.

"I'm good," he said automatically, running a hand through his hair.

Reyna hummed, turning back to the coat rack to empty the pockets of her jeans into the pocket of her coat.

"Can I kiss you?" he blurted.

It wasn't often that Reyna was rendered speechless. Her lips parted slightly in surprise, and her brow furrowed as her eyes searched his.

"What for?" she asked, finally.

And there were hundreds of reasons Leander could give—because he'd been wondering since he was fifteen, because she'd brought him chamomile, because it felt right to be back here on Great Cranberry—but he settled on a version that was no less true than the others.

"Because I don't know what tomorrow's going to be like," Leander admitted. "And I want to have this before it takes over."

Reyna's head tipped to the side, as she mulled over his words.

And Leander supposed that was the cruelty of this weekend: that his wolf could know exactly what he wanted, but Reyna couldn't comprehend his wanting her independently.

Reyna nodded slowly. "Yeah, that makes sense. Sure."

Not exactly the overture Leander has been hoping for, but it would do.

He could tell she was nervous, but he couldn't for the life of him think why. He could see it in the fluttering pulse in her neck, the way her hands were deliberately still by her side, though Reyna was constantly a creature of motion. Yet she stood still, like a statue, rooted to the spot as he crossed the room to her.

He only got one chance at this.

One first kiss, one moment that Leander knew the rest of his life would hinge on— before and after her.

He should be terrified, should be nervous, but all he felt was anticipation.

Reyna's head tilted back, just slightly, to look up at him from this close. He could see the freckles on her nose, the faint flush in her cheeks that betrayed that she was affected. Maybe not as much as him, but she didn't have a wolf under her skin that was chanting *finally, finally, finally.*

Leander lifted a hand, his finger brushing her cheek as he tucked an errant curl behind her ear. Reyna's eyelashes fluttered as her eyes closed, her face tilting sweetly, further upwards to him, and Leander wanted to freeze this moment, remember it forever.

She was so beautiful.

Her smooth, warm, skin, the gentle lines of her face, the almost purple pink of her lips. The scent of bergamot surrounded him, and Leander trailed his hand loosely over her hair to cup the back of her head, and lowered his mouth to hers.

She was so soft.

Leander loved it, that for the steel in her spine and the sharpness in her eyes, like this, for him, she was soft. Her lips were full under his, and when they brushed, he felt it through his whole person.

He kissed her slowly, carefully, could feel his heartbeat slowing as he absorbed her. Gentle presses against her lips, sharing the same air, tasting her breath and when he pulled back slightly he felt her follow him.

"Reyna," he whispered her name like a prayer, against her lips, and she made a small sound in the back of her throat before she rose up on her toes, reaching for him.

Reyna's arms wound around his neck, pulling him back to her, and Leander went without a moment's hesitation. Her body curved into him and Leander's hand fell from her hair to the small of her back, pulling her closer as her lips parted.

He felt her tongue trace his bottom lip and Leander moaned against her mouth. He heard her sharp inhale, remembered she liked to hear him, and stored the revelation away before he delved into her mouth.

God, she was sweet.

He was trying to take this slow, be gentle for this first kiss, but it was impossible when she tasted this good.

Leander was overwhelmed by slow slide of tongues against each other, the soft brush of lips, the way the air in the cabin was just oranges, only Reyna. He could feel her breathing, the way her chest expanded as she pressed up against him, and his arms were full of her but he wanted more. Her hands were in his hair, around his shoulders, and Leander's splayed over her—his— sweatshirt, as the kiss deepened.

He felt ravenous, drunk, and it was only heightened by the fact that Reyna was meeting him.

She whimpered into his kiss, a sweet, delicate sound that went straight to Leander's cock. He wasn't thinking, only feeling, and when their hips pressed together, he could've died happy in that moment. Reyna's arms tightened around him, and he felt her kiss change to something more charged, more needy. She felt so good, warm and welcome and perfect, in his arms, but when she rocked her hips into Leander again, he choked down a groan.

How had he thought he could survive this?

His rut still wasn't here, he was still mostly in charge of his mind, and he could feel himself going feral. Needing more of her taste, more of her touch, more of those soft sounds she was making.

His hands tightened on her waist, his thumbs rubbing soft circles as he gentled the kiss. A kiss was what he had asked for, and they'd talked boundaries already, but it was too soon to get carried away. He made himself slow down, fighting against every instinct that told him to take more, more, more, until he was consumed by her.

Leander kissed the corner of Reyna's lips, the bridge of her nose, the freckles on her cheek, before he straightened. He pulled her into his chest before he could see her expression, wrapping his arms around her and resting his chin on the top of her head.

This felt right.

All of it, every bit of it. Reyna in this house, in his arms, her heart beating against his. He realized they were swaying slightly, and Reyna's arms had wrapped around his waist. He could feel her hand rubbing up his back lightly, a soothing gesture that was familiar, if only in memories.

It warmed his heart, pierced him through, that she would give him this, trust him with herself, and then comfort him as they stood afterwards.

The cabin was quiet, their heated breath returning to normal, but neither of them stepping away. After a couple minutes, Leander loosened his arms, and, as he expected, Reyna followed his lead. He stepped back, and Reyna looked at him, her expression inscrutable, as her head tipped sideways. Leander was sure she was going to ask about the plan for the weekend, putting away their bags or something, but instead, she pulled in a deep breath, pushed back her shoulders.

"Okay," Reyna said, and Leander thought he might never forget how her voice sounded after he'd kissed her, and that was even before she said, "I think we should have sex."

Ten

Her words seemed to echo in the room around them, and Reyna couldn't read Leander's reaction.

"I mean, we're going to do it anyways, and by the same kiss logic, I think we should—" Reyna broke off with a shrug, "I don't know, just do it now, instead of later."

In her defense, she wasn't thinking clearly.

Leander tasted like ginger soda, and the kiss had been incredibly good. Devastatingly good. I'm-not-going-to-survive-the-weekend good. Her dormant crush seemed not at all dormant, and this weekend was probably going to wreck her in a number of ways.

So, she figured, why not just confront that reality head on?

Leander frowned, a worried look in his eyes. "Are you scared of how I'll be?"

Reyna blinked; she hadn't even thought of it like that.

"I trust you," she said, shaking her head. "I know it'll be a lot, but I'm also here for you."

Leander shifted on his feet, looking nervous. "Obviously, I'm game, but I don't want you to feel pressured or anything."

Reyna took a deep breath, as it settled over her shoulders.

This, she could do.

Be there for her best friend, convince him it wasn't pressure, be what he needed, help him through the rut. All but that last, she'd done before, and she could do it again.

"Kiss me again," she asked, and Leander didn't hesitate.

Of course he was a good kisser.

Of course someone as sweet and pretty and kind as Leander also kissed like he liked it, like it wasn't an obligation before sex. She smoothed her hands over his tshirt, her hands coming up to run through his hair. The strands were longer than normal, curling down at the base of his neck, and she loved the feeling of it through her fingers. She followed his lead, bowing into him when his hands on her waist pulled her closer, and then she broke off.

From this close, Leander was wide-eyed behind his glasses, fogging up slightly from how hard they were breathing.

"Take me to bed, Lee," Reyna said, enough of a request and an order both, the kind Leander responded best to.

His eyes fluttered closed, and then he grabbed her hand, walking her into the bedroom.

She'd never been in this room.

It'd always been closed off for Leander's grandmother when she came over, and Reyna looked around curiously. It was simply appointed, like the rest of the cabin, light walls, linen sheets, open windows. The moon was nearly full, that'd been the impetus of all of this, but it was a fresh reality as moonlight streamed through the windows, illuminating Leander sitting on the bed. Reyna walked over to him, her heart pounding.

She could do this.

Just sex between friends, just a favor between besties. She smoothed her hands over his tshirt, resting on his shoulders, stepping between his legs.

"Thank you," Lee said quietly, and his voice drew her eyes back to his.

He was looking at her intently, something hidden in his blue eyes, obscured by something other than the thick glass over them. Reyna wanted to know, and then again, she didn't. She wanted this, wanted him, enough to damn her future self to sorting out the mess.

So she smiled a close-lipped smile at him, shrugging like this wasn't a big deal.

Maybe one of them could believe it.

Before she could lose her nerve, Reyna pulled off his sweatshirt, dragging her shirt off with it. They fell beside her, and the room felt suddenly cool, except for the heat in Leander's eyes. He reached for her, and she stepped into his arms, amazed at how quickly a kiss had become something comfortable. One of Leander's hands was at the back of her neck, his thumb stroking her jaw, and she leaned into his touch.

He was so gentle with her.

She pulled back, looking at him, smiling at the image. Hair ruffled from her fingers, color rising on his cheeks, and she wondered if that continued down his chest.

She could find out.

She tugged at the hem of his tshirt as soon as she made the realization, and then it was just Leander in the moonlight, broad shouldered and gazing up at her. He was so tall that she often forgot he was strong too. Thankfully no abs, but strength corded across his chest, down to thick biceps, veiny forearms. His hand on the back of her neck squeezed, and Reyna followed the unspoken prompt, leaning down to kiss him again.

He kissed her nervously, unhurried, like he was also aware that they only had one first time, and wanted to do it right. His lips were gentle and Reyna could feel herself getting into her own head about it, so she broke the kiss and climbed around him to lay on the bed.

He followed her a moment later, his body carefully arranged on his side next to her, so as not to crowd her. Which she could appreciate, except the whole purpose here was to crowd, to be together, and she reached for him again.

Reyna's hands slid up his arms, her nails skimming through the coarse hair on his forearms. It made her curious and she reached for his chest, smoothed her hands over the hair there. Leander hummed as she continued the perusal, and Reyna liked how it felt under her palms, like a cat purring.

She explored soft skin and scratchy hair, broad shoulders and bunched muscles. He shifted, held himself above her, and she could feel him waiting for her, but instead of meeting his eyes, she curled her arms up his back, over his shoulders, pulling gently so he'd lower himself.

When his body settled over her, she sighed, her eyes falling shut.

He felt so warm, and she didn't know what her face was doing, but it made him kiss her again. This time she opened for him, eager for the heat of that first kiss. When Leander's tongue stroked into her mouth, Reyna sucked on him. His hips punched forward and his head dropped to her shoulder.

"Sorry," he panted, and Reyna wanted to know what the hell there was to feel sorry about, when he felt how he did. She hadn't...call her old fashioned, but she'd never looked. In the moonlit room, she was curious, and she lifted her hips slightly, her clothed core brushing against him.

That couldn't be right.

Reyna pressed her lips together, moved her hips again, and nope, that was right—he was huge.

The feel of him, half hard but so thick already, hot and heavy between his thighs, made her throat dry in anticipation. Reyna reached down, slowly. Her hands skimmed down his sides, playing with the belt loop on the front of his jeans so he knew where she was going, and Leander shifted onto his side. He pulled his boxer briefs off with his jeans, kicking lightly so they fell off the edge of the bed.

And there he was.

Flushed and heavy against his thigh, his cock was thick, pooling pink and just begging to be touched. Reyna reached for him, her eyes darting up to find Leander already watching her, an expression of rapt interest on his face.

"Lee," Reyna breathed, "Can I—"

"Fucking please," he gritted, and Reyna's mouth dropped open. She could count on one hand the amount of times she'd heard Leander swear, and now he was naked in bed with her, and it slipped out of him like the most natural thing. The man had the audacity to blush, looking flustered like he wasn't the sweetest man with the biggest cock.

And it was in that moment that Reyna realized how good this could be.

Through her complicated feelings for Leander, she'd known it was something she'd wanted, regardless of how it went, but looking at Leander beside her was something else.

She reached for him.

She trailed her nail up the side of his dick and it bobbed at her, like he was eager, and she pressed her lips together before she did something embarrassing like coo at him. She brushed her thumb over the head of him, smearing a drop of precum that was beading at the tip, and Leander's head dropped. She closed her fist around him, and when she realized her fingers barely touched, Reyna couldn't stop the breathy gasp that escaped her.

He felt heavy in her hand.

Hot and soft and so hard and she pulled her hand loosely up the length of him, mindful of that fact that there wasn't any lubrication. Leander pulled in an audible breath when her grip tightened, and when she looked over at him. His eyes were squeezed shut behind his glasses.

His glasses.

With the hand that wasn't playing with his dick. Reyna reached for his glasses, pulling them off his head and placing them on the nightstand. Lee blinked at her slowly, his eyes readjusting, and Reyna's heart twinged at the sweet expression of trust on his face.

Moonlight crested over him like a halo, his blond hair highlighted in the pale light, and Reyna focused on his cock before she did something stupid like comment on it. She spit into her palm, reaching down to grip him again. As he got harder, he swelled thicker, and Reyna felt herself grow warm at that knowledge.

This was going inside her.

She squirmed, just trying to imagine it. The heavy cock in her palm was going to stroke into her and she found that she wanted it, rather desperately. She pulled her hand over him, curious how long she could continue exploring him, and when her thumb snagged under his head, Leander moaned.

Reyna froze.

It was such an unguarded sound, honest and raw and hungry, and she was done with curiosity, she wanted more.

"Sorry," Lee muttered, and Reyna needed him to stop apologizing. Not letting go of his cock, she turned into him, kissing him. His mouth was soft and warm, and Reyna licked Leander's bottom lip, tasting his gasp. She felt his hips push into her hand as she kissed him harder, trying to pour how much she wanted him into the kiss.

"Stop apologizing," she whispered against his lips. "I like how you sound."

Like a reward, he groaned, something tortured and low, and then a moment later, he was pushing her hand away, and pulling closer to him.

"You have no idea," he muttered, and he nudged her chin up with his nose, kissing down her neck. Reyna's breath caught as his lips closed over her pulse point, and teeth brushed against sensitive skin.

"How you smell," he whispered, and his tongue flicked out against her neck, "how you taste, how you look, how you sound, hearing your breath catch and go thin because of me — *like* doesn't begin to cover it, Rey."

It was a nickname he'd given her years ago, but like this, with his mouth hot against her, settled differently over her skin. She reached down for her jeans, undoing the closure and pulling her panties down with them as they slid over her thighs.

Leander looked like he was barely keeping it together.

His hands were shaking, and Reyna knew it was the rut, knew it wasn't him, but it was a hell of a confidence boost for a girl. He looked at her like he was starving, like he couldn't wait to dive in. When his hands settled on her thighs, she felt like he was burning her, and she wanted more. She pulled him back on top of her, and they both stilled as he settled between her thighs.

Fuck.

It felt *right*.

How they fit together, the weight of him over her, how easily they fell into place...first times didn't happen like this. But when Reyna rubbed herself against him, chasing the friction she knew she needed,

Leander moved like he couldn't help himself either. He pushed that thick cock between her folds and Reyna couldn't stop the whimper that escaped past her lips.

Leander grunted, pulled back and pushed over her again and Reyna felt dizzy. She reached between them, trapping his cock in her hand and guiding him towards her center. She wasn't ready enough to take him, but she knew how to get herself there.

Leander groaned as she rubbed her clit with his cock, prodding against her and Reyna felt warmth spreading through her. How he sounded, how he moved, how warm he felt, how good he would fill her...soon she was rocking against his cock, grinding her pussy against him, panting as she imagined him pushing in.

"Careful, Rey," Leander said, his voice low, and Reyna opened her eyes to see his face poised over hers. His eyes were hooded, glowing silver in the low light, his jaw slack. She couldn't stop moving, shifting her hips and feeling herself growing more and more wet for the promise of her best friend fucking her.

"Careful?" she asked, shocked by how breathless her voice sounded.

Lee was too, his eyes closing briefly and his hips punching forward. They both swallowed moans as his cock slipped through her folds, now an easy glide for how turned on she was.

"If you keep working that pussy against my dick—" Leander broke off, "I want it to be good for you, but I need you too bad."

His words settled around her, dirtier and sweeter than she'd expected, and Reyna adjusted her grip. She pushed him through her folds, whimpering as she felt his cock gather collect her arousal dripping out of her.

"Feels pretty good to me," she whispered, and Leander huffed a laugh, shaking his head. A moment later, he reached between them, and his smile fell as he pushed through her folds again, this time guided by his hand.

"You're so beautiful," he murmured, and Reyna shook her head, fisting the sheets on either side of her.

Hot sex she could do, hot sex with her best friend, she could manage. Hot sex with her best friend who said things like that? She had to shut that down.

She shifted her hips, trying to catch him inside her, but Leander held steady.

Almost there, a breath away, watching her squirm for him. With his hand around his cock, he reached his thumb up, exploring. When he found her clit, Reyna jolted. Fuck, had his fingers always been this wide? He stroked over her, humming as he learned her reactions, the touches she liked—gentle strokes around her clit, rather than direct pressure over her.

"Can't wait till I can taste you here," he mused, almost to himself, and Reyna's eyes flew open. Not that he was looking at her; Lee was talking to her cunt, and that was somehow even more devastating. "Bet you taste so sweet, don't you? I need you too bad right now, but fuck I'm tempted, it's so pretty. Would you let me eat this pussy, Rey?"

Reyna was pretty sure she was gaping at him. She had no idea Leander had this kind of mouth on him but yeah, she'd let him do whatever he wanted.

"Please," she whispered, rather than saying that. "Please, Lee—"

She broke off when he pushed a finger inside of her. Her mouth dropped open and she clenched around his finger, his thumb still playing with her clit, and she whined.

"Honey, you sound so good, fuck," Leander murmured, his voice wrecked, and Reyna shook her head; what was happening? He sounded so hot, and when he added another finger, she wanted to cry. It was so good, it wasn't enough, she needed him.

"I wonder how you like it," Leander said softly, that gentle voice dangerous. "Slow and gentle? Fast and hard? What positions—shit, sweetheart, I have so much I want to know." Reyna's head was spinning, her world centralizing on the two fingers Leander was slowly pumping in and out of her. He curled them slightly, teasing her, and she bowed off the bed. Were her thighs shaking? Was the room moving? She couldn't tell, she just needed more of whatever witchcraft he was weaving.

"And I get to learn it, don't I," Leander was saying. "I'm the luckiest man, fuck. I have this pussy all to myself, get to learn just how my best friend likes it—"

Reyna moaned, his words whipping up a frenzy in her mind. This wasn't fully him, but he sounded like he was still there, and she couldn't even figure it out because she was so distracted by the fire he was stoking between her thighs.

"Lee, I swear to God, if you don't hurry up and—"

He pulled his fingers out and Reyna's next words died as his cock pressed into her.

Holy. Fuck.

He was so big.

The stretch burned, but in the best way. It was like he was molding her, shaping her in the best way to cradle his dick, and Reyna's head completely emptied. All she could think, feel, want, need was Leander.

The way his breath got shallow, like this was overwhelming to him, too.

The way his hands found hers, pulling on her fingers till she let go of the bedsheets and tangled her fingers in his.

The heady, overwhelming press of his cock, the way it was perfect and the way she felt like she was being remade.

She cried his name, trembling. Fuck, he felt so good. He was so deep, she was so full, and she couldn't lay still.

"I know," he said, his voice strained, as his head dropped to beside hers. "Fuck, I know, Rey, I'm almost there…"

He trailed off, and Reyna's head thrashed from side to side as she realized he wasn't even fully seated in her. She felt like a live wire, like she needed everything but had no idea where to start. His hips spread hers, pressing her flat into the bed, and when he finally stopped moving, Reyna wondered if she could get away with never leaving this bed.

"So good, sweetheart," he whispered into her hair, and Reyna felt him twitch inside of her as they got used to the feeling of each other.

Like she could ever get used to this feeling.

Like dick this good was normal, like him calling her sweetheart was average. Like his voice wasn't sending her into orbit.

Leander started to pull out, she could have wept for how perfect the slide of his thick cock felt against her walls. He went slow, controlled, and it drove Reyna's need higher, that he was so in control of it.

"I wanna watch you," he mumbled, and Reyna thought she might be drunk on how his voice sounded, like he was slurring to speak. "Ah, that's so pretty, look at you."

She felt him lifting off of her to look down to where they were joined, but Reyna didn't know if she could handle it. Just in her mind's eye, it was too much — the contrast of his skin against hers, the way he'd be hard where she'd be soft, the trembling that seemed to overtake both of them.

"Move," she gasped, "I need to feel you move."

"Yeah," Leander said, somewhere between magnanimous and awed, "yeah, I can do that for you."

This time, when he pushed back in, it was smoother, easier for having already been there. Reyna felt it work over her like a shock, the way her body opened for him, the way he was already learning her. No less overwhelming, no less earth-shattering, but more familiar.

He kept it slow, a gentle easing in and out of her, and Reyna could weep from it. It was so good, so much, and she knew he was also just trying to warm her up.

She was so warm, she was burning.

Reyna clenched around him, rewarded by another low moan from Leander.

"Look at me," Leander said, his voice tense.

Reyna pried her eyes open, her heart slamming in her chest as she looked up at Leander. God, he was pretty. So known and dear and then to see him like this—eyes hooded, chest rising quickly, a flush on his skin from her—she'd never forget this.

"There y'are," he murmured, and his tongue darted out to wet his lips. "Keep those eyes on me, honey, I need to see you."

Then he needed to not fuck her so good.

Reyna fought to keep them open, but the punishing push of his cock was so tempting. She focused on the glowing in his eyes, the pink of his lips, trying desperately to keep from falling back into her own pleasure.

She failed when he slammed into her.

Shoved his thick cock into her hard, and her head fell back, her back arching as he pushed into her. He moaned her name, and Reyna thought she'd never heard another person sound so beautiful. She locked her ankles around his ass, pulling him to her, needing him exactly like this—deep, moaning, needing her.

He understood.

He braced their hands on the mattress and built a steady rhythm. She felt his mouth on her neck again, his lips clumsily brushing over her skin, too desperate to be a kiss. Reyna felt like she was floating, felt like the only thing that was maybe ever true was the driving pressure of Leander's cock into her. The sound of his hips hitting her ass, the taste of his sweat on the air around her, the feel of his breath puffing against her neck, it was perfect, it was divine.

"Lee," Reyna whimpered, not even sure what she was asking for. He pulled back, not breaking his rhythm, and she could feel him watching her but couldn't make herself look at him.

"Fuck, you're so pretty, Rey," Leander said, his voice rough. "You feel so good, sweetheart, so fucking tight and warm and all for me—"

He broke off on a groan and Reyna felt her spine tingling. His words and his fat cock, his body all around her, his words brushing over her, it was building and Reyna wanted it.

"You're getting close aren't you?" Leander asked, and Reyna nodded weakly. "Yeah? What am I gonna do, knowing what you look like when you come? Please, Rey, I wanna make you feel good, come on, baby—"

It was the petname, one she'd never heard in Leander's deep, wrecked voice, that sent her over the edge. Reyna keened as her orgasm broke, as the world shattered and heat exploded over her skin. Leander didn't stop, his body over hers like a caress, working her through it, murmuring soft praises in her ear.

Reyna wanted to hear them, wanted to bottle them up, but her mind couldn't process them, so she just clung to him. Leander seemed to approve, and when he felt her coming back, she felt his rhythm change, speed up, as he chased towards his own release.

For how vocal Leander had been through the whole time, he was now suddenly quiet, choked gasps escaping him at the top of each thrust and Reyna coveted each sound. She rolled her hips weakly, and a moment later Leander let go of her hand. His hand curled between her neck and the bed, clutching her nape as his thumb stroked over her cheek. She felt his thrusts growing frantic and when Reyna realized this was the hand he'd used to feed his cock into her at the start, she couldn't help herself. She turned into his hand and captured the end of his thumb in her mouth, moaning when she tasted herself on his hand.

Leander groaned, a strangled sound, and then his hips jutted forward once, twice, and stilled. Reyna preened, feeling his warm release pump into her. He yanked his hand out of her mouth, replacing it with his lips, kissing her almost angrily as his hips thrust into her. Reyna kissed him back, just as greedy, sharing her taste from his touch, soothing him.

He moaned, and she felt it through his chest, on his tongue, perfect. Perfect.

It was late, Reyna knew, probably close to tomorrow at this point, but the world continued to turn. There were still groceries to be put away in the kitchen, their bags discarded and forgotten by the door, but all Reyna could think about was the way Leander still clutched her to him. Like he wanted her, needed her, craved her.

She felt it when he came back, a slow return to consciousness, and a sudden jolt of self consciousness as he realized he was lying on top of her.

He pulled back slightly, his arms still firmly around her, and a part of Reyna relaxed as he looked down at her. The fact that he hadn't rolled away, immediately pushed off of her, told her this was still her best friend. He still knew what she needed, how to comfort her.

He'd always been better at that than her.

"That was..." he said, and the dreamy, dazed expression on his face could've saved Reyna thousands in therapy bills.

"It was," she agreed.

Leander smiled, something broad and beautiful and Reyna's heart slammed in her chest.

He looked *happy.*

He looked like this was exactly what he'd wanted, like she was it, and just as quickly, Reyna's heart sank.

It wasn't all real.

Sure, the gratitude, and the ease of interacting, anticipating each other, that could all be real. But the needing her, the wanting her, that was the heat. But the expression on his face, the trust in his soft blue eyes, it had Reyna wanting to be delusional.

How the hell was she supposed to survive this weekend?

Eleven

T he cabin was filled with soft light that made Leander wonder how late they'd slept in, since it was too bright to be morning. He felt different.

Leander felt like he was burning, like he'd been laying in the sun for hours and Reyna was the closest thing he had to shade. When he inhaled, he could smell her, but more than that, he could smell his touch on her skin. The room carried the scent of the previous night, and Leander wanted more of it, more of her, and he was pretty sure it was more than just want.

Pretty soon, he was going to need it.

She was on her side, her back to him, and her skin was cool as he traced his hand over the slope of her shoulder. He watched her skin prickle under his touch and a part of him wanted to pull the blanket up over her shoulders, keep her wrapped up and protected in his bed. The other part of him wanted to yank the comforter down, settle between her legs and *make* her warm.

He got to do neither, as Reyna stirred.

"Morning," Reyna mumbled, sleep clogging her voice, and then she drew in a deep breath. "Is it still morning? It's too bright."

"I don't know," Leander said, which was true, because he knew nothing except that she sounded amazing, and he needed to know what else she would sound like, with sleep this close. He shifted closer, his lips grazing the curve of her shoulder, and Reyna sighed, leaning back into him.

"You're warm," she sighed, and then she winced. "Ow."

Leander stilled. "You okay?" he asked into her skin.

Reyna sighed, then huffed a laugh. "Sore, but don't get in your head about it."

Too late—he was already cataloging every sigh, every compliment, every whisper as assurances that he would unpack later. After the weekend, when he didn't have her this close, didn't have her at all.

"I'm sorry," he mumbled. Leander's fingers pushed under the blanket, tracing down her body to the softness of her waist. The room beyond Reyna blurred, which Leander knew was because his glasses were still on the beside table, but in a much realer way, it was that she was truly all he could focus on.

Her shoulder lifted as she shrugged, nestling deeper into the pillow, as if fighting off the brightness of the day. "I don't suppose you want to kiss it better?"

She asked it so lightly, clearly intended as a flippant remark, but the offer lodged somewhere deep inside of Leander and yes, absolutely yes, that was all he wanted to do.

"Wait, Lee," Reyna protested as Leander shifted, pulling the sheets over his head and moving down the bed. "I was kidding, you don't have to—"

"I do," Leander said, and hoped she could hear the need clinging to his voice. She was soft and warm beside him, already so enticing and sweet, but he wanted her to overwhelm his senses—and now he knew where to start.

It was warm under the sheets, and Leander felt cocooned in the soft light. He could feel the tension radiating off of Reyna, her surprise that he had taken her offhanded suggestion as an instruction, but he could sense something more—an anticipation. Like she was nervous but willing, ready but hesitant, and he couldn't wait to assuage her.

He kissed his way down her body, and he wanted to bask in the surrealness of the moment but a strumming heat pulsed under his skin. Hidden by a canopy of white linen, his hands prompted her to switch from her side to laying on her back.

He meant to be patient, meant to tease her with it and slowly work her up but when he settled and Reyna's pussy was right in front of him, Leander found that restraint was no where in sight. He leaned in close, dragged in the heady scent of her, and kissed her where he'd been craving.

Reyna moaned.

A beautiful, broken sound, and then her hand was under the covers, reaching for him and tangling in his hair. Her fingers wrapped into his hair as Leander's tongue slipped between his lips, licking into her, tasting her, feeling her.

And, fuck, the taste of her.

Leander groaned as he licked up the length of her cunt, wondering how the hell he was supposed to wake up any day, for the rest of his life, without immediately tasting her. And it wasn't just that, it was the breathy gasped that escaped from her lips, like she was just as shocked as he was. Her pleasure washed over him, and Leander wanted to be patient, wanted to learn what she liked, but first, he was starving.

He licked into her hungrily, chasing the taste of her arousal. His tongue lapped at her, caressed her, tasted her and claimed her and Leander had to remind himself to breathe. He spread her with his fingers, pulling her apart so he could drink from her. God, she tasted so good, so sweet, and her fingers pulled at his hair as his tongue speared into her core.

His cock would be here soon.

His cock had been here, the night before, and now his tongue was; Leander moaned as he licked into her, and it made her thighs shake around his head. His fingers still stroking through her folds, Leander propped himself up on his elbows and traced his tongue upwards.

Reyna pushed her hips up towards his face, riding his face as best she could, as he flicked his tongue over her clit, circled it, closed his lips over her and sucked.

Leander groaned as her arousal coated his face, soaked his chin, slid down his throat. He pumped his fingers into her, he pulled her arousal out and ate it from his fingers, he dove back into her cunt when she pulled on his hair. He felt when her whimpers became more frequent, when her thighs clenched more tightly around his head, and when she bowed off the bed, crying out and shaking for him.

She tasted even sweeter when she came.

Leander meant to relent, but once he tasted her as she came, it wasn't enough. Even as she writhed and whimpered that it was too much, he stroked through her folds and teased her and chased every last drop of her release. His wolf was unleashed, was drowning in Reyna's pleasure, and needed more of her.

A wave of cool air rushed over him as Reyna pulled back at the sheet, her hands grabbing at his shoulders, pulling him. A part of Leander considered fighting her, pushing her hips into the mattress with his shoulders, continuing to eat her cunt until they were both mindless from it, but he realized she was saying something. It reached his ears through a fog of arousal, and Leander let himself be pulled up the bed, bracing his arms on either side of her as his eyes focused on her face again.

"I need you in me, Lee," Reyna was gasping, and she kissed him before he could respond.

Her tongue swept into his mouth, chasing the taste of her release on his lips and Leander moaned into her kiss. Reyna whimpered when she heard him, and it went straight to Leander's cock. He settled over her and nearly shivered with relief as her body welcomed his. She felt soft and warm under him, all curves and sweetness, and Leander felt his kiss go lazy as he was overwhelmed by her.

"Rey," he mumbled into her skin, kissing down her jaw. The spot where her neck met her shoulder was inviting, smelled strongly of her, and Leander buried his nose there. "Fuck—how you smell, how you taste, it's driving me wild, I need—"

"It's okay," Reyna soothed, her voice thick enough it made Leander's hips thrust against her. They both moaned at the contact, his throbbing cock brushing over where his mouth had just been. "It's just the rut."

Her quiet conviction cut through the haze of lust and if he were more himself, maybe Leander could've fought it. Maybe he could've pulled back and told her he'd want her no matter when, no matter the moon, just her, but as soon as the thought crossed his mind, it was overtaken by the fact that he could have her now.

Leander's wolf growled, and he had to clench his mouth shut to keep himself from replicating the sound. He'd tell her how she'd accept it—like it was just chemicals, like it was just biology, like he was mindless from the moon, and not her.

Propped on his elbows, Leander shifted his hips over hers slowly. Reyna's head fell back as his cock brushed against her warm center, and he couldn't help but drop his face back to her neck. God, she smelled so good here. Warm and sweet and earthy, and Leander tasted blood before he realized his fangs had distended, and had nicked his tongue. He pressed his lips shut and pulled in a deep breath through his nose, a hand reaching between them to part her thighs further for him.

Reyna sighed softly as he guided her open, and Leander swore he could taste her, just on the air. He knew he couldn't turn her, and a bite would just hurt, but his hips pushed into the cradle of her thighs at the thought of it—her blood on his tongue, her scent sharper and fresher than between her thighs, coating him...

Leander pushed himself up, needing clearer air, needing to focus on something other than the pounding need running through him. He shoved at the sheets, pulling them away from her until she was bared beneath him, and her skin prickled as cool air rushed over her. Leander needed to see her, feel her, and if he couldn't taste her how his wolf wanted, her could still devour her.

He reached between her thighs, his fingers coming back shiny with her arousal as he trailed them up her torso, higher.

The brown of her nipples turned glossy from her slick, and Leander had to taste them, leaning down and laving his tongue over her. Reyna bowed off the bed, her back arching as she pressed into him, and Leander moaned as he lapped her come off her nipples.

"Lee," she panted, and she was pulling on his wrist. Leander relaxed his grip from the base of her breasts, where he'd been holding her steady, and saw indents from his claws in her soft skin. A frisson of worry shot through him, but Reyna only whimpered when he kissed the scratches, pressing herself further into his touch.

He nipped and licked his way up her breasts, his mouth latching onto her pulse point. Reyna moaned as his teeth nicked across her skin and Leander knew she didn't bruise easily but god, he wanted her wearing his marks. She writhed beneath him, and Leander reached down to soothe over her clit again, playing with her as he sucked loved bites over her neck.

Shit, he wanted to actually bite her.

He wondered how he'd taste, he wondered how they'd smell together, needed her to smell like him.

Like his.

Need took over as his hands roamed over her desperately, harshly. Everywhere he had dreamed of, for years now, and when he realized her hips were rising into him again, that her pussy was begging for his cock, Leander pushed back to line himself up.

She looked up at him like a dream.

Last night had been incredible, overwhelming, with the moonlight lending an aura of mystery. But today, the sun was warm and bright, and from this close, Leander could see every detail of Reyna's reaction when his cock pushed into her.

Her mouth fell open as her eyes shut, her jaw hanging slack as he pushed into her. He felt her around him, pulsing and warm, and Leander knew he should go slowly but she was here, in his arms, dripping for him and wanting him. He wanted to ease into her, remembering how she'd already been sore, but the scent of them was in the air.

"You feel so fucking good, honey," Leander mumbled, needing to do something with the energy pulsing out of him. "First you tasted so good, and you came for me so pretty, and now I get to feel you around my cock—shit, Rey, I'm tryin' to go slow, but it's so hard, you feel so good."

He was barely halfway, but he felt like he could feel his heartbeat pulsing over his skin, every inch of him throbbing with awareness.

He moaned, his arms fully shaking from the effort of holding himself back. He pressed up to kiss her, distracting himself with her lips and her mouth, anything to keep a hold of his sanity. Another slow inch, and Reyna gasped into his mouth before she pulled back.

"Leander," she whispered, and she waited for him to open his eyes and look into hers, "stop being gentle."

Leander didn't even think to react, just did as she asked and thrust hard into her.

He almost came.

Reyna cried out, her knees lifting off the bed at the strength of the push, but Leander barely heard it as his hips met hers and he drove home between her thighs. This moment was what he'd been craving since he woke up. He could feel it thrumming in his blood, beating across his chest, the need to be this close to her, to claim her, to have her.

"That's it," she sighed, the most contented he'd ever heard her, and her praise spread over his skin like a caress. "Fuck, I feel so full...oh my god, Lee, it's so good."

Leander had been prepared for a wince and a sigh, but her reaction—it broke something in him.

He kissed her, tasted her gasps on her lips as he started to pump into her. Almost immediately, Reyna was moaning, and Leander swallowed the sounds, greedily.

Each stroke made her breasts bounce, each press of his cock pushed her body up the bed. Reyna seemed unable to be still, her hands running up his sides and down his back, clinging to him and caressing him. His claws were shredding the sheets but he didn't want to know what they'd do to her skin so he dug into the bed and used the leverage to push deeper, harder, claim more of her.

"Yes, Lee," she moaned, and Leander groaned as his hips worked even faster.

"That's right," he gritted, his cock slamming into her. "Fuck, honey, it's like all I can do is get closer, take more. And you keep letting me, don't you? Shit, how you feel around me honey, it's so good—"

He broke off with a moan, surrendering to the sensation of fucking into her. She matched him stroke for stroke, rewriting every definition of pleasure he'd ever known. She was warm, she was safe, she was his.

The thought lodged in the back of his mind and Leander growled, needing her mouth against his.

He wasn't normally like this.

Normally sex was sex, and it was good, and that was it. But he felt like he needed the air from her lungs, needed to hear and feel and taste the way she was gasping for him. Leander dropped to his elbows, bracing himself over her as he claimed her with his cock and his kiss. She tasted so good, she felt so good, and the way she was welcoming him made him feel absolutely feral.

She was his.

His everything, the sweetest thing and he heard himself grunting with every thrust, like he couldn't even find the words to claim her, but couldn't be silent.

"Holy shit," Reyna broke away from the kiss, her eyes widening, "is that...?"

At her astonished question, Leander realized what was happening, and he made himself pull back. As he sat up to rest on his thighs, he looked between them, fighting what his body was trying to rush.

Reyna's chest was heaving, her eyes blown wide, and at the place where they were joined, his knot was forming. Blood was pooling at the base of his cock, like nothing he'd felt before, and Leander pressed forward slowly, tentatively.

He nearly collapsed with pleasure as the sensitive skin of his knot brushed against her cunt. Reyna moaned, a drawn out, breathless sound, and it took everything in Leander to not slam his knot into her.

"Look what you did, baby," he murmured, and he barely recognized his voice.

Reyna whined, fully whined, and Leander could feel his heartbeat pounding in his temples. He curled his fingers around her thighs, careful of his claws, and his own thighs trembled as he pressed into her slowly. Leander's mouth fell open as he fed her inch after inch of his swollen cock, and when his base reached her, the pressure compounded around his knot.

"Fuck, Lee," Reyna cried, her head falling back.

Her nails scraped up his back and Leander realized his knot could press up against her clit while he fucked her. He pulled back and pressed into her again, feeling every inch of the stroke and the way her cunt seemed to pull him in. He would never grow tired of her wanting him, craving him, the way her body was cradled around him and calling him home.

God, she felt so good. So tight around him, and he was never going to leave. He only ever wanted to be between her legs, pressing himself into her, close enough that she couldn't deny that she needed this, needed him, and that he was the one bringing her pleasure.

"How's it feel, Rey," he panted, his hips slapping into hers as his cock pressed against her inner walls. "God, you're working me so good, feels like you were made for me—"

"I know," she gasped, and Leander groaned. Of all the things she could say...

He could feel his knot teasing her entrance, getting closer to slipping inside of her with each thrust. It was a blinding pressure and he didn't know how he'd survive it, when just his cock inside her had him feeling close to divine.

"I want it in me, Lee," she panted, and Leander groaned. He lowered himself over her, trying not to preen with the way her arms immediately clutched him to her chest, like she needed him this close too.

"Not yet," he grunted, not even caring how close to the edge he sounded.

At this rate was going to come as soon as his knot pushed into her, and he mouthed at her breasts to distract himself. His lips closed around a nipple and Reyna moaned as his tongue stroked over her. He teased her as he worked into her, tongue and cock wringing pleasure from her, working her body and pouring adoration over her, into her, the only way she'd accept.

She groaned his name when his fangs pricked over her nipple, and Leander pulled back before he gave into the impulse to nip at her.

He should tell her she was beautiful, that she felt good, but all he could feel was the warm clench of pride, that she looked like this, sounded like this, tasted like this, because of him. His knot slipped, almost in, and Leander couldn't slow down. He licked the valley between her breasts, his cock punching into her when she whined a response.

"You want my knot, Rey?" he growled into her skin, feeling his voice vibrate across her chest. "You want your best friend's cock lodged inside of you, nowhere to run, stuffing you with his come?"

"Lee," Reyna whined, her voice breaking, "let me feel it, I want to feel you..."

"But you already have me," Leander teased, though it would've been a hell of a lot more convincing if his voice didn't sound completely wrecked. They were both trembling, and Leander knew that that final push would be devastating.

"Please," Reyna whispered, "Need you so bad, need your knot, let me have you, please—"

Her babbling left him defenseless, left him unable to do anything but exactly what she wanted, because if she asked him like that, he'd do anything. Leander pulled back so he could watch her face, his heart leaping to his throat at the sight of her. Her mouth was slack, her eyes wide and desperate and when he started to push into her, her lashes fluttered closed.

A part of him wanted to demand she open her eyes, look into his, see how gone he was for her, but he couldn't wait.

He pushed into her.

Leander couldn't tell who was shaking, who was moaning, he was pretty sure it was both of them but also that the room was ringing.

He should stop, he should slow down, but all he could think was *finally*, he was here. His hips pushed deeper into her, and Reyna gasped, her hands tangling in his hair as she clung to him.

"Baby," she whispered, and Leander nearly passed out. She'd never called him that, he'd never heard it from her, but now she was breathless, stretched on his cock and clenched around his knot and she meant him. "It's so big."

Leander tasted blood again as he bit down, hard.

Pleasure like he'd never known curled over his skin like heat, but what he wanted more than anything, was the soft contentment in Reyna's voice. He hadn't come yet, and every inch of his body was on fire, but he would stay like this forever if it meant she would stay here too. Like this, with him, wrapped in daylight and heat and each other.

She rolled her hips.

Leander hadn't been expecting it, had been lost in sensation, so when she clenched her pussy around his cock, all Leander could do was thrust into her once more and come.

He shouted with it, felt it rip out of him, felt destroyed and incinerated as he unloaded into his best friend's cunt, and his knot held his come there. He felt like it might never end, like he was swimming and drowning and lost in an overwhelming tidal wave of completion and he came back to himself as he realized he was clenching her hips. Reyna's thighs were soft and she moved her pussy against him, milking him.

"That's it, baby," she was cooing, a fondness in her voice that made him want to pull her to his chest, bury his face in his neck and never let either of them out of the bed. "God, Lee, you came so hard, that was...oh my god, that was so much. You feel so good, you feel...shit."

She broke off on a gasp, and Leander heard her. He was so sensitive, but he realized it was her hips pushing up into his, that she was clenching around him and he looked up at her in wonder as he realized that his orgasm was beckoning hers.

"You gonna come on my knot, Rey?" he asked, his voice hoarse, and Reyna moaned.

He reached between them, his fingers brushing over her swollen clit, and they both moaned when she tightened around him.

"I'm so full, fuck," she gasped, her hand closing around the wrist that was working over her clit. "Lee, I can't stop—"

"Don't stop," Leander muttered, rubbing circles over her clit. He couldn't breathe from how raw his cock felt, but he would do anything for the way Reyna was chasing her own pleasure, reacting to his.

"Keep working on my cock, keep fucking yourself," he told her, and Reyna's legs jolted as he pressed on her clit, "on that werewolf cock. You did so good for me, honey, letting me fuck you and fill you. Now I want to feel you come so hard on my knot, Rey..."

She was sobbing, her legs shaking and her hips pushing weakly up into him. He could tell she was exhausted but it was so beautiful, how she was chasing it.

"Let me feel it, honey," he whispered, and Leander felt when it worked over her. Pulsing heat spreading over her body as she trembled around him, cradling him, clinging to him. And though he'd just come harder than he'd ever come, Leander couldn't stop the way his hips pushed into her—meeting her, soothing her, fucking her through it. He felt a smaller, lesser, orgasm pulse out of him, and Reyna moaned as she settled, feeling him spurt even more into her.

The sun was still too bright.

The day was too far gone, and yet Leander knew that even if they weren't joined, he wouldn't have gotten up.

He knew this was just the first, just the beginning of the weekend but Reyna didn't protest as he turned her into him. Exhausted and depleted, Leander wrapped Reyna in his arms, and the wolf inside of him purred as they curled into each other.

Twelve

Reyna stared at the ceiling of the small room, wondering if she should stay here or go to join Leander.

Or even if she could, if her body could remember how to move after two orgasms before food or water or even 'good morning'.

Not that she'd minded.

Her body was thoroughly exhausted, warm and sated and like she could go back to sleep even though daylight streamed through the windows. She could hear Leander puttering around the kitchen, pulling bowls down and starting to prepare food.

There was a clicking sound, then a whoosh, as the flame of the gas stove caught in the kitchen, and Reyna's curiosity got the better of her. She tried to remember where she'd put her bag...she hadn't put it anywhere; it was probably still by the door, where she'd dropped it when she first came in.

Before Leander kissed her.

It was just her in the room, but Reyna still felt guilty as she smiled. How could she have known that this is what Lee would be like? Exactly how he always was — attentive, intent, sweet —but then just more. Like the intensity he always kept carefully locked away had just bolted out of him.

Again, not that she'd minded.

Reyna knew she was moving slowly, almost lethargic, and she considered just pulling the sheet off the bed before she saw Leander's sweatshirt crumpled at the foot of it. She pulled it over her head; it didn't quite afford her modesty, but it did cover all the important bits. She used the restroom quickly, avoiding looking in the mirror as she washed her hands—she didn't need to know what she looked like in her current state of unmade exhaustion.

The hardwood floor was warmed by the sun, streaming uninhibited through the eastern-facing windows of the house, as she dragged her feet across it towards the kitchen.

There was no way he hadn't heard her coming, not with nearly ever step causing the wood to squeak in protest, but Leander didn't look up as she stepped into the kitchen.

"It's gonna take a minute," Leander said softly. "I don't mind bringing you a plate."

Reyna leaned against the doorway, watching him as he ladled pancake batter into a nonstick pan.

"I don't mind standing, either," she told him, and it was true. She wasn't going to bust out stretches or anything, but it was good to be moving her body.

Well, moving her body, *vertically*.

Leander made quite the picture.

His hair was mussed, and he was half dressed, in sweatpants and not much else. A dishtowel was hung haphazardly over a shoulder and his glasses were perched low on his nose, giving him an attentive air that countered the slow way he moved around the kitchen. His skin looked so soft in the sunlight. It looked almost golden under the rays of sunshine that cut through the window.

She'd never really noticed his back before.

The broadness of his shoulders, the way skin wrinkled at his side when he leaned over to open the window over the sink. And since when had Leander had an ass like that? Reyna knew she was exhausted, because what the hell kind of thought was that to have? She was ogling her best friend as he paraded around in literal sweatpants, flustered at the sight of his ass like he hadn't come inside of her last night. Or an hour ago.

Leander flipped the first pancake onto a waiting plate, and finally looked over at her.

Reyna had never understood the expression 'his eyes heated', and maybe she still didn't, but her skin felt warmer the longer he looked at her.

"Y'look nice," he said, almost gruff.

Reyna was too drained to start the *no I don't* fight that the comment warranted. She looked fucked, not nice, but she supposed the rut made them synonymous.

"Thanks," she said instead, and Lee smiled lightly, like he was pleased she allowed it.

He turned back to the stove, poking at the pancakes still in the pan with the back of the spatula. Every few moments, his eyes would flick back over to her, dart to the hem of his sweatshirt, then avert, and Reyna watched the hand that wasn't flipping pancakes tighten on the edge of the counter.

"Everything good?" she asked, and Leander nodded, shortly, and changed out the pancakes. He started another batch, his movements deliberate and slow, and Reyna waited for an explanation.

But the kitchen was still.

The stove hummed, the batter sizzled, and Reyna noticed Leander was breathing through his mouth. He flipped the pancakes, then again, then deposited them onto the plate.

If he wasn't going to tell; she wasn't going to guess.

Determined to be helpful, Reyna went to cross the kitchen to grab the clementines from their spot by the fridge, but was startled when Leander took a full step back from her.

She raised her eyebrows, pointing to the refrigerator, and Leander swallowed heavily, letting her pass. She noticed his jaw was clenched, his nostrils flaring. Reyna hadn't thought sleep deprivation made him jumpy, but maybe the rut affected him differently?

"Sorry," he rasped, his voice hoarser than it'd been minutes ago, as he repeated, "sorry."

"It's okay," Reyna said, hoping it was reassuring. She grabbed the bag of clementines, ripping it open, and heard the spatula clatter to the ground behind her. When she turned around, Leander was running the spatula under water.

She lifted the bag demonstratively. "I was just gonna peel a couple oranges...is that okay?"

"Uh," Leander clenched his teeth together like he was trying to stop the words, abandoning the spatula and grabbing another from some drawer. "No."

Reyna stopped in her path across the kitchen. "No?"

He nodded, sharp, and Reyna stood still, considering her options. She set the bag down by the sink, backed away from it slightly, re-treating to the doorway where she'd stood before. Once she was there, Leander's nostrils flared again, but he went back to the stove. He lifted the mixing bowl, pouring the rest of the batter into the skillet, like he needed to be busy rather than say what he was thinking.

"I'm trying to just make pancakes," he said, "because we really need to eat, you especially. I know it's a lot, so you need to eat, but you—" he broke off, eyes darting to her again.

Reyna crossed a leg in front of her.

"But you smell really fucking good, Rey," Leander said, his voice low, "and I need you to not be any closer to me, before I forget there's an active gas flame."

Oh.

Reyna felt her skin flush at his words, even as she wished he didn't have to sound so upset about it. The day had already been a lot, she shouldn't be feeling any type of way, but she was only human. A man in sweatpants and glasses was cooking her pancakes, and telling her he wanted her; how was she supposed to be unaffected?

"So, again," Leander said, after a moment, "I don't mind bringing you a plate."

His earlier offer made sense now, as did why he'd reacted when she crossed the room, and when the door had opened to the fridge. He'd mumbled something about that earlier, in bed, about her scent, but now she could see that it was a tangible thing outside of bed, too.

Leander looked at her for a long moment, both of them realizing she hadn't left yet.

"It's burning," Reyna said, lifting her chin at the skillet. Leander looked down quickly, flipped the pancake onto the plate and then switched off the burner, pushing the skillet to a colder part of the stove to cool. He staued by the stove, his shoulders tight, and Reyna could leave.

Could go back to bed, wait for him there, let him feed her breakfast he'd made for them like it was normal.

None of this was normal.

And that was why she was here, wasn't she, to help him through this? Even though he was doing his best to look after both of them

"I'm still wet, Lee," she told him quietly. She didn't have to check; with how hard she'd come and how much he had, it was an empirical fact.

He was across the room in a heartbeat, his lean body caging her in, pushing her back against the door frame in a way that would've stolen her breath if his mouth hadn't beaten her to it. He licked into her mouth and Reyna whimpered when she realized he still tasted like her, like hers. Leander moaned against her lips, his body pressing tightly against hers and Reyna loved how he felt.

It wasn't lost to her that he hadn't told her to leave, hadn't demanded that she get out of the room so he could focus, just bore it. Just continued steadfastly to make her food, and didn't surrender to this until the meal was ready, and the stove was off, that he cared so much about looking after her that he'd driven himself halfway feral for wanting her.

His hands were already under his sweatshirt, reaching up for her breasts, holding onto her as he devoured her mouth.

"You smell so damn good, Rey," Leander panted against her lips, "and taste even better, standing in my kitchen like this…"

He kissed down her neck, and she felt claws drag against her skin as he pulled his sweatshirt off of her. Why did she love it so much? He was still Lee, still here with her, but seeing that darker side of him excited something in her. She lifted her arms to help him, and when her hands pulled free, he captured them in his. He turned her in his arms, his mouth grazing her neck again as he guided her hands to the doorway, bracing her against it before his hands trailed down her body again.

His fingers traveled over the tops of her arms, up her shoulders, where he gathered her hair into his fist. Reyna's head lulled, turning her face when his hand in her hair guided her, promptly rewarded by a searing kiss when his lips met hers.

He hadn't taken her from behind yet.

If she'd thought about it before this moment, she would've expected it to be impersonal, distant. But those words were the farthest from her mind as Leander arranged her body in the doorway—bracing her hands, caressing her ass, nudging her knees farther apart. She was absolutely pliant in his grasp, and Leander's hand slipped between her thighs. They both broke away from the kiss as his hand glided between her folds, teasing the wetness there.

"Fuck me," Leander groaned, as his fingers spread through her. "You're ready for me already?"

Reyna rocked into his touch, chasing the sensation of his fingers over her clit. He obliged and she nearly choked on how good it felt as his finger pushed into her.

Another finger joined the first, a broad stroke through her folds and Reyna's mouth fell open.

She didn't know what'd come over her.

Somewhere between Leander cooking for her and looking at her like he would die if he wasn't inside her had her somehow feeling like that also might be the end of her. She felt him back away, only for a moment, and then his hot cock teased over her folds.

Reyna rocked back into him, trying to ease him into her with just the motion of her hips.

"Easy," Leander chuckled, had the audacity to laugh like it wasn't the sweetest torture to feel him so close, and not be filled.

Any litany of responses vanished as he angled his cock against her entrance and began pushing in. Reyna's back bowed and her grip tightened on the door as she arched to accommodate him, and she focused on the hitch in his breathing as he pushed into her.

He kept pushing and Reyna's mouth fell open weakly.

She kept expecting him to stop, work himself into her in thrusts, or pull back to gain leverage. But instead he just pushed in, steadily prying her walls back, remaking her with his certainty. She was on her toes, her back arched to help the angle as much as she could, and she could only wait for him to go deeper.

"Thatta girl," Leander breathed, his cock sliding another inch into her, and Reyna felt a whine building in her throat. "How's that feel, hmm?"

"So good," she managed. "Lee, shit, you feel so good."

"That's all you, baby," Lee panted, another glorious inch deeper into her. "It's that perfect pussy, taking me so well, fitting my cock like a glove. We're almost there, honey, breathe for me."

Reyna hadn't realized she'd stopped breathing.

She pulled in a breath obediently, her grasp on the world feeling tenuous at best. There was only the brilliant, burning pleasure of Lee stretching her out, and when his hips finally rested against hers, she felt like collapsing in a heap.

But he was holding her up, with his hand in her hair and on her hip, and his cock so damn deep inside of her. Reyna clenched down on him, relishing the way he filled her so completely, and Leander swore behind her.

"Tell me it's as much for you as it is for me," he said, his voice hoarse. "Tell me it feels this unreal to you, too, because I'm losing my mind here, baby."

Reyna's thighs were burning and she realized that everything was shaking, it felt *so much*. She needed more.

Leander stopped only a moment at the top of his stroke, fully seated, before he pulled back again. It was devastating, how steady he was. And she knew it was intentional, that this morning had been so frantic that he was trying to counter that, but she might ignite if he kept with the slow pressure. Reyna let go of the door to reach for his hand in her hair. He released her hair as soon as her fingers touched his, but she didn't let him go, pulling his hand to her jawline, and then lower.

Reyna felt when he understood.

His breath hitched as his fingers closed around her throat. He didn't grip her, didn't do anything more than hold his broad palm there, pressed against her, checking in on both of them. Leander pulled her more tightly to him, away from the doorframe, and Reyna's back arched as he pulled her back. His glasses scratched at her face and she reached back to pull them off, setting them on a counter so she could press their faces together. She was on her toes to accommodate his length inside her, but she braced herself on the doorway, as Leander crowded behind her.

"Lee," she whispered, her body shaking. God, she couldn't believe she needed it so bad, needed him so bad.

He pulled in a slow breath, and she felt something sharp prick at her neck, where his lips and fangs teased her skin. His fingers covered her neck, his thumb flexing up to brush against her jaw. She wondered if he could feel her pulse, wondered what his was doing, but then he moved his hips again and Reyna bowed forward.

Which pushed her neck into his palm.

Reyna's eyes closed, her jaw dropping open as the pressure increased on her throat.

"Fuck, look at you," Leander mumbled, either to himself or to her, Reyna couldn't tell. "You need it that bad, honey? You're gonna choke yourself for it?"

Reyna felt her thighs growing wet as arousal literally dripped down them as she squirmed.

Leander's fingers curled slightly around her as he understood how much she wanted this—wanted him, like this, hard and choking her and desperate, so she didn't feel insane for wanting it too. He stroked into her, his cock pressing into her and Reyna scrambled against the door. Leander chuckled darkly as his hand on her hip tightened; Reyna could feel the press of his blunted claws pressing into her as he held her tightly, and then his breath puffed against her shoulder blades.

"Now you know how I feel," Leander said, his voice somehow soothing and also clipped, and Reyna's head fell back against his shoulder. "Driving me crazy, Rey, but it's okay; I've got you."

He repositioned himself so he could fuck into her, and Reyna's knees nearly buckled as he found a rhythm. His hips rocked up into hers, the angle making an impossibly tight fit. The stretch of him eased, and she felt his teeth graze the back of her neck, as he nuzzled against her shoulder.

"Fuck, honey," he mumbled with his lips against skin, "you smell so good. You feel so tight around me, taking me so well…"

Reyna loved how his words slurred like this, like he was just as out of it as she was. His nose met the crease of her neck and she heard him inhale, and his hips thrust deeper into her.

How was that so hot?

Reyna didn't know what it meant that he was so obsessed with the scent of her, but she felt his fingers tighten slightly around her throat. He wasn't anywhere close to blocking airflow, but the pressure of him there was enough to reminder that he could. It was the perfect balance, like she was driving him wild but he'd never act on it, but he *could*.

Hazy pressure coiled through her body and she turned back to him, and he kissed her, his hips slowing. His tongue matched the pace of his thrusts, slow and deep and overwhelming, and Reyna felt the back of her hands against her cheek before she realized she was almost falling into where she'd braced them on the door. She felt Leander let go of her hip, and a moment later, a she felt him between her thighs. Like his claws on her neck, he was careful as he brushed over her clit with the pads of his fingers.

The intensity of it shocked her; she was practically drowning in sensation. His cock was so deep inside of her, and his fingers were rubbing methodically over her clit, and Reyna felt her legs start to shake.

"Look at you," Leander said against her lips, "taking it so well, letting me into that tight pussy and holding me there like it's where I'm supposed to be. Are you gonna come for me, baby? Fuck, you feel so good—please, Rey—"

Like the sweetest, blinding relief, she felt her body surrender to Lee's hands and soft voice as he coaxed it out of her. Her ears were ringing and she felt like she could finally breathe, *finally*. She was practically dead weight in his arms, locking her arms against the door to keep from sending them both toppling over. Leander was running a soothing hand over her hip, as he mumbled into her skin. She couldn't hear his words over the way her pulse was pounding, and as she came back to herself, she realized he was still hard inside of her.

"Lee," she whispered, her body shaking. She wasn't sure what she was asking but he heard it, reaching to pry her off the door. He kissed her forehead softly, and then grunted as he pulled out of her. Reyna was surprised at first, but then she realized there was no comfortable way to knot her while they were both standing, bent over like this. She followed him into the bedroom, trying not to notice the way her come was dripping down her thighs, or that his cock bobbed with each step.

"How do you want me?" she asked, a logistical question rather than a seduction, but from the look that crossed over Leander's face, he didn't hear the difference. He reached for her with a growl, a soft sound rumbling from his chest that Reyna found frankly devastating, and they tumbled onto the bed. He rolled her onto her stomach, pulling her hips off the bed before he knelt behind her. Reyna cried out as he pushed in, feeling every inch of his cock push into her, and Leander's grip on her hips tightened enough that he could feel his claws.

"Fuck, Rey, how you feel…" Leander groaned, and he lifted a leg to plant his foot on the bed. He fucked into her sharply, falling quickly into the rhythm they'd found in the kitchen and Reyna wondered how a person could feel so overwhelmed and so ready at once. The push of him was so filling, so deeply satisfying, and she arched her back to take him deeper.

She felt his knot.

It swelled at the base of his cock as it pressed against Reyna's core, and she whimpered at the thought of it filling her. Being even more full of him, being more overwhelmed, with nothing to do but take it. She was too overstimulated to come again, but he felt so fucking good, and she wanted to take it, wanted him to take her. She spread her knees wider, and Leander moaned as she deepened the angle.

"You want my knot, honey?" he asked, his voice gruff. He was pulling her back onto his cock, slamming into her and shaping her to him, and Reyna spread her palms on the bed, a semblance of pushing back against him.

"That's it, baby," Leander gritted, his voice breathless. "Push back on it, I know you want it—fuck, that's so hot, Rey. I'm so close, but you know what'll get me there?"

He didn't wait for her response, just reached between her legs to find her clit again.

Reyna was so oversensitized, so overwhelmed by him, so she didn't expect more than a reflex, but he was less careful this time. As his fingers rubbed over her clit, his claws pricked at her, and the soft pain was like an electric wire through Reyna.

"Shit, there it is," Leander praised, and Reyna felt it roll over her. "God, you feel so good. Taking me so well, and still so fucking tight around me. Let me feel it again, Rey, come for me again."

Reyna felt like she was an endless circuit of sensation, reacting and whimpering and begging for something she wasn't sure she could take, but unable to stop it. As she clenched around him, she felt his knot pressing closer and closer, and Reyna surrendered to it. She stopped pushing back at him, stopped arching her back or trying to do any type of thing that wasn't just taking him. She felt boneless against the mattress, like she was molten and accepting, and Leander pulled her hips back and fed his knot into her.

It was so tight.

Reyna moaned into the bedsheets and Leander's hand stuttered over her clit. He rubbed her sharply, his knot forcing any remaining thoughts to flee, and Reyna came again.

"Fuck, that's it, gorgeous," Leander groaned. "This pussy, Rey, it's like you don't want me to do anything else but fill you. I'm gonna...I need to—"

Leander buried his face in her neck as he came, his moan vibrating across her body, as he continued to pump into her. He collapsed on top of her, but his hips continued to work as he came, driving into her like he couldn't stop any more than she could. Reyna trembled as her orgasm worked through her, piercing and nearly harsh, emotions and adrenaline rushing through her.

It was too much.

Reyna didn't know why or how things shifted, but it was too much, and no longer in a sexy way. She couldn't stop trembling, and it wasn't pleasure, it was just shivers, working over her body.

Fuck, what was she doing?

Alarm pounded through her, her body's signals no longer registering. Reyna frowned as she tried to burrow deeper into the bedlinens, wincing when she realized Leander was still wedged inside of her.

She couldn't go anywhere.

And that was the whole point of it, why they were here and what she'd agreed to do, but Reyna's mind clouded as tremors worked over her. She felt exhausted and knew she was dehydrated, so she was probably overreacting, and what a selfish time to overreact, because Leander had just made her come twice, so hard, and here she was not even sure what she was going on —

"Reyna?" Leander's voice, shot with concern, pierced through the haze. Reyna gasped, pulled a breath of air in that felt piercing cold. She felt like she was vibrating, useless and needy, and confusion turned to shame in the pit of her stomach.

"I don't know," she whispered, not even sure if he could hear her over the chattering of her teeth, or the way they were pressed into the mattress. She wasn't even certain what she was trying to tell him, and that made it worse.

"I'm here," Leander said, his voice soft as he shifted them. He lay beside her on the bed, turning her from the mattress into him. They both felt twinges of discomfort as the movement pulled at his knot, but he stayed lodged inside of her, and as he wrapped his arms around her, Reyna waited for the feeling to go away, but it didn't.

He must be so annoyed with her.

She knew what she was here for, and he'd taken good care of both of them, and she was here feeling what, needy? What, did she expect compliments? She couldn't think clearly, couldn't breathe clearly, but she could feel the beating of Leander's heart against her cheek, and she focused on that.

"You smell scared," Leander said. His voice was gentle, and he seemed to know that she needed him to keep talking. "Normally it's oranges, but greener, but you...it's not bitter, or aggressive, it's just soured."

That made sense.

He was still talking, explaining how her scent was normally, but Reyna only listened so much as to hear he was still speaking. She liked how his voice sounded, and what he was saying mattered less than the fact that he didn't sound annoyed. She shook her head against Leander's chest, feeling the hair there scratch against her face. She knew the answer to overstimulation, or whatever the fuck this was, wasn't more stimuli, but the unfamiliar texture grounded her.

Or maybe it was Lee.

She was pretty sure her sense of smell was normal, with just regular human nose, but he smelled like sweat. He smelled like they'd gone for a run, not whatever they'd just done. She felt like a cat, but she didn't think Leander minded, just let her soothe herself against him, and kept talking.

After a couple more minutes, he pulled his hips back slightly.

"This is gonna...sorry," Lee muttered, and he pulled out of her as gently as she could.

Reyna whimpered as his knot pulled out of her, followed by a gush of fluid.

"I'm sorry," Leander repeated, and then a moment later, he was gone.

Reyna waited for panic to surge again, but it didn't.

She felt fuzzy.

Groggy, clouded, like there was something she was supposed to be catching but wasn't. Lee was back, then, prompting her to spread her legs. The washcloth was warm, courtesy of the scalding tap, but Reyna thought that his hands were somehow warmer. She curled into him, too tired to fight the impulse to cuddle against him.

Annoyingly, he rearranged her.

He sat behind her on the bed, his knees spread as she sat between them. Reyna frowned, registering that she was chewing a slice of a clementine.

When had that happened? How? She meant to ask Lee, but then he was coaxing her to take a small sip of water, which she managed, and it felt good. Soothing. Not as much as his voice against her back, the way she could feel it rumbling through him into her. She took another sip of water, another bite of clementine, another piece of a pancake as he offered them to her.

She could feel his cock, hard and hot, pressing against her back, but he wasn't doing anything about it. Anytime she tried to ask, he pushed a bite of food into her mouth.

Lee was a good nurse, she decided.

He knew that, probably. Hopefully. She just hadn't often let him take care of her. Maybe that was nice too, every now and then.

She pressed her lips together to decline another clementine slice, holding Leander's arm around her chest instead. The sun was bright and he was so warm, but she closed her eyes against all of it, and when sleep crept in, she let it claim her.

Thirteen

The sunlight on the ceiling turned orange as the sun set, and Leander lay still, listening to Reyna breathe.

He turned his head on the pillow, looking at where she lay curled next to him, where he'd coaxed her to lie down after convincing her to eat something. She still had one of his arms, clutched against her chest like a teddy bear, with her knees curled up slightly. He could see the rise and fall of her breathing, the way her upper body shifted with it. He'd wanted to fall asleep with her, but when he closed his eyes, all he could see was the glazed, unfocused look in hers, and the panic when she'd realized she couldn't get away from him.

He'd heard enough surgeons in the hospital staff locker room to know what sub drop looked like; even if they hadn't been in a scene, that had been pretty intense. What he didn't know was if he handled it right.

The moment that he'd realized her shaking wasn't from pleasure, his heart had nearly stopped. He'd tried to soothe her as best he could, reassure and comfort her and then start taking physical care once she'd steadied, but he still wasn't sure.

That'd been hours ago, but neither Leander's need nor his anxiety had calmed.

It was everything he'd been afraid a rut could be: overwhelming and overpowering, something that could hurt Reyna if he wasn't careful.

Even now, she was calming him.

Asleep and close, soft and near, just her proximity soothed him. Hell if he deserved it, but her nearness and her scent settled something in him. He ached for her, but even more he felt a deep protectiveness over her. She wouldn't have reacted how she had, if she wasn't in this deeper than she was letting on.

Reyna hummed in her sleep, her hips shifting backwards.

Leander grunted as her ass brushed against his pajama pants, the light touch feeling like it had burned him. He'd known this would be intense, but he'd never experienced prolonged need like this. But it was more than impulse, it was a heightened intensity, like all the impulses he could normally curb were magnified. He also was someone who was used to having a normal refractory period, so the fact that his body was consistently primed, was a lot.

Reyna must've been dreaming, because she moved again, a soft sound in the back of her throat.

Leander clenched the fist that she didn't hold, making himself lie still. His best friend was deep in exhausted sleep, her body entirely worn out from helping him through an unfamiliar physiological transformation, and he was here reacting to her. The sunshine was morphing from orange to a deep red, and Leander watched through blurred eyes as leaves outside the cabin cut through the sun shadows.

Reyna moved again, innocently unaware of the way she was grinding into him, the way her soft hips were pressing back into him.

The way his body was reacting.

Leander held his breath and tried to move away from her, but Reyna only pushed back, and Leander winced, wishing he didn't have to wake her.

"Reyna," he whispered, "hey, you have to wake up…"

Her response was a breathy laugh, soft and faint, and he realized she was already awake.

"I don't know if it's your fault or mine," Reyna said, but she didn't sound upset.

Her voice was thin, distracted, and Leander didn't know he'd reached for her until his hands settled on the warm skin of her hips. He'd meant to hold her still, but then she sighed, almost like a relief, and his fingers tightened, kneading her soft skin.

"Whose fault for what?" Leander heard himself ask, heard it like it was someone else. All he could focus on was the way Reyna's hips flared under his fingers.

"I had a dream," Reyna said, almost laughing. "And normally it's fine, you know, I can brush it off, but then I woke up and you were right here, and you felt nice and—"

Reyna broke off when Leander's hips pushed forward to meet her. He knew he shouldn't.

They still had to talk about earlier, but right now she felt nearly irresistible, and to know she'd been thinking about him too, in a dream, was almost too much. He could smell her now, her arousal perfuming the air around them, and then he realized what she'd said: *normally*. Had she dreamt of him before?

"How is that my fault?" Leander asked, to distract himself. And he was curious, but it also didn't sound like Reyna was actually looking to place blame.

"Probable cause," Reyna said, like her ass wasn't rubbing against the front of Leander's pants, like she wasn't breathless from how good it felt. "We've never had sex before yesterday, and I've never taken a knot, so of course that's what my subconscious latches onto."

Leander gritted his teeth. "I'm trying to find a way to interpret that, that isn't you telling me you're dreaming about taking my knot."

Reyna gasped, her head falling back and almost knocking against Leander's.

"Why is that hot?" she asked, sounding both fascinated and needy. "It shouldn't be, but how you say it…"

She trailed off as Leander ground against her again. He'd say anything if she thought it was hot, but as it was, he was losing focus fast.

Their bodies were pressed together from sternum to knee; with her body molded against his, Reyna felt like temptation personified—but Leander couldn't shake the image of her curling in his arms, panicked and unsure what to ask for.

"What do you need, Rey?" he made himself ask, even as his hands guided the motion of her hips.

She sighed softly, letting him move her, letting him match the rhythm of their hips together. Even through the thin material separating them, Leander could feel how warm she was. The way she was grinding her ass against the bulge in Leander's pajamas was obvious, but he needed her to say it.

"Make me feel good," Reyna whispered, a request and a command.

Leander ground his hips into her again and Reyna arched her neck, an irresistible invitation, and Leander leaned forward to skim her neck with his lips.

"Honey," he said, his voice coming out softer than he'd intended, and Reyna's skin prickled, like she knew what he was thinking about.

"I don't know what that was, earlier," she said, and one of her hands reached back to wrap around the back of his neck, "but it's gone. You…I didn't even know what to ask for and you took care of me. Let me do that for you."

It was a blind reach, but her fingers curled through the hair at the base of his neck, pulling him back to her neck. Leander kissed her obligingly, keeping his touch light, but unable to refuse her.

Reyna hummed as his kisses grew stronger, less like a caress and more like a mark, her hand tightening in his hair. He believed her, and he could tell she was being honest, but she'd also wanted everything they'd done before, and she still wound up shaking in his arms.

"I don't want to hurt you," he said, hoarsely, and Reyna's hand tightened in his hair.

"It hurts now, Lee," she whispered.

Leander broke away from her, pressing his forehead to the space between her neck and shoulder, fighting desperately to retain control. His fingers were shaking to stop from reaching between her legs, and thrusting between her thighs.

How was he supposed to function, hearing his best friend tell him she was aching for him, that it *hurt* to not be with him?

"You'll tell me if it's too much," he insisted, hearing the desperation threaded through his voice, "and we'll stop."

Reyna turned in his arms to press a quick kiss to his mouth.

"It won't be," she said simply, as she resettled back against him, "but I will."

He wished he could see her more clearly, but her confidence and confirmation were enough. He had to trust her in this; in the same way she was trusting him with her body, he had to trust her with her consent.

Leander reached between them, tracing down towards her core, and Reyna's gasp was drowned out by his groan as he felt the moisture gathered between her thighs.

"Fuck, honey," he moaned, his finger tracing through her folds. "You're so wet already."

"I wasn't—" Reyna broke off when his finger brushed over her clit. "Shit. I wasn't being coy; I need you."

The feeling of her wetness on his fingers, her whispered words, the way the room smelled more and more like her, Leander wanted to get drunk off of it.

"You're so soft here," he murmured, pushing two fingers through her folds, careful with his claws, savoring the way her breath caught, and her back further arched. He wasn't in control enough to tease her how he wanted, but Reyna's hips were moving like she was impatient too. Leander shoved his pajama pants down his thighs, pressing back to her as soon as he could, but it wasn't soon enough. Reyna reached between her legs, rubbing slowly at her clit while she waited for him, and Leander paused for a moment, admiring the way her fingers and thighs were shining with her arousal.

At the first press of his bare cock between her dripping thighs, they both moaned. Reyna's hand dropped from her clit to brace herself on the bed, her fingers tangling in the sheets as her thighs tightened around him. Leander rocked over her cunt, his cock dragging against the soft skin of her thighs and Reyna's head fell back against his chest.

"Lee," she whispered, "you feel so big, it's—"

"I know," Leander gritted. It was so good, it was unreal, he had no idea how he was going to handle being actually inside of her.

Just the thought of it reminded him that he had a wolf that desperately, unequivocally, needed that.

He listened carefully, waiting for the change in her breathing or her body that he'd seen earlier, something that would take this from overwhelming to overburdening. But Reyna's body was languid, and she was whimpering softly as his cock rocked between her legs. She even shifted slightly, working her hips how she'd take him, like a promise, and Leander answered her.

"Let me..." he prompted, his hand curling around her thigh to lift her upper leg. Reyna reached a hand between them, guiding his cock into her waiting cunt as he parted her thighs to press into her.

She was so warm.

Leander's grip on her thigh was tight, and he buried his face in her neck, kissing the spot he knew was sensitive as he fought to control his pace. Even so wet, even so worked up, it was a tight fit, and he didn't want to rush her.

"More," Reyna breathed, her hand still between their thighs, like she needed to feel the inches of him that weren't inside her yet.

"Easy, honey," Leander promised, his throat tight as he pressed further into her. Each inch felt like it took hours, as her body remembered how to take him, and accepted him into her tight warmth.

Reyna was fully panting, her upper body limp as he pushed the final stretch into her.

"Yes," she breathed. "Fuck, Lee, I'm so full."

Her voice was soft, awed, and her thigh was shaking in his hand. At some point her hand had lifted from between their legs to clutch at his arm, her nails digging into his forearm, and Leander focused on the sharp sting rather than the way being inside her felt so *right*.

They lay still as they adjusted, their breathing syncing as their chests rose and fell together.

Leander lifted his head to kiss her cheek lightly.

"How're we doing, Rey?" he asked, his voice hoarse. "Can I move?"

"God, *please*," Reyna moaned, and Leander's hips pulled back immediately. She keened as he pumped into her slowly, the delicious slide of his cock through her tight walls just as overwhelming for her as it was for him.

When he reached the top of the stroke he needed more, needed to feel every inch of her cunt, every warm, sweet sensation. Before he knew it, he was rutting into her, each stroke pushing a beautiful moan past Reyna's lips. She felt so good around him, and Leander felt himself recentering around her. Knowing she was here with him, that she felt something close to what he did, even though neither of them knew what to name it.

He propped himself up on his elbow looking down at her. Her eyes were scrunched shut, her mouth gaping open in pleasure, and her skin was flushed darker. Leander felt dizzy with how good she looked in his bed, in his arms.

"Fuck, Rey, look at you," he whispered, and Reyna shivered. "Taking me so good, asking me so sweetly, you're driving me out of my mind."

When he adjusted his grip on her thigh, her leg lifted slightly, changing the angle, Reyna cried out.

Leander's eyes rolled back as she clenched impossibly tighter around him. She sounded so good, and she felt even better, and he angled his hips to hit that same spot again.

"There, fuck," Reyna whined, reaching back for him, "right there, yes—"

Leander groaned as her hand rested on his ass, pulling him into her. Like he was going to go anywhere. But she held him tightly, like she needed him, like she wanted him as close as she could have him, and fuck, if that didn't do something to him. Her neck rolled weakly, and each breath seemed to be a gasp, and Leander knew she was getting close.

"This what you were dreaming of?" he asked and Reyna shuddered, her grip on his ass tightening. "Being this close, taking me into your pussy, clenching down on my cock like you want me to stay?"

"Yes," Reyna practically sighed the word, even as her hips worked desperately over his cock, chasing her orgasm. "Yes, Lee, and you feel so good, I can't—I need—"

She broke off on a whine, as Leander fucked into her. She was so close, and he wanted her to come so hard, to know she felt half as mindless with pleasure as he did.

"I've got ya," Leander panted, "right there, yeah? You're doing so good for me, baby, are you gonna come for me?"

Reyna nodded, frantically, her eyes screwed shut and Leander loved that she knew he was watching her, that that was enough of a response. He kept his pace, kept doing exactly what she asked, thrust his cock as deep as he could into her. She was getting louder and then she was quiet for a long moment, both of them holding their breaths, before it broke over her.

Reyna arched off the bed, letting go of Leander and then her hands were scrambling again, needing to feel him, wherever she could reach. Leander held her tightly as she worked through it, as her gasps melted into soft sighs as she finished, collapsing back against him. He felt a drop of moisture on his chest from where her head was resting and a bolt of panic went through him.

Was she crying?

Had he missed something, had it been too much? He reached over to brush at her face, tracing the tear track back to her eye.

"Shit, are you okay?" he asked.

He wished he could see her expression more clearly in the low contrast of the fading light.

Because she went still, and then a moment later, she was pulling away. Leander blinked at her, wondering what was wrong, but then Reyna had pulled herself off of him with a soft grunt, and was standing up. His heart sank, but then she was turning back to the bed, her hands shoving his shoulders back to the bed.

Leander rolled onto his back, trying to understand what was happening and then Reyna was on top of him, her thighs spreading around his.

"Reyna, wait—"

She did not wait. She grabbed his cock and sank herself onto it, her head tipping back as she sank onto his length.

Leander's hands shot out, clenching her thighs as she sank determinedly onto his cock. She braced herself on his chest, holding herself up and holding him down. He couldn't see her face clear enough, but could sense the determination radiating off of her as she worked herself down on his cock.

Leander couldn't breathe.

The room felt freezing without her in his arms, but he was burning where they were joined. This was exactly what he *hadn't* wanted—he needed her close, needed to hear and feel and smell how she was reacting to him, but this far away and in the shadow of twilight, it was a mystery.

Until she sighed as her hips met his, and he was fully seated inside of her.

"Leander," she whispered.

Leander couldn't make his tongue move, which was just as well, because Reyna was still talking.

"You feel so fucking big," she said, and swirled her hips over him in a move that had Leander crying out hoarsely. "You look so pretty, sweet and strong and so *big*, and you made me cry because you fucked me so good, and you're asking me if I'm okay?"

Leander shut his eyes, understanding washing over him with her praise. She didn't like that he was questioning her, questioning them.

"How do I feel, Lee?" Reyna panted, her fingers smoothing up his chest as she pushed herself off his cock. She slid down slowly and Leander heard a wrecked moan before he realized it was him.

"Perfect," he managed, and Reyna laughed softly.

Leander choked as one of her hands fell between them to trace the base of his cock, her fingers gently probing at his knot.

"It feels perfect," she agreed. "So I need you to stop second guessing yourself, and fuck this into me."

She pressed lightly on his knot and Leander's hips thrust up. His hands went from her thighs to her waist, clinging to the soft flesh there, mesmerized by the blur of colors that was their bodies joined together.

"Fuck, yes, like that," Reyna moaned as he thrust into her.

Her fingers traced over his knot, feeling how it was pressed against her entrance. Feeling how her pussy was already stretched around him, and both of them knowing she'd stretch to take even more.

"Reyna—" he protested, but she shook her head.

"I'm good, Lee," she said, "I promise, and I want this."

Leander reached for her, his hand curling around the back of her neck to pull her down to him. She braced herself on his chest again, and something in Leander felt like growling *yes*. That was how she should be—in his arms, resting on him, her cunt wrapped around him. He needed her on his tongue, all around him, everywhere, and he palmed her breasts before feeding one into his mouth. He moaned at the taste of her sweat on her skin, at the way her skin prickled as he breathed over her, at the way her nipple stiffened as he flicked his tongue over her. He could feel himself turning frantic, his hips working up into her, the need to rut and to claim and to knot her overwhelming him.

"Tell me," he panted, switching to her other breast and cradling her ass to pull her closer to him. "Tell me how we look together."

Reyna moaned when his mouth closed over her other breast, his tongue laving and teasing and licking at her. He felt her back bow as her head dropped to look at where they were joined, and he felt when she saw them together. She tightened around him, accepting his fervent pace, trembling all over, or maybe that was him.

"Lee, it's so good," she whispered. "I can—shit, I can see you in my stomach. You feel so big, and it's so deep, oh my god—"

Leander groaned, closing his lips to suck on her nipple, savoring the way she cried out. She sounded so good, she felt so warm, and he couldn't get enough of her taste. Reyna moaned, and then her hand was in his hair, her nails carding through his hair as she pulled his head up, her lips finding his in a desperate kiss as he fucked into her.

"Baby, it feels so good," she whined, her lips against his.

Leander's head was spinning, his world was reorienting. Reyna so close, Reyna around him, Reyna over him. Kissing him, feeling him, praising him...

"I—" he started, but he couldn't say it. Not like this, not this weekend, he couldn't risk her thinking it wasn't real. So he swallowed the three words that threatened to rip out of his chest, tried to think of something, anything else to say, but then Reyna cried out again.

"Oh my god," Reyna moaned, "it—it's pushing against my clit. Oh my god, Lee, please, it's so good..."

He could feel his knot pressing against her entrance. The most tortuous pleasure, each push reminding him how tight she was, how he was too big, how he couldn't fit—

"Let me have it, Lee," Reyna whimpered, and Leander had no choice.

His hips slammed into hers and they both moaned as his knot stuffed into her tight cunt.

"Fuck, baby, it's so good," Reyna said, "thank you."

Leander groaned, his own cry echoing around the room as he reached clumsily between them. Reyna's thighs jerked when he found her clit, and when he circled it with his thumb, her hips started jolting into his.

"Take my knot, Reyna," Leander grunted. "Milk my cock, let me feel you come—"

Reyna gasped as her orgasm washed over her, stronger and more sudden than either of them expected. She broke away from him, burying her face in his hair and wrapping her arms around his neck tightly as she shattered. Her cunt tightened rhythmically around Leander, but it was the way that she clung to him in her release that pushed him over the edge.

Leander came with his arms banded around her waist and his face in her curls. He was pretty sure he was leaving claw marks on her skin, but she was too perfect for him to do anything else. He came hard, like he knew that when it was over, she'd crawl out of his arms and didn't want that yet. Primal as it was, he wanted a part of him deep inside of her, still with her, even when they left the bed.

She was petting him, he realized, as he came back.

Just soft, gentle brushes of her fingers through his hair, over his shoulders, as he came down from his orgasm.

Leander wanted to tighten his arms around her, tuck his head into the crook of her neck and wait until his body recovered so they could go again. But he loosened his arms around her, enough for her to pull away if she needed the space. When she relaxed into him, Leander felt his chest expand in relief.

He liked how she felt, resting on top of him, a closeness that he wasn't often afforded. They stayed there, with soft touches and shared air, as twilight faded, but when the room was pitch dark, Reyna still hadn't moved off of his chest.

Fourteen

The wave curled in, a wall of saltwater pushed her underwater, and Reyna opened her eyes to admire the sunrise filtering through the Atlantic. The world above the waves was wreathed in the shadows of dawn, but underwater, the light crested over the horizon, and it all seemed glitter and gray.

Reyna watched a stream of bubbles trail its way to the surface, and gave herself a moment longer before she followed their ascent.

The small beach on Great Cranberry was empty, with none of the surfer crowd that was likely gathered in Port Cadie. The shallow water was considerably warmer than the larger harbor, but Reyna knew she couldn't stay out as long without her wetsuit.

She broke the surface and rolled onto her back, staring up at the sky.

It was the faintest blue—pale, and streaked with the pinks of a sunrise, interrupted by seagulls flying overhead. Even so, it was beautiful and still, and Reyna closed her eyes, willing some of the serenity to soak through her skin.

Leander had looked peaceful when she'd left him this morning.

She'd woken warm, softer than she had any memory of being, with Leander's arms wrapped around her. For a moment, she'd felt fine. She'd felt cared for, cared about, and she knew she was those things.

But it had felt different when he'd whimpered it into her skin, when she'd read it in his eyes before they glazed over in pleasure.

Reyna's body lifted as a wave buffeted under her, and she pulled her legs under her to tread water.

In another day, the moon would wane.

Leander's eyes would lose the spark that looked dangerously like something neither of them had ever dared voice. She wasn't imagining it, and she believed he believed it, but she was fairly certain it was the wolf in him that felt that way. And that didn't mean it was true, any more than it meant it was lasting.

The edge of the cove had a small outcropping of rocks and Reyna swam towards it. She pulled herself over the small waves, enjoying the cold of the water, the strain of her limbs against the sea. Salt burned her eyes and when she licked her lips, she tasted it, and she breathed deeply when she reached the rocks. Her toes felt distant; she needed to head in, so she gave herself a moment at the rocks before kicking back to shore.

Reyna didn't know how long she'd been out in the ocean.

She'd been so content when she woke, and she knew when Leander woke, his body would want her again. And she'd give herself to him, it was what she was here for, but she needed a moment to remember she was more than that.

She felt at peace here, with the briny sea, the calling gulls, the foam on the tide; that wasn't a peace that could go away when a man woke up.

The wind stung her skin as Reyna walked across the pebbled beach, towards her small pile of things, trying not to think too hard about the scene she'd left this morning.

Leander had stirred when the bed shifted as she got up. He'd mumbled something, nestled deeper into the pillow, and it had taken more willpower than she'd thought to leave the room. She'd stepped carefully across the old wooden floors, grabbed a dress, a swimsuit and a towel, before slipping out into the morning, and refusing to look back.

Reyna shook the towel out, drying herself off brusquely before spreading her towel over the pebbles so she could dry a little before she got dressed. She fingercombed her hair absently; it would dry quicker for lack of a product, albeit at the price of frizziness. Still, she only had to impress Leander, and she had the feeling he'd barely notice.

Reyna tipped her head back, already feeling the warmth sink from the sun to the stones to her hands. The sea had been bracing, numbing, but now she had to think about it.

It being sex with her best friend. *It* being the fact that *it* felt like a hell of a lot more than just sex. Enough so that she'd snuck out of the house while he was still asleep, to go lose feeling in the ocean for a while.

Reyna blew out a long breath, listening to the sound of the tide lapping at pebbles down at the shoreline.

She supposed absently that it'd always been an option.

That she and Leander cared enough about each other that as soon as sex was introduced, it'd tip into something that made so much more sense. The problem was, this wasn't anything more, and couldn't make sense, because he was in a rut, and she was in over her head.

Reyna pushed herself up to rest on locked elbows.

This weekend wasn't about her.

It wasn't about how easy it was to fall asleep in the circle of Leander's arms, or how good it felt to tease him, see him chuckle or blush like he couldn't help it. It wasn't about how precious she felt with him, how he read and worshipped her body better than partners she'd been with for months. And it certainly wasn't about how gently he kissed her, or how well they fit, or how good, and right, and perfect, it all felt.

Reyna pulled her knees up to her chest, wrapping her arms around her shins.

The first night had been her mistake.

Because as much as she wanted to blame the adrenaline and endorphins on the rut, that first night in the cottage had been entirely lucid. It'd been sweet and exploratory and when the light of the full moon had crested into the cabin, Reyna had felt like it was her first time seeing moonbeams, and then she'd buried that revelation in a full day of orgasms and suppression.

But now it was daylight, now her skin was salty from the sea, and Reyna had to reckon with the fact that it wasn't just the moonlight.

It was Leander.

The way he seemed amazed that she'd bring chamomile, like bringing him peace wasn't something she'd tried to do for most of their friendship. The way his touch felt at once reverent and familiar, the way she'd known his smile for most of her life, but know she knew how it felt when he smiled into a kiss. It was the way his expression was entirely unguarded without his glasses, how he'd let her look at him without fully being able to see her, like he had nothing to hide.

There was nothing Reyna would do to break that trust.

If it meant burying the fact that she was feeling a hell of a lot more than she was expecting to, then so be it.

When the sun had dried the seawater into salt in her hair, Reyna pulled the sundress over her head. Her suit was mostly dry, but her dress was thick enough for her to untie the strings under it, wrapping the two-piece in the towel.

She wondered if Leander had woken up yet.

She wondered if he'd woken every time she'd stirred during the night, holding his breath to see if she'd pull back, and falling back asleep when he'd realized she was still there.

She wondered if he had any inkling of what she was feeling and she wondered if that would make a difference, before she reminded herself it didn't matter, and slid her feet into sandals and left the small cove.

It was a quick walk to the grocer's, a small cottage crammed with industrial refrigerators and a few tables of island-grown produce. The screendoor slammed behind Reyna as she grabbed a wire basket from a stack in the front of the shop and turned sideways to navigate around the other islanders. She wasn't actively working off a list, just grabbing things that felt like they could work together for a meal—cabbage and paper-wrapped haddock, flour tortillas and fresh bread. As she made her way up to the register, stepping into the small line, Reyna felt something prickle on the back of her neck.

Unsure what she was looking for, Reyna's eyes wandered through the small store. The same islanders as before, the same small setup, but through the screen door, she recognized a pair of wide shoulders and golden mop of hair outside.

Leander couldn't see her, she was fairly certain, not with the high sunlight and the obfuscation the screen door provided, but it felt like he could. It felt like he could see through the walls, through her, and when he crossed the street to come into the store, his stride didn't break as he came to stand in front of her.

He looked good.

In the mid morning shadows, his chest heaving like he'd rushed here, needing to find her, like something from a Jane Austen novel. And Reyna almost said as much, but then she noticed there was an unfamiliar glint in Leander's eyes, almost unfocused, like he was processing too much and not enough at once.

"You're okay," he whispered, almost to himself, and then he pulled her into a smothering hug.

Reyna frowned against his chest, her arms uncertainly coming around him to hold him back. His hands hadn't stopped moving, running over her upper arms and he pulled back to cup her face with his hands.

It was like he was scanning for an injury of some sort, and Reyna felt a stab of guilt as she realized he'd been worried something had happened to her.

"I'm fine, yeah," she said softly, as Leander's eyes flicked across her face. "I went for a swim, and I knew we needed groceries so I figured I'd swing by here on my way back to...on my way back."

She snapped her mouth shut, wondering why she'd almost said *home*. She'd never lived on Great Cranberry, and had only visited a few summers with Leander. But it'd almost slipped out, and she couldn't help but feel like Leander knew.

Reyna wasn't sure what he needed, but he winced, turning away from her slightly.

"You needed a break," he mumbled, and the guilt in his voice sounded too much like what she'd heard last night. And Reyna had no idea how to get it through his head that she wasn't being coerced here, wasn't overwhelmed by something he was doing; it was her own mind that was too loud, that she'd needed to be in the ocean to quiet.

"I needed to be at the sea, Lee," she said, and she ran a hand over his arm on impulse.

It was a light touch, meant to be soothing, but Leander jolted like she'd shocked him. She looked back up at his face, noticing the color high on his cheeks, and the way his eyes were still unfocused behind his glasses.

She slid her hand down to his fingers, tucking his hand into hers, and tried to ignore the way it felt right to be connected to him like that. Maybe she could've, if his shoulders didn't dip in relief, like her touch was grounding him, somehow, despite the fact that he was clearly distressed because of her.

The older woman behind the counter cleared her throat.

Reyna looked over at her, then back at Leander. His nostrils flared as he looked at her—not the hot way they had in the kitchen yesterday, but like a spooked animal, sensing danger in every direction.

She had to get him out of here.

She didn't know where to, or how to calm him down, but she'd never seen him like this, and didn't know what it was going to look like if he suddenly switched from nervous to threatened.

"Is everything okay, dears?" the woman asked, curious and concerned.

Reyna pasted a smile on her face, hoping it was convincing.

"Yes," Reyna said, casting about for a solution. "Well, actually, no. We've, um, we've just got some news we're trying to process. Do you think—could you hold these for us?"

She put the wire basket on the counter, her smile widening reassuringly.

"We'll just be a minute," she said, tugging Leander behind her, as she walked out the door, "and we'll be right back to check out."

The sun that had seemed muted during her swim was now bright, directly overhead and glaring. Reyna winced slightly, knowing Leander's blue eyes were more sensitive to the light than hers, but to her surprise, when she looked at him, he was just staring at her.

"Okay," she said, pulling him around the grocer and down a path that led down to another cove, "I'm not sure if that was the right move, but I felt like you needed to be out of there."

She felt the moment he stopped following her, and started leading. Reyna couldn't read his expression, but she could feel the tension radiating from where their hands were joined as he pulled her further down the lane, towards the cove. No one was out, and rentals were closed for the season, but Leander pulled sharply on the padlock of the boat shack and it cracked open. Reyna's mouth went dry as she realized he hadn't unlocked it, had simply shattered it with his grasp.

Leander was still silent as he pulled open the door, pushed her into the dark shack.

It wasn't a big structure, a double wide shed made for storing canoes, kayaks and life vests. Near the back, there was a wall of paddles and a back door, and Leander crowded her towards the door. The metal was cool against her fingers and Reyna knew they should probably talk about what specifically was bothering Leander, but his body covered hers as he pushed her into the wall, and thoughts fled.

Fifteen

Reyna's head tilted back against Leander's shoulder as she reveled in the feeling of his long body pressed against hers, and she felt Leander nuzzle into her neck.

One of his hands folded over hers against the metal door, the other held her waist, like he needed to press her somehow closer to him. She felt his nose nudging aside the straps of her dress, and then he pressed open kisses along the line where her shoulder met her neck.

"I'm sorry," he whispered against her skin. "Fuck, I'm sorry, I just need a minute."

He was shaking, she realized, his body vibrating with need, and Reyna felt a frisson of concern.

"Lee?" she asked, and his hand on her waist tightened.

"You just—" he broke off, and his hand on her waist tightened, like he couldn't bring himself to even think of it.

"It's okay," she soothed, and Leander made a sound like a growl, his teeth scraping over her skin before he tried to explain.

"I needed you so bad, and you weren't there, and it just—" Leander broke off with a choked sound. "You weren't here and I...I just need to feel you for a second. Then we can get the groceries and go."

His voice was breathless, and Reyna felt her concern fading as understanding dawned. She'd thought that with the intensity of the previous night, she'd have enough time to step out, but the way he was clenching her tightly, she'd been mistaken.

Leander's body was covering hers, pressed close enough that she could feel the heat of his skin through the layers of clothing they wore. She shifted her hips slightly, and felt the hardness between his legs, prompting guilt over leaving him alone like this.

"I'm sorry," she whispered. "I didn't—"

Leander let go of her waist, reaching to grab her chin and turn her face towards him. He kissed her hard, his tongue delving into her mouth in time with the rhythm of his hips, and just as sudden, he pulled back, trailing kisses over her cheeks, her nose.

"Don't apologize," he said roughly, against her skin, "I can't...please don't."

Reyna nodded, turning her face back up to his, and sighing when he acquiesced, kissing her again. She didn't think she'd ever be tired of it, the soft press of his lips, the sweep of his tongue, the taste of him. They both released their guilt into the kiss, trading it for something more heady, more immediate.

"I didn't know," Reyna tried again, when he'd quieted enough to hear her. "I wouldn't have left if I'd have known it'd get that bad."

Leander drew in a deep breath, his hips still sliding determinedly against hers.

"You wouldn't have left..." he mumbled, reassuring himself, and then he groaned again. "Fuck, I'm trying to calm down, but just thinking about you leaving—"

"I'm here," she promised, turning around in his arms.

He looked truly haunted when she met his gaze, and her heart stammered at the sight of him. It was just his rut, just biology that told him he needed her, but that rationale didn't make her want to reassure him any less. His eyes roamed over her, desperately flitting across her face, down her body, like he was committing the sight of her to memory.

Like he was afraid she'd vanish again.

Reyna reached down to cover his hands in hers, and guide them to her body. She placed his hands over her breasts, and his fingers tightened instinctively over the thin fabric of her dress. He was teasing her through the cotton, and his hips rocked slightly, as if in reaction. The glide of his clothed cock against her core made them both gasp softly, and Reyna knew how to apologize in a way he'd accept.

"I'm here," she repeated, sliding down his body.

Leander groaned when she got to her knees, his hand gathering her curls at the base of her neck, even as he shook his head.

"Shit, Reyna, you don't know how long I—" he broke off when her hands closed on him over his jeans, his hips pressing into her hand.

Reyna tilted her head to the side, her fingers undoing his belt, then his fly, and reaching into his jeans. Leander's breath punched out of him, his other hand banging against the wall as he tried to hold himself upright.

"You don't have to–" he tried again, and Reyna shook her head at him. Couldn't he tell how badly she wanted this?

"I'm here now," she repeated, and pulled him out.

He was so thick in her hand, heavy, no less intimidating for having taken him as much as she had already. A drop of precum pearled on the tip of his cock, and Reyna adjusted her grip to aim his cock at her mouth, her tongue licking flat over the tip of him.

He was salty, heady, and she was already hungry for more, but then Lee opened his mouth and fucking moaned.

It was the most beautiful sound.

Reyna had a couple tricks up her sleeve but they all went out the window the moment she heard that gorgeous sound. All her focus, all her intention, was just to make him make it again.

She licked up the length of him, marveling at the scent and feel. She suckled the tip of him, kissing the part of him that fucked her so damn deep. She fondled his balls, and his knees bent before he could catch himself.

Lee's glasses slid down his nose and she nearly swooned; he was such a dream.

She settled into the rhythm of the blow job, teasing him down her throat, hollowing her cheeks. Pulling him deeper, seeing how deep she could take him, releasing him with a slurp and kissing him back down.

He sounded so good.

Each hitched breath, each choked moan, each grunt as he hit the back of her throat had Reyna obsessed. Her own core was pulsing, but she ignored it. She decided she would have to do this again, a million times, and see how each of those sounds looked when he was naked. She wanted to watch every contraction of his stomach, notice every tremble in his fingers, and see the flutter in his eyelashes, magnified by his glasses.

His jaw tightened and Reyna thought that might've been her favorite yet.

"You're so good," Leander moaned softly, fighting to keep his voice down. "Fuck, I don't deserve you, you feel–"

She sucked him harder, and he broke off with a groan.

When his hips started canting towards her spread lips, Reyna nearly sobbed in relief. Her hands settled on the front of his thighs, and she imagined she was holding his soft skin, scratchy with his fair hair, instead of coarse denim. Leander was tentative in fucking her mouth, but Reyna tilted her head back, wanting more of him.

Her mouth was burning, her eyes were streaming, but she needed him to finish, needed to show him she was here. The ache between her thighs was pulsing, but she wanted him to come down her throat, his thighs trembling against her face—Reyna swallowed in anticipation and Lee's hips shot forward and he came.

"Fuck, fuck!" Lee groaned, as she swallowed his release, and he reached down a massive hand to hold off his knot.

Reyna whined, knowing he was right, but she half-wanted to see if she could take it. She wanted him to stretch her, use her, test her – hell, break her. She'd let him.

"Reyna," Leander breathed, reaching down for her to haul her up to her feet, bracing her back against the wall of the shed. He wasted no time in pushing up the fabric of her sundress, spreading her legs and stepping between them, his hand falling to the apex of her thighs.

"Fuck, honey, you're so wet," he whispered, a thick finger running over her soaked folds.

Reyna nodded, lost for words. She felt languid, dreamy, even as her thighs rubbed together, desperate for friction. He was so big, he'd felt so good, she needed him—

"You're okay, honey, I've got you," Lee murmured, and she felt him lift her, prop her against the wall.

"Lee," she panted, her hips canting towards him, his touch.

"I'm here," it was his turn to promise, rubbing his hand over her. Reyna whimpered when he brushed over her clit, but it wasn't enough, she needed to be filled.

"Need your cock," she whimpered. "Please, Lee, I feel so empty–"

He shifted her higher, and she felt her body slide up the siding of the shack, her toes barely able to reach the ground.

She opened her eyes and the sight of him nearly undid her.

Lee's glasses were fogging up from how hard he was breathing. His beautiful mouth was panting, because she'd undone him. His fat, heavy, cock rested against his stomach, still just as ready to knot her as she was to take him.

"Please," she tried again, and Lee laughed, the most stunning sound.

"Anything, sweetheart," he said softly, and he reached between them to feed his cock into her weeping pussy.

When he fit into her, Reyna's eyes rolled back.

Fuck, would she ever recover from the stretch of him?

He was so broad, and he filled her so steadily, and from this angle, gravity was pressing them impossibly close. Reyna's head lolled and she didn't know she was making sounds until Leander's hand clapped over her mouth.

God, why was that so hot?

"Gotta be quiet, honey," Leander said, his own voice a hoarse whisper. She made her eyes open to meet his, and she whimpered from behind his palm.

Leander had her impaled on his cock, held against the wall by his strong thighs, and yet he looked at her like she was the miracle.

She watched his lashes flutter as she feebly rolled her hips.

"Reyna..." he warned, but Reyna shook her head.

Gentleness wasn't what she wanted and it wasn't what he needed, and they both knew it. She hadn't been there and so now he needed to claim her. Needed to fuck her, knot her, remind his wolf that she was his and she wasn't going anywhere.

Reyna saw the moment Leander accepted it, when his eyes hooded further and he pulled back. His hips punched forward, sheathing himself in her, and Reyna thought maybe she'd never been so full. When he started thrusting, his driving rhythm was a declaration, a promise, and it was everything Reyna had wanted. She dug her fingers into the fabric of his shirt, her moan blocked by his palm over her mouth.

"Yeah?" Leander asked, and Reyna could cry, it was so good. "Like that, that's what you needed?"

His voice held a thread of pride, like he knew how tight she was wound and knew it was all for him. Reyna nodded weakly, her legs bouncing in the air as he thrust into her. She was pretty sure she was drooling behind his hand, but what else could she do? His cock was so deep inside her, and each push of his hips ground against her clit so perfectly. It was rough, it was hedonistic, it was exactly what she wanted because it was the claim he'd needed.

Reyna whined, leveraging her grip on his shoulders to swivel her hips slightly. She was rewarded by Leander's rhythm faltering, his mouth falling open.

"Shit, sweetheart, that's so good," he groaned, and his thrusts got somehow deeper.

Reyna didn't know how it was possible to ride him from this angle, but her hips worked into him, and she needed him to come. She wanted his claim, his touch against her skin, his knot in her. Reyna was whining with each thrust, desperate for him, desperate to be his.

"It's mine," Leander growled, like he could hear her thoughts, and his voice brought Reyna's eyes back to him.

A possessive, primal look was etched across his features, and Reyna nodded her response as best she could manage.

Leander hummed.

"This is my pussy, isn't it?" he asked, punctuating the question with a deep thrust. "My cunt to play with, to fuck, to knot, to have waiting for me when I need it—fuck, honey, I feel you getting tighter around me. You like that? Knowing how this is all mine?"

His thrusts got sharper, and Reyna moaned when she felt the base of his cock swelling. She wasn't sure she could take his knot like this, but she wanted to try. She could feel her legs trembling but she circled her hips again, hungry, and Leander's eyes fluttered again.

"It's all fucking mine," he growled, and he moved his hand away from her mouth so he could kiss her.

Reyna keened into his mouth as his knot pressed against her, begging for entrance, the tightest pressure. Leander held her there as she cried against him, her body shaking and needing him, and his driving and needing her.

"Fuck, that's so good," he moaned against her lips. "My pussy, my girl, fuck—say you're mine, Rey, please–"

Reyna sobbed his name, her body overwrought.

Lee fell forward, one hand bracing against the wall and the other clutching her ass to him as his thrusts grew sharper. "Need you closer, need to be so fucking deep in you, need you–"

"Yours," Reyna managed, breathless, "I'm all yours, Lee."

Lee's hips rutted up, shoving his knot into her and the sudden give pushed him over the edge. He came with a hoarse cry, and he staggered closer to the wall, pressing ever closer even as his legs gave out.

The feeling of his come streaming into her pussy sent Reyna over the edge, and she buried her face in his wrinkled shirt as she came. She felt his hands tighten on her, moving her body into his as she finished, like even her orgasm was his.

They slumped against the wall, exhausted.

They were wrapped tightly around each other, like even if the knot slipped, they couldn't be more than a breath apart. Each gasping breath Reyna drew reminded her of where they were joined, of the way he was pulsing inside of her. She came back to herself, mindful of her tangled hair, and the fact that Lee was mumbling something into her chest.

"You can't leave me, please, I need you too much," Lee was whispering, pressing mindless kisses wherever he could reach. "I'm so sorry, Rey, you can't leave me like that, please don't..."

It broke her heart, that he could apologize in the same breath as promising something so beautiful to her. And she knew he didn't mean it, not all the way, but his wolf did.

And that part of him deserved comfort as much as any other.

Reyna summoned her strength to brush her fingers through his soft hair. She soothed him as gently as she could, wordlessly so his wolf would understand. With calming touches and gentle acceptance, she kept him pressed to her breast long past when the knot had gone down, and when she could deny that this moment was just for him.

Sixteen

The walk back to the cottage was quiet, and Leander kept stealing glances over at Reyna as they went.

She'd pulled her hair back into a ponytail, in an attempt to hide what they'd been up to in the boat shack, but her dress was wrinkled pretty condemningly, and Leander was pretty sure the ladies at the grocer knew anyways.

He appreciated that Reyna was doing her best to keep herself within arm's reach. He couldn't quite believe how intense his reaction had been earlier, but she had stayed within his line of sight since.

Even when they got back to the cottage, she kept the bathroom door open when she showered. It wasn't for seduction, it wasn't anything other than making sure he knew she was there, and she was mindful of how much that mattered to him.

As it was, the domesticity of it settled differently over Leander.

As they put away dishes and took turns in the shower, it felt like the perfect kind of routine, the one he'd wanted so bad from outside the grocer's. The afternoon passed quietly and without flourish, and soon enough it was time to get dinner started.

Leander poured oil into a dutch oven, managing to attach the thermometer to the side of it, and wondering what temperature fish fried at.

"You can chop that," Reyna lifted her chin to indicate the head of cabbage sitting on the counter. Leander found a big enough knife and wondered if there was a wrong way to cut cabbage for coleslaw.

"Just start," Reyna said, not quite laughing, and Leander started.

Reyna worked her way through an onion, tomato, and cilantro while he hacked away at it, adding them to a large mixing bowl and leaving it by Leander's cutting board.

"How's Chesa doing?" Leander asked, when the cabbage finally lay in a chopped mountain, as he swept it into the mixing bowl.

From the corner of his eye, he watched Reyna hesitate, before she physically tossed her hair over her shoulders, releasing the tension, and starting in on a bunch of cilantro.

"About that," she said, "I should probably tell you something, but you can't get mad."

"Great premise," he said, reaching for a jalapeño.

Reyna hummed, the chopped pile of cilantro growing, before she quietly announced, "I paid off her business loan."

Leander waited for her to further quantify the statement, but nothing happened. He dropped the jalapeño stem in a pile with the onion skins, trying to process that.

"You did?"

Reyna nodded slowly, her expression intentionally blank, as she pushed the cilantro into the mixing bowl, and starting to toss it all together. "I may have used the money I was saving for a house down payment."

Leander froze.

Technically, it wasn't his business. Reyna was fucking smart, had a job that paid her well for it, and had a sense of indebtedness to her family was frankly foreign to him. He had no doubt she'd figure it out, and she could have a house she wanted in another couple of years.

"Limes, please," she said, her voice tight, indicating for the limes on the counter beside him.

He sliced them and handed them to her, and she squeezed them over the slaw, starting to mix it again. He watched her carefully, the deliberate way she was moving, the way she had phrased this news, and he knew what he knew about Reyna—she wasn't asking for advice. She was asking for affirmation.

And, technically, it still wasn't his business. But the last few days had been just good enough for him to try pushing his luck.

"You'll sort it out," Leander said, a compliment and the truth, and he saw her shoulders deflate slightly, confirming what he'd expected.

That Reyna knew she could carry it, and trusted in nothing but her ability to bear impossible burdens.

A moment later, she pushed her shoulders back.

"Right," she said, brightly. "I can keep renting, it's not that big of a deal, and this way, Chesa just has to worry about operating expenses, and she can help with mom's bills. So, really, it's an investment in both of our futures, you know?"

"You figured it out," he said, and she nodded sharply.

"Yep," she said. She finished stirring and wiped her hands on the back of her dress, reaching for a towel, but Leander intercepted her.

He pulled her to him, a gentler embrace than they'd shared in days, and he felt her surprise. He wound his arms around her shoulders, his chin resting on top of her head, and waited.

After a moment, Leader felt her shoulders relax, her face nestling into his shirt, her arms joining around his back, and he felt twelve feet tall. This, this was who he was supposed to be to her. When Reyna was conquering everything in her life, figuring out how to answer everything, he could be the one she turned to. When she held everything together, he'd hold her.

Her arms tightened around his waist when he didn't let her go, and he moved one hand to rub up and down her back.

"You did good," he said quietly, and he felt her shiver.

She wouldn't cry; he knew better. In a couple moments, she'd decide she'd indulged enough, but for a minute, she'd let him be this for her.

"Thank you," she mumbled into his shirt.

He nodded, and she pulled back, tipped her head up to look up at him.

"You don't think it was impulsive?" she asked. "Or just me being controlling?"

"I think it's definitely both of those things," he said, and grunted when Reyna swatted at his ribs. Leander smiled, couldn't help himself, and she was grinning too, so it was worth it.

"Come on," she sighed. "We did, like, one step of seven, to make fish tacos."

He let her go, stepping around her as she moved around the kitchen.

The afternoon sun cast long, golden shadows across the kitchen. They cracked open some windows to let the oil smell out, fried haddock in beer batter and heaped it in cabbage slaw and more limes.

Reyna was still mostly within arm reach, but it felt different.

It felt like maybe it was for her as much as him, and Leander was pretty sure he was drunk on the feeling. They ate standing around the kitchen, leaning against the countertops, as the sun faded from golden to twilight.

Reyna took the dishes and pointed Leander to the old wood stove in the living room. He wasn't sure the last time he'd made a fire, but he accepted the task, trying not to think about how anxious it made him to not physically have Reyna within his line of sight.

He could hear her humming, loud enough over the dishes, intentional. Just another method of reassurance that settled him, and threatened to overwhelm him.

He knelt beside the stove, cracking the sticks that were piled behind it, and arranging them into a tent. The faucet switched off in the kitchen and he ripped up strips of a newspaper, crumbling them and fitting into the tent of sticks. The lighter had a bit of juice left, and he watched fire catch in the stove, giving it time to breathe before he closed the door, resting back on his thighs.

Leander watched the flames dance behind the glass cover, listening for the sound of Reyna stacking porcelain in the kitchen.

He heard the floorboards creak, and Reyna padded back into the room. She held a colander of blueberries, which she wiggled in his direction as she headed for the sofa. Leander meant to join her, but as he turned to watch her, his heart caught in his throat for a moment.

How many times had he dreamed of this moment?

Reyna back at this home, with him, her features softened by firelight, waiting for him on the sofa.

She pulled her sock-covered feet up underneath her on the sofa, looking surprised that he hadn't moved to join her yet.

"Um," she said nervously, looking down at herself and then back at him, before determining to not call attention to his lovesick stare. "You have a book around here somewhere, right?"

Leander shook his head, pushing himself to his feet and dropping onto the couch beside her. She shrugged as he sat down, shifting over to make room for him, and as he reached for a book, she snuggled into his side.

Leander wondered if it would ever be normal, if Reyna's hair brushing his chin when she settled her head on his shoulder would ever feel unlike a miracle.

He could tell himself it was just the day they'd had.

Just a continuation of her comforting him, being near him and loud about it to quiet his wolf. He tried to be calm about it, his arm extending over the back of the sofa, but as Reyna settled against him, Leander couldn't deny it felt more than that.

It felt like he needed her in a much more permanent way.

Making dinner together, pretending it wasn't the most profound trust to share her day and hold her after. Putting away groceries and risking indecent exposure because he needed her that badly, he'd take all of it. He wanted all of it.

He started reading his book aloud, picking up the middle of the chapter, knowing it was more about winding down than comprehension. God knew he wasn't retaining any of what he was reading. Even as he spoke, he was mindful of the soft exhale against his shoulder as Reyna breathed, in and out. How a gust of wind would brush some of her hair off her neck, and the room would smell faintly of bergamot for a moment. The amused huff she'd give when something amused her, how it made him want to keep reading if it would bring her more joy.

Eventually, the fading light was gone enough that he couldn't read anymore. Reyna had been still for the last few pages, but Leander knew she was still awake.

Sure enough, she shifted as he closed the book, her cheek pressing deeper into his shoulder as she wrapped her arms around herself.

"Comfortable?" he asked, and Reyna hummed.

"You're a good height," she said, her voice sleepy, and Leander's heart tripped. It wasn't like when he first started dating, when people asked him conspiratorially how tall he actually was. Instead, with Reyna, it felt like she'd left off two words at the end of the sentence.

Like he was the right height *for her*.

The thought of which, unfortunately, Leander was still not immune to. Though they were both tired, though the day had made him weary, Leander's body registered that Reyna was soft beside him, resting against him, leaning on him. Registered the warmth of her body, the way it fit so well against his, the other ways and places he knew fit well...

"Comfortable?" Reyna parroted his words back to him teasingly, having taken notice of the new tension in his frame.

"I knew it'd be constant," Leander admitted, "but I'd kind of hoped we'd get a night off."

He heard, rather than saw, Reyna smile. "I think if people had figured out how to temper ruts, there wouldn't be the PTO policy we're currently taking advantage of."

She was right, but it didn't make it easier. Leander knew he was pouting, but he just wanted it to be simpler. Why couldn't they just have a night? Why did it have to be about fucking, claiming, needing?

"Do you want me to..." Reyna trailed off, looking up at him. It was a tempting idea, a really, really, tempting idea, but truthfully that wasn't what Leander wanted.

He wanted what they'd had—a quiet moment, together, fire crackling and shared breaths, and nothing more complicated than that.

But it was more complicated, because of what this weekend was, and despite the satisfaction he'd found in her over and over again, his wolf was greedy, and wanted more.

"I know," Reyna said, her voice soft, and Leander couldn't read her expression, but she sounded like she understood. Like they both knew the reason for this weekend, but a part of them wished for the respite that it could've been, if it weren't for the rut. She hesitated for a moment, then patted his leg gently as she pushed off the couch.

She was back a few moments later, holding lube, a thoughtful expression on her face.

"Do you think cockwarming would, like, pause it?"

It took Leander a moment to process her question, because apparently when it came to Reyna, a part of him was still sixteen, and got overly excited to hear her say 'cock'. Then her words sunk in, and he didn't know right away.

"I'm not sure," he said, trying to think through the technicalities of what Whit had told him, plus the lived experience they'd been through so far. "I think the end goal of the rut is breeding, but in terms of permanence and possessiveness, it could work."

Reyna nodded, a pleased expression on her face. "That's what I was thinking. Can't hurt to try, right?"

It definitely could.

The fiasco of his earlier panic was proof of how much it could hurt to try to delay it, but with how proud Reyna looked of herself for coming up with a workaround, Leander could bear it.

They got undressed quickly.

It was more a matter of efficiency at this point, and Leander imagined the appeal of cockwarming was the intimacy. He'd never done it before—hated feeling sticky, or trapped to another person, or too self conscious of everything—but if they could handle knotting, maybe this was similar?

Reyna crawled back onto the coach, lowering herself gently to sit on his thighs, and Leander had to stop a myriad of responses to her position.

How natural it had been for her to sit there, how he loved the weight of her in his lap, how her facing him this way meant they were almost eye level, and he kind of loved looking up at her. Reyna shivered, and without thinking Leander reached for a blanket off the back of the couch, wrapping it over her shoulders. It closed the room around them, wrapped them in a cocoon of closeness, just the heat of their bodies, so close together. Reyna smiled at him appreciatively, and reached for the lube again.

She uncapped it and then paused, before hesitantly reached for his hand. She pulled it slightly, until it was hovering between them, and then she paused.

"I think this might be easier if I'm..." she trailed off.

Leander didn't have to be asked twice. He pulled his hand free, lifting his fingers to his mouth to wet them, before lowering his hand to between her thighs. Reyna didn't look away and Leander didn't want her to, wanted her to see how much he wanted to do this, how much he wanted to do whatever she asked.

He loved that she was asking him anything, especially this.

He brushed his fingers through her pussy, and she swayed slightly, like it was intoxicating for her how it was for him. He knew it wasn't. She might get turned on, but she was in his blood. He felt like he was orbiting around her, worshiping her, how he'd wanted to for years.

He was obsessed with how she felt on his fingers.

The way it'd only been a matter of days, but that she was familiar to him. That he recognized her reactions to the patterns his fingers traced, that he knew what each gasp and shaky exhale meant. He felt when she grew slippery under his touch, felt when she got somehow warmer, when her thighs parted under his touch. He felt her opening for him, bore it like his greatest pride.

Reyna hummed, her voice breathless as she spoke, "I love how your fingers feel."

And Leander could've said a million things—how she felt, what parts of her he felt, how hot it was, how perfect she was — but his mind stalled on her first two words, and it took everything in him to not say what he knew she wasn't going to want to hear.

So he leaned forward, pressed his mouth to her neck. Tasted the salt of her sweat, the way her pulse fluttered against his tongue. He lapped at her skin, his tongue pulling the way his fingers moved over her clit, and Reyna sighed.

God, the noises she made.

Every sigh, whimper, gasp, cry, was perfect. He felt them all, stored them all, an ever-mounting pressure at his spine. He wanted more, was desperate for more, but at the same time he hated it, because they were only in this situation because his wolf refused to be sated. Leander felt like his lungs were crowded, only inhaling eucalyptus and bergamot and he wanted to drown in her scent. He tried to breathe deeply, only to realize he was already panting, his hand moving more quickly over her. He felt her grow slicker, wanted to stop, needed to keep going, wanted to lose himself in her and drive her to mindlessness too.

"Hey, hey," Reyna's hand on his wrist stilled him, and she was frowning slightly in concern when he looked up at her. "You're okay."

She said it like a promise, how she always meant it, like if she had anything to do with it, it would be. He trusted her. More than his blood burned and his skin singed, he trusted her.

"Okay," he whispered and she smiled.

She reached for the lube again.

It was cold on his cock, but her hand was warm, and he was already throbbing for her. The first glide of her clenched fingers over his dick had Leander's head falling back against the couch. He'd been in her, he knew how tight she was, but her hand still felt so good. It was her, it was just that it was Reyna, that had him reacting.

He wanted to flex his hips, flip them both onto the couch, rut into her until she was sobbing his name. Hear her as desperate for him as he was for her, taste her need on his tongue, feel her tremble with it. But as she looked at him, her dark eyes trusting, Leander knew he wouldn't do it. He'd been holding back everything he felt for her for long enough to train a wolf.

"There you go," Reyna soothed him, pulling her hand back up. The motion reminded Leander that he could move, his fingers spreading around her clit again. He felt her grip slacken as he moved and he tried not to let it get to his head. He continued to play with her, work over her, savoring her and following her instructions and the room was quiet as they built it.

It was so intimate.

The sunset was almost gone, and the room was lit only by the wood stove, and the shadows it cast. Leander memorized the way the light of the flames danced off Reyna's skin, the way her motions seemed an extension of it. The way they moved around each other, with a new familiarity, and Leander was wondering how much longer he could hold on when Reyna shifted back on her hips.

Her knees were planted on either side of him, and she rose up to take the tip of his cock into her cunt. Leander refused to let her go, his fingers slipping from her clit to part her folds, and they both moaned when his hot skin met hers.

It was so good.

She was soft everywhere he was hard, all welcoming and warm and Leander was practically shaking with the effort of staying still. He wanted to claim her, could remember all too well how good it had felt just hours ago, but they needed this slow. They needed a rest, needed a moment of understanding, and damn everything else, he was going to do it.

Reyna let out a soft moan.

It was an unintentional sound, like it'd ripped from her, and Leander couldn't help when his hips pushed up in response. What else could he do? Hearing her make sounds like that, knowing it was just from his touch, his body?

Her eyes were closed, and she was biting her lip. Reyna's brow furrowed in concentration as her body bore down on his and Leander hoped to god she didn't open her eyes because he couldn't hide what he was feeling in that moment.

She was everything.

Just an absolute gale force of a human, so fucking beautiful, and it was unreal that she was with him. Now, like this, or ever. He wanted to worship her, savor her, lavish her and he thought he might burst from it.

The back of her thighs met the top of his, and Leander realized she was seated. He was fully inside of her, and she felt unreal.

She was so tight around him, warm, and fluttering slightly. He guided her arms around his neck, and his own hands wrapped around her back, pulling her front flush against his. He could hear the beating of her heart. Steady and even, unlike his galloping pace, but so close to him. He knew they were just delaying the inevitable, but it was more than enough for now. To be here, to not rush into that yet, to hear her heartbeat and feel her arms around him, it was plenty.

He'd make sure of it.

Seventeen

Reyna hadn't meant to sleep.

But the day had been a lot, emotionally and physically, and when Leander's arms had wrapped around her lower back, it'd been too much temptation to avoid. She'd let herself rest on his chest, hoped she could hide the depths of what she was feeling from him as easily as she could hide her face. And now she was blinking awake, hours later, and she thought that maybe she'd never felt so held.

The room was dark, the fire burning low in the stove. She couldn't see what time it was, but it had to be late at night, technically morning. No dawn crested through the windows, and the room was simply shadows and heat, and she pulled back slightly to look at Leander.

He looked like an angel.

An artists' rendition of one, fair skinned and light eyed. His head was tilted back against the headrest of the sofa, exposing the long column on his throat, and Reyna noticed the soft flicker of his pulse right at the base of his neck. His pink lips were parted, just slightly, a rhythmic sleepy exhale pushing between them.

His glasses had fallen down his nose.

Reyna reached up to pull them off his face, folding them carefully. She leaned over to put them on the end table, and the motion wasn't much, but it was enough to make her gasp as she became extremely conscious of Leander inside of her. She held her breath as she deposited the glasses, letting out a slow breath as she came back to him.

He felt good.

Of course he did, he had the last—five? six?—times; it shouldn't have been a surprise. Reyna flushed, thinking over said previous times, and her mind snagged on how he'd woken her up yesterday.

She thought of how, earlier tonight, he'd shaken with the effort to not make this more, and that maybe she should return the favor.

Leander was still sleeping, his long blond lashes fluttering, and Reyna let the blanket slip off her shoulders as she braced herself on the back of the couch, on either side of his head. She shifted slightly, pulling her thighs in tighter from where they'd been spread. As she rested on her shins, she relished the way that each movement seemed to remind her that she was connected to Leander in the most intimate way, and she could feel her own need rising to match the way he was hard for her.

She pushed up on her knees, rising up to as far as her thighs would let her, while still keeping him in her.

She tried not to think about how much she needed him in her.

It was a slow slide, but it left Reyna breathless all the same. Leander fit her so well, stretching her just right, and she worked herself up and down his cock slowly. She licked her lips as she repeated the motion. Whether it was lube or the fact that her body seemed perpetually primed for him, it was a heady, smooth, drag over her walls.

Her thighs were burning, and Reyna couldn't tell if that was because of how much of a workout they'd gotten in the last few days, or the fact that Leander was so fucking thick between them, and even while she was sleeping, he'd been stretching her out.

A part of her rationalized that maybe she was out of practice, that she hadn't been with anyone for a while and so anyone would feel this good, but Reyna knew that wasn't true. As she lowered herself back down, accepting every inch of his thick cock, she knew it was all so painfully Leander.

As if on cue, his arms tightened around her rib cage, hands flexed on her lower back, as he woke up.

"'m I still dreaming?" Leander mumbled, sleep thick on his voice, and Reyna smiled as she looked up to find him watching her. His face was still relaxed and rested, but there was a sharp hunger in his eyes that made Reyna's stomach tighten. He was so beautiful. Soft and strong and perfect in the faded firelight.

She rocked up again, lifting herself off of him and savoring the thick slide of him against her walls.

"Do I often make an appearance in your dreams?" she asked, holding herself at the top of her arc for a moment, and looking down at Leander. She'd meant it to be cocky, slightly teasing, but it didn't feel like a joke, not with how he was looking at her. Leander's hands slid down her back, cupping her ass to help guide her movement, and Reyna wasted zero time in leaning back into him.

"You have no idea," Leander said, his voice low. Some of his hair fell across his eyes as she worked herself back down, and Reyna leaned deeper onto one arm so she could reach for his face. She brushed his hair off his forehead, her finger trailing down his jaw.

She knew he didn't mean it, knew it was just this rut that had him looking at her like this, but it was still sweet of him to say. His eyes were glowing that soft silver in the low light, and she crooked her finger under his chin, lifting his mouth up to meet hers. Leander pulled in a deep breath through his nose as he pressed up to kiss her.

God, how he tasted.

Like memories and longing, like gentleness and summer, and his tongue immediately slipped between her lips, like he wanted her taste just as much.

For a moment, they stayed like that—her resting in his arms, drinking from his mouth, rocking slightly into him, treasuring the closeness. Reyna could feel the lingering heat of the fading fire at her back, but all the warmth in the room was coming from Leander, she was certain.

His hands, his arms, his nose bumping hers, the soft way he hummed when their tongues brushed each other. Then he shifted, just slightly, and his happy trail pressed between her thighs, and Reyna broke away with a gasp.

Just a simple touch, but it reminded her that her whole body was thrumming, filled with him, and her hips spread slightly, wanting him deeper.

"You're so beautiful," Leander mumbled against her skin, his words muffled as he trailed light kisses down her neck.

Reyna tipped her head back, letting his lips wander, her eyes falling closed as he kissed her almost tenderly. One of his hands trailed up her sides, his touch so light it almost tickled, closing around her breast and lifting her so he could take her into his mouth. Reyna sighed as his hot mouth closed over her, tongue stroking, and her hands closed over the back of the couch so she could rock against him again.

Everything was warm.

His mouth, the fire, his cock, her pulse, everything, and when Reyna started to move, Leander groaned. The sound sent vibrations over her nipple, sensitive and strong, as she worked herself over him.

"You feel s'good," Lee murmured, as he pulled back to switch to her other breast.

A string of saliva stretched between her nipple and his mouth and Reyna whimpered. She loved that he was messy, loved that it felt like desperation and a dream and when his lips closed over her other nipple, her hips started moving faster.

She wanted everywhere messy.

She chased the friction of his cock dragging against her walls, the spongy spot deep within her that he brushed at the top of each stroke, the way his thighs started to flex to help her. One of her hands tangled in the hair at the base of his neck, anchoring her, as she ground against him. She could feel her arousal building, and Leander was grunting with each bounce of her hips. Her thighs were burning, her mouth hanging open as she panted, but Reyna couldn't bring herself to care.

"That's right, beautiful," Leander said, his voice curling around her like another caress, "take it. Riding me so pretty— feels so fucking good."

Reyna looked back down at him, and her heart stuttered as her eyes met him. They were close enough that he could see her, even without his glasses, and the bright blue of his eyes felt like it was burning her. The corners of his mouth turned up, like her eyes brought him the gentlest joy, and Reyna couldn't look at him, not when he was looking at her with a mix of pride and wonder that she knew would only last through the next few hours.

"It's so good, Lee," she whined, her eyes falling shut. When she said his name, his hips punched up into her, and Reyna cried out, her hands clenching on the couch. "Fuck, how is it so good—"

She broke off when Leander readjusted his grip on her waist, his fingers digging into her skin as he started to work her over him. She surrendered to his strength, welcoming his lead, her body going heavy as he brought her down onto him as he pumped up. She could feel the tips of his claws digging into her skin as he clenched at her, trying to be gentle, but still scraping her, and she loved the urgency, the desperation, in his touch.

"It's cause it's you and me," Leander whispered, his lips trailing over her clavicle, breath huffing against her skin as he lifted her on and off of his cock. "Was always gonna be this good, Rey, never could be anything but. You're taking me like you're meant to, so sweet and warm, and it's fucking heaven because it's right—that's why."

Reyna's hand tightened in his hair and Leander groaned, like he was just as overwhelmed and needy as she was, like her hand in his hair was anything like the relentless rutting of his hips. Like her body was driving him half as mad as his words were driving her.

As her body welcomed him deeper and deeper, she reached between them to rub at her clit. When her fingers brushed over the sensitive nerves, she clenched and Leander drew in a choked breath. The sound echoed around them and Reyna whimpered as she worked over her clit.

"I'm gonna come," she warned him, and she felt Leander nod against her shoulder.

"Please come, gorgeous," he panted. "You're so beautiful when you come, let me see it, please. Waking me up with this hot pussy—fuck, I want to see you come. Come for me, baby, let me have it."

His words and her fingers pushed her over the edge and Reyna came with a cry, everything tensing. She registered Leander's choked moan as she convulsed around him, her cunt clenching him even tighter. He kept fucking her, kept that beautiful rhythm and it stretched her orgasm out.

"That's it, Rey," Leander whispered, his hands stroking up her back. "How'd that feel, hmm? You did so good for me."

Reyna whimpered, the warm heat spreading out to her fingertips and she realized she was still pulling his hair. She loosed her grip, carding her fingers through the blond locks, feeling boneless and sated.

"Feel warm," she mumbled, and Leander chuckled, low.

"You don't know the first thing about warm, baby," he said, and his fangs scraped the shell of her ear, teasing. Reyna smiled to herself, grateful her face was hidden. How could someone be all that he was at once? Dorky and sweet, a dirty talker who teased her, the best dick she'd had and her best friend who encouraged her to find hers first?

She pulled in a deep breath and rolled her tired hips, rewarded by the breath that punched out of him.

"Yeah?" she teased back, and Leander's hands tightening was the only warning she got.

A moment later, he was moving, lifting her while she was still around him, turning them both. Her back hit the couch, and then a moment later, Leander covered her. He bent down, capturing her mouth in a searing kiss, even as his elbows hooked under her legs. He lifted her, bending her, pumping into her spread thighs with a heightened intensity, until he had to break off their kiss to be able to breath.

"Yeah," Leander said again, his voice hoarse. "I'm losing my mind, honey. I just want to live in this tight cunt, stretch it out till it's all mine. Wanna knot you and stay in you, fuck, need to keep you full and filled with me—"

He broke off, his hips pistoning into her and Reyna's head fell back against the cushions as he rutted up into her. There wasn't a better word for it, sharp and deep and with one end. She could tell he was getting close, could hear the tightness in his throat as he drew in shallow breaths, but his rhythm never faltered. Steady and deep, and she'd already gotten hers, but it felt so good to be here for him.

Leander pushed himself back. One knee was between her and the back of the couch, his other leg flexed on the ground to balance them both. He braced himself on her raised knee and thigh, and both of them moaned as they watched his cock slide out of her. He was so thick, shining with her come, and the slow glide of it after the frantic pace was intoxicating.

Now that there was space between them, Reyna could see his knot.

Swelling at the base of his cock, thick, and it made her mouth water. She knew how it'd feel, knew the stretch of it would burn and yet she knew how Leander whimpered as he pushed it into her, and Reyna needed that.

"I want to feel it, Lee," Reyna told him, wondering why it felt like a secret. His eyes flickered up to hers, and his jaw slackened at whatever he saw.

"Fuck, Rey," he whispered.

He slowly pushed forward, his gaze unblinking as he fed his cock back into her weeping hole. Reyna's eyes fluttered shut as she stretched around him, and Lee's panting breath echoed around the room as he fucked her slowly. Agonizing slow, both of them achingly aware of the pulsing heat at the base of him, pressing up against her whole cunt, begging for entrance at the top of each stroke.

Reyna felt like she was empty, like she needed it. She needed *him*, needed him to need her, wanted to feel him lose himself in her. She felt mad with it.

"Please," Reyna gasped, squirming under his steady pressure. "Fuck, please, Lee, need you to come, need you to knot me, need—"

"You can't say shit like that, Rey," Leander groaned, but she heard the longing in his voice, and she felt the hand on her knee tremble. Reyna arched her back, the motion pushing her breasts up, and on the next stroke, Leander sunk deep into her.

Reyna held her breath.

The pressure was intense and concentrated, but she wanted to hear him. Past the push of his hot flesh against hers, past the frantic beating of her heart, she heard Leander's soft moan as his knot slipped into her. He sounded satisfied, he sounded beautiful, he sounded like hers, and Reyna's orgasm hit her by surprise.

She shook as she came, silently and writhing. Everything was Leander, everything was on fire, and she surrendered herself to it. She was floating, she was trembling, and she registered spreading warmth a moment later as he came inside her.

She was cock drunk and sated, thanking him for his knot, for his come, and Leander was shaking over her. He braced his arms over her head as he rode his orgasm out. His hips kept pumping into her, his knot clasping them together tightly. Reyna floated back to herself, registering a lethargy in her bones, the rich smell of their sex in the air, and Leander was still moving.

With each thrust, a whimper punched out of his throat, and Reyna ran her hands up his back, soothing over his sweat-slicked muscles.

"I can't stop," he moaned, and Reyna thought she'd never heard anything more beautiful than his voice. He was shaking, over sensitized, but he kept his rhythm like he was possessed. "Fuck, Reyna, baby, it's so good. It's so good, I can't, Reyna—"

He shouted, wrecked, and Reyna whimpered as another splash of come painted her inner walls. She felt like she might burst from holding him and his knot, but it was so, so good. Leander collapsed over her, spent, his second orgasm exhausting him, and Reyna felt a flash of pride settle over her.

She kept smoothing her hands over his back, soothing him, relishing this chance to comfort him. His shaking calmed after a couple of minutes and as he relaxed, Reyna focused on the echo of his heart through his chest. His head was thrown on top of hers, his chin pressed to her cheek, and Reyna loved the weight of him, the absolute abandon with which he'd given himself to her. Her nails scraped over him and Leander shivered, his broad shoulders shaking at her touch, and it made Reyna feel soft.

A couple minutes later, she felt his fingers start to twitch, as he came back to himself.

"Am I crushing you?" he asked, his voice hoarse, and Reyna shrugged, but it was ineffective under his weight.

"It feels good," she admitted. Like a Leander-sized weighted blanket, the kind that quieted her anxiety and maybe let her sleep a solid night.

She could tell he didn't believe her, but let her have it, shifting to settle slightly on his side. He was still covering her, but she could breathe a little easier, even as they couldn't pull apart from the knot. Reyna resigned herself to sleeping on the couch, snuggling deeper into his chest and the cushions. She hesitated for only a moment before lifting her chin to press a kiss to the cheek over hers. It felt silly, cheesy and romantic in a way that she didn't have an excuse for, but it felt right.

"Goodnight," she murmured, lamely.

Leander hummed as she adjusted, his arms tightening around her.

"You might be perfect," he mumbled. She could hear exhaustion sinking into his voice, the darkness and the fact that he'd come twice calling him back to sleep.

"That's what I'm here for," she reassured him, hoping he couldn't hear the note of longing in her voice. She knew why she was here, knew it was fleeting, but something about this moment made her want it for real. Want *him* for real.

"I said 'you'," Leander said, his voice uncharacteristically grumpy. "The sex is hot as hell, Rey, but I said 'you'."

Reyna's lips parted as she stared at his chest.

A moment later, she heard his breathing even out as he fell asleep, but Reyna stayed awake till dawn seeped through the curtains of the living room, torturing herself with the knowledge that it was his rut talking, but it'd felt dangerously close to real.

Eighteen

It'd been decades since Leander had first learned which boards creaked in the little cottage, and this morning, he was grateful the knowledge was still somewhere in his subconscious.

He'd woken with soft morning light seeping into the living room, and Reyna asleep beside him on the couch. He felt around for his glasses as he listened to her breathing. He knew enough of her sleep patterns to know she was out for the count, and had wanted to move them both before they fell into a repeat of the last few mornings.

So, Leander stepped by memory through the cottage, a sleeping Reyna in his arms. His feet padded heavily over the old boards, knowing the warped ones to avoid, as he bore them steadily towards the bedroom.

Reyna didn't stir as he laid her down on the bed, and when he pulled the thin comforter up over her, her fingers curled around it automatically. Her legs pulled up and she nestled deeper into the pillow, and Leander rubbed a hand against his chest as he looked down at her.

This was right, he knew it so deeply, *felt* it so deeply. That she would be with him, that he could care for her, that she would let herself rest with him.

He thought about joining her for a moment, but he knew he was awake for the day, and if he stayed with her, they'd probably end up doing something much less restful.

He ran a finger down her cheek, brushing a curl behind her ear, and smiling to himself when her nose wrinkled, even in her sleep. His sweatshirt was still beside the bed and he pulled it over his head gracelessly, trying not to think about how it'd been Reyna's for the weekend. He grabbed his phone and let himself out to the stoop, watching as dawn painted the sky.

It was so still on the island.

Birds cooed from their hidden perches in trees, auburn leaves falling as the wind moved through them. The ocean wasn't close enough to see, but the briny smell of it blew through on the breeze.

Leander sat directly on the stoop, pressing his back against the sliver of entryway that wasn't the screen door. The sun wasn't high enough to be bright, and he closed his eyes to the world, letting his thoughts drift back to the real world.

He wondered if Esther had rescheduled the board meeting, and if Mateo had decided to take an intern after all. He wondered if Whit took time off on weekends like this, or if he did suppressants, and if he should look into them, or if Whit ever had to leave a meeting, or a room, with pitying glances for his rut.

It might've been thirty minutes or a couple hours, but eventually the sun was high enough that it was too bright for him to continue resting. It was warm, and it was the first time Leander had noticed it since coming out to the cabin.

His rut had broken.

As he was processing that it was done, his phone buzzed on the stoop beside him, and a picture of the Mendler sisters flashed on the screen. He wasn't surprised Chesa was up this early; she'd probably been up for hours at the shop, but still, she didn't normally call him.

"Hey, Chesa," he answered, and he could hear Chesa shutting a door and the shop quieting around her.

"Oh, good," she said, "so it's not that there isn't reception on Great Cranberry, it's that my sister just isn't taking my calls."

Come to think of it, Leander hadn't seen Reyna on her phone for most, if any, of the weekend.

"She's asleep right now," Leander said loyally.

"All weekend?" Chesa asked archly, and Leander didn't know what to say to that.

Well, when she hasn't been asleep, she's been otherwise occupied.

Actually, said other occupations have meant she has been sleeping/recuperating a lot of the time.

Instead, he cleared his throat and asked, "So, everything okay? What's up?"

"Got a call from my bank this morning," Chesa said, a hundred unspoken things in her voice, "and an Account Closed email from my lender, too."

Leander bit the inside of his cheek, trying to remember what Reyna had told him in the kitchen last night.

She always made decisions singularly, but he'd assumed she'd at least have given Chesa a warning call. From the weighty silence on the line, it sounded like that had not happened.

"That sounds like good news?" Leander offered.

There was a long pause.

"Unbelievable," Chesa muttered. "So she told you before me?"

She asked it, but it wasn't a question.

"She worries about you," Leander said carefully, and Chesa scoffed.

"I worry about *her*," she said. "She's a workaholic who hasn't let herself feel a feeling in decade, who refuses to accept help from anyone that isn't you—but being worried doesn't mean that I have the right to make decisions for her."

"She should've told you," Leander said, and Chesa sighed into the phone.

"She should've," Chesa agreed, resignedly. "I just wish she trusted me half as much as she tried to fix things for me."

Leander thought about the union presentation Reyna had re-drafted for him, the groceries in the fridge, and almost smiled. "That's never been her forte."

Chesa huffed a laugh. "Yeah, I guess not."

The line was quiet for a moment, and Chesa sighed again.

"Sorry, I didn't call to yell at you," she said. "I just hadn't heard from her since the start of this sexcapade weekend, and then all this stuff with the loan..."

She trailed off, and though there was no one around to see, Leander still blushed. "I mean, it's not like that, we—"

"Come on, Stetson," Chesa said, an edge of humor creeping into her voice. "You get bit by a werewolf, and suddenly my sister's taking a vacation she's never had time for before, to run off with you, oh, and coincidentally it's a full moon? I know Reyna thinks I can't handle my shit, but I'm not a complete idiot."

There was a sound like a crash that echoed through the phone and Chesa pulled the phone away from her ear to resolve whatever situation was around her. A minute later, she was back.

"I gotta take care of this," Chesa said, "if Reyna's phone magically starts working again soon, can you have her give me a call?"

"Will do," Leander said.

"Thanks," Chesa paused for a moment. "I know I'm not really one to talk, in terms of having my life together...but did either of you guys think about how this weekend ends?"

Leander rubbed at his chin with the hand not holding his phone.

"Yeah, not so much," he admitted.

Chesa hummed. "While I appreciate that you're too preoccupied with trying to pretend you aren't in love with her, please remember that paying off my loan means that Reyna just bought herself out of a place to live. So, maybe both of you start having these conversations in front of other people, and not just in your heads. And be gentle with her okay?"

Leander smiled slightly, recognizing the same 'no matter what, she's my sister' protectiveness in Chesa that he so often saw in Reyna. It looked different, but it was still there.

"Okay," he agreed.

"Okay," Chesa repeated. "I'm gonna deal with this. I'm running some day-old pastries by the hospital when I close today; let me know if there's anyone I should mark a box for."

She hung up before Leander could say goodbye, and he tapped the phone against the palm of his other hand. The sun had turned the morning from pale blue to bright, and he had to squint to look out over the island, but he remained on the stoop, mulling over Chesa's advice.

The pride both sisters bore, the tangle of their good intentions and mixed messages...and the way Chesa had clocked his feelings for Reyna, and dropped it into the middle of a sentence to prove a point.

Leander heard stirring in the house, and hoped he hadn't woken Reyna by being on the phone. He heard her walking around, and he found himself smiling to himself. Waking up with her was one thing, but the domesticity of just hearing her go about her morning in a space that was theirs, was pretty special too. After a couple minutes, he heard footsteps getting closer on the hardwood and then the screen door squeaked as she opened it.

When he turned to look at her, his vision was blocked by a mug of chamomile tea, held through the crack in the door.

"Thanks," Leander said, accepting the mug and looking up at her. She looked beautiful.

Tired, definitely, but with an honesty in her features that normally was wiped away by her day job, or whoever else people needed her to be. But in the morning light, she just looked like Reyna. Her hair was slightly frizzy, her skin bare, and there was a crease on the side of her face from where she'd slept on a seam on the pillow.

She was watching him closely, and Leander took a sip of the too-hot tea, his glasses fogging immediately. As they cleared, Reyna tilted her head, her eyes narrowing, and an unreadable expression crossing over her phase.

"So it's over," she said, her expression unreadable, "isn't it?"

Leander pressed his lips together and nodded. "I think so, yeah."

This was where he said something, he knew it. The moment that he told her he wanted more than this weekend, more than the unreachable thing they'd always avoided. But Reyna's brown eyes didn't soften any with his words, and he wondered if now was right—if he should wait or rush ahead, if either would ruin his chances, if Reyna would listen more, one way or another.

When he didn't say anything, something ticked in Reyna's jaw, and she nodded shortly to herself.

"I'm gonna shower," she said shortly, turning back to the cottage before he could say anything. He heard her step retreat across the floor, and she'd closed the bathroom door by the time the screen door swung shut again.

Nineteen

The water was cold as Reyna stood under it, waiting for it to heat, trying to put a name on her feelings. She showered quickly, wincing at the unfamiliar soreness in her body, refusing to recall the memories of how she got the bruises and aches.

Reyna pulled on another sundress and was tying her hair into a braid at the base of her neck when she smelled coffee.

She nudged the door of the bathroom open with her hip, still braiding, and a glance out the screen door confirmed that Leander was no longer on the stoop.

A clatter came from the kitchen then, and Reyna followed a thumping sound to find Leander trying to fling the coffee grounds from the bottom of the French press into the waste bin via gravity.

A steaming mug filled with hot coffee sat on the counter.

If Leander noticed her entrance, he didn't say anything, just retreated from the waste bin to the front of the sink, where he was doing dishes. Reyna padded across the kitchen to the coffee. It was the perfect temperature to wrap her palms around the mug, while Leander busied himself beside her. She lifted herself up to the counter, absorbing the quiet sounds and the soft sunlight, sipping her coffee and watching Leander move around the kitchen.

It was the closest they'd been all weekend, without being on top of each other.

Leander's glasses were pushed higher as he wrinkled his nose, a flinch from a shaft of direct sunlight through the window. The window over the sink was open, the wind gently blowing the linen curtains open, and lifting Leander's hair off his forehead. He flicked soapy water off his hands and Reyna admired the line of his shoulders in the sweatshirt. He'd pulled on jeans, but was barefoot, a quiet dichotomy that was endearing. The kitchen was quiet, just the soft smell of coffee and the lemony dishsoap and a pang of longing went through Reyna.

Taking care of each other was something they did so easily, but this weekend had somehow made it complicated, because something in Reyna wanted to stay. And she couldn't, she had work to get back to, and Chesa to be honest with, and an apartment to find, but in a sunlit kitchen with Leander, it dimmed. It seemed like maybe it didn't have to be so hard, maybe it could just be this.

"Hey, what's going on?" Leander said gently, and Reyna blinked, realizing he'd come to stand in front of her, an expression of concern on his face.

His eyebrows were bunched and he pushed his glasses up nervously, like he wanted to reach for her and Reyna felt all the more how he *wasn't* reaching for her. She was appalled to find him swimming in her gaze, her eyes filling with unfamiliar tears that she couldn't explain any more than she could justify.

"Shit," she mumbled, wiping at her face aggressively, and Leander made a soft sound somewhere deep in his chest as he reached for her coffee cup, to free up her hands. Reyna rubbed at her eyes, hiding them, wishing Leander was back across the kitchen and not right in front of her, looking for all the world that he wanted to just pull her into his chest.

"I'm okay," she sniffed, after a moment, "just tired, you know?"

"Sure," Leander agreed softly, and she realized the hand that wasn't holding her coffee was on her knee, rubbing little comforting circles on it.

It made her want to actually sob, that gesture, that she would be emotional in front of him with zero explanation, and all he'd do is reach to soothe her. Reyna gave herself another few moments to revel in it, before she pulled in a deep breath, and made her smile easy before she dropped her hands.

He was so close to her, his blue eyes wide and concerned, his hair practically brushing against her forehead. As he saw her smile, she watched his grow, nervously, like he wasn't sure he believed her, but wanted to. Reyna couldn't bring herself to push him away, any more than she could push herself down, and she reached up to trace her finger down the side of his face.

"It's stupid," she told him, "but I wish it wasn't over."

A dozen emotions flitted across Leander's face, and then he shook his head, just slightly. "It doesn't have to be."

It did.

It did, because this weekend had been so intense, and it'd fade soon enough. When they were back in Port Cadie, back in the normalcy and without the needing of the full moon, they'd be in too deep to untangle themselves without getting hurt. And Reyna knew that however much it stung in this moment, that awakening would be devastating.

"It does," she said, but he didn't move and she didn't make him.

She felt him lean forward slightly, till his forehead was resting against hers, and she could taste his breath on the air. His thumb on her knee curled around to stroke up her thigh, featherlight and warm, like he couldn't help it. Her hand on the side of his face curled to the side of his neck and something unfurled in her stomach, a longing she barely recognized.

"Lee," she whispered, wondering why she couldn't finish the request. To ask him for more, to say they should stop, to walk away or give them one more time, but she couldn't find the words.

"Need to know what you want, Rey," Leander said, his voice nearly hoarse. "But I can't let you go unless you tell me too."

Reyna opened her eyes to find his closed, clenched tightly like he was holding himself back. The sun spilled around him like a painting, and his other hand was in a fist, pressed against the counter, as he braced himself.

This was a bad idea.

It was a bad idea, and she knew the only hope she had at a clean break was to stop this now. But what she knew was right was different from what she'd needed, and that was what he'd asked.

"Kiss me," she asked, and before she had finished speaking the words, Leander's hands were in her hair, tipping her head back to meet him.

He tasted like chamomile, like flowers with too much sugar, sweet enough to make her forget. He kissed her like he knew how desperately unmoored she was feeling, and that he could ground her in a way she didn't know to ask for. She tasted salt in their kiss, and Leander pulled back to wipe her eyes for her.

His thumb was tender on her cheek and then his hand curled around her knee, pulling her to the edge of the counter. Reyna grabbed at his waist, his back, loving the feeling of his broad chest pressed against hers. Leander's fingers curled into her hair, the tension as he pulled reminding her that he was here, with her, that he needed her as badly as she needed him.

Reyna didn't know when her knees had spread, pushing her dress up to around her waist, but she shifted to be closer to him and she whimpered as she pressed against the denim of his jeans. Leander's hand in her hair tightened, and she rocked against him, chasing the friction of the rough denim against her cotton panties.

Leander deepened the kiss and Reyna felt herself go breathless at the combination of his mouth, and the way the friction between them eased as she grew wet. She could feel his cock straining against the denim and she reached down, her breath catching as she felt the outline of him through his pants. Leander's hips pushed into her, and then he was grabbing her hand, pulling it away from him as he reached between them.

His breath ghosted against her cheek as he ran a finger over her panties, and Leander sighed when his fingers snagged on the wet fabric.

"Reyna," he whispered her name like a prayer, and she shifted her hips forward, panting. "Shh, I've got you."

His thick fingers trailed down the soft cotton, and he nudged them to the side to touch her directly. When his fingers, broad and gentle, brushed over her, and then pressed into her, her fingers curled around the back of his neck, clinging to him.

Reyna's head fell back against the cabinet, and she pressed her lips together as she worked herself onto his fingers. She was still sensitive from the night before, but even though his fingers were smaller than his cock, she felt every digit.

"That's it, honey," Leander soothed, stroking into her gently. A moment later he pulled out and Reyna whimpered as she lifted her head to look at him.

He was already watching her.

His blue eyes were dark as he lifted his fingers to his mouth. His tongue was already out, like he couldn't wait until his fingers were past his lips to taste her. He moaned as his lips closed around his fingers, and Reyna's hand tightened on his nape. He made her feel so wanted, so desired, and it was overwhelming.

One moment, they were eye level, panting close to each other and hips shifting closer, and the next Leander was gone. He sank to his knees on the hardwood floor of the kitchen, pulling her panties farther to the side and leaning into her cunt.

The first brush of his tongue made Reyna shudder, her head falling back to the cabinet again. His tongue was broad, licking up over her, through her, like he wanted her taste coating him. He lapped at her, and Reyna's hand wound into his hair, encouraging him. He hummed his approval, and Reyna whimpered as she felt the vibrations work through her. He was messy, his mouth open and tongue pulling through her cunt, and then he flexed his tongue, fucking it into her where his fingers had been.

"Yes, baby, please," Reyna whined, her hips pushing back to meet his mouth.

Leander pulled her thighs over his shoulder, allowing him even closer access, like he was drinking from her. He reached around her, his elbow hooking around her thigh to nudge a finger under her panties to stroke over her clit. Reyna's back bowed, and she felt like she was dripping onto the counter. He felt so good, his hands on her, his tongue in her.

She could come like this.

She could fall apart on his tongue and on his face and it would be stunning, but she needed more. Needed him closer. The fabric of her panties was digging into her hip as Leander pulled it tightly to give himself full access to her cunt, and she needed him closer.

Reyna's hand tightened in his hair, trying to pull him up. Leander resisted and she felt her thighs trembling, undone by the thought that he was fighting to stay with his face in her pussy.

"Not yet, sweetheart," he mumbled into her, his words muffled by her thighs, and Reyna felt them against her skin. She was close, she was so close, but if this was the last time, she wanted to come with him.

"Lee," she gasped, and she felt him falter when he heard the desperation in his voice. He tilted his head back and looked up at her through foggy glasses. He refused to back away from her, his tongue teasingly stroking over her as he met her eyes, and Reyna moaned.

Leander heard her acceptance, his mouth returning to her pussy as he held her eyes. It was a million times more intense like this, the way his mouth was working over her without looking, the way his eyes were feasting just as greedily as his mouth.

"Come for me honey," he asked, his voice thick, sending vibrations through her. "Let me see it, please, Rey, wanna see you come on my mouth again."

He readjusted his grip on her panties and the motion wrenched the cotton across her clit, and Reyna shattered. She felt tears falling as she came, the sharpest pleasure and profound terror, hating how good it felt when she knew she couldn't have more. Pleasure streaked over her and as she came back to her body, she realized she was babbling.

"Didn't want to come without you, Lee," she was crying, "Wanted you with me, wanted to feel—"

"Sweetheart, don't cry," Leander was whispering, replacing her panties and standing again, his hand cradling the side of her face. "Fuck, Rey, please don't cry."

He sounded gutted, like he believed that trying not to hurt her wouldn't do just that. His lips were soft as he kissed away her tears, a gentle touch, but he smelled like her, and it just made her more determined.

Reyna pulled back to look at him, his kind eyes and earnest face. She felt boneless, exhausted, and didn't know why she was fighting for something that was going to hurt them both. What she knew was that she felt empty, and like she wanted to feel *with* him, and that she could deal with all of her tears later.

She kissed him, and tasting herself on his tongue and only made her lonelier.

She reached down, shifting her hips to pull her ruined panties off, and then pulling him back towards her. She kissed him as she fumbled for his fly, unbuttoning him with trembling fingers and shoving his jeans down his thighs.

"Rey—" he protested against her lips, and Reyna shook her head when she pulled back.

His glasses were foggy, and her eyes were still cloudy with tears, but she was certain.

"Then make me stop crying," she told him. "If you want me to stop, fuck it out of me."

Leander's eyes searched hers for a moment, flitting between her eyes before he reached down and pushed down his boxer briefs. Reyna's breath caught in her throat as he took himself in hand. He was so hard, the tip flushed and leaking, like he also needed this. Leander leaned forward, bracing himself on the counter with one hand, which his other hand rubbed his cock into her cunt.

Reyna whimpered at the soft caress of his head over her dripping pussy.

"You want me as bad as I want you, don't you," he asked, and when Reyna glanced up, he was staring at where they were touching, just as entranced as she was. She could feel herself shaking, aching for him to fill her, her stomach quavering as she held herself still, waiting. He circled his cock around her clit, the blunted head tracing over her, making her whine for him.

"So bad, Lee," she whispered, "please, fuck me, need to feel you—"

He pushed into her, his hips slamming into the countertop as he thrust his cock into her. Reyna moaned loudly, her body throbbing as it welcomed him in. Even without his knot, he filled her so fully, so deeply. Her knees were bent and she braced herself on the counter as she adjusted to his size.

She didn't want to think about how it quieted her.

How her panic faded, how Leander was deep enough to assure her that he was here, that he felt this as much as she did, as hard as she did, but he wasn't running from it. She squirmed on his cock, pinning her in place, one of her hands splaying across his back to press him to her.

"It's not because I want you to stop," Leander said, his voice tight. She could see his arms were shaking, trembling to hold himself still as he waited for her to stretch around him. "It's because when you're like this, when you're this tight on my cock, you start actually saying what you want."

Reyna couldn't look away from him, from the quiet conviction in his eyes, in his voice. He looked back at her, unwavering, and when he pulled out, it was slow. It was a devastating retreat, careful and slow, and she felt every inch of it, her eyes falling shut.

"So you can cry, baby," Lee grunted, and she could feel that he was still watching her, still refusing to back down. When he reached the top of his stroke, he started again, pushing slowly back into her, stroking against her, claiming her. "You can cry, you can just feel it, you can scream, because I can take it. And when you're like this, I think you let yourself believe it, too."

Reyna's head fell back; she couldn't look at him, couldn't let him see he was right. She was feeling too much, every nerve ending aflame with his steady press, with the push of his cock into her and his words washing over her. A moment later, she felt his mouth at her neck, his tongue licking at her sweat there, and sloppy kisses pressing over her skin.

"It's not that simple," she panted, and Leander scoffed, a huff of hot breath against her skin.

"It's exactly that simple, Rey," he said, and he sucked at a spot that made her gasp. "So be honest: what do you want?"

And then he didn't move.

He was so deep in her, so close that she could feel his cock throbbing within her, could hear his breath shaking from holding himself still, waiting for her. She was pulsing around him, clenching around him, desperate for the friction he withheld, and she felt her resolve weakening.

"You want me to start?" Leander mumbled against her skin, his mouth traveling up the other side of her neck. His hands trailed down her arms to catch her hands, and Reyna knew he felt it when she nodded.

"I want to keep you," he said, and she felt his cock nudge deeper into her. "I want...fuck, I want so much, but I'll start with I want more of this. Slow mornings and your cunt stretched around me."

Reyna felt like she was gasping for breath, as his fingers curled around hers. He lifted their joined hands, braced them on the cabinet above her head, stretching her out beneath him.

"I want your tears and to scandalize the neighbors. I want every gasp and whimper, I want your pussy to be used to taking me, used to stretching for me. And I want to make you breakfast after, or coffee, or to sleep in together, and not feel like it's borrowed time."

Reyna shook her head, pressing her lips together.

It sounded so good when he said it, but it wasn't real. He didn't know he wanted that, he'd just had biology-driven, mind-blowing sex for a weekend, and it rewrote him. And when they got back to Port Cadie, and it faded, then someone would have to pick up the pieces, so Reyna would rather they break now, than then.

She felt his lips traveling up her neck, but she still wasn't prepared when he kissed her.

It was sweet, it was longing, it was like he was promising everything he said. And when she whimpered into his kiss, Leander groaned, and his hips started moving again.

Reyna could feel tears squeezing out the corners of her eyes, but she couldn't stop, never wanted to. She clenched around him, rewarded by the moan that ripped from Leander and his thrusts sped up. He held her hands tightly, kissed her hungrily, almost angrily, and she was trembling from the intensity of it all.

His cock was so deep inside of her.

His hips slammed into hers, thrusting up against the counter like if he chased her far enough, hard enough, she'd turn back to him. And it was working; she felt herself unraveling. Reyna worked her hands free of his, wiped at her face angrily and reached for him. She framed his face in her hands, kissing him as he thrust up into her. His cock was nudging against a spot that had her unable to sit still, and Leander reached for her thighs to hold her open. His fingers dug into her hips as he pressed her open, his groin grinding against hers, and Reyna broke away from his kiss on a moan.

She knew what he was doing—there was no knot.

She knew what he was doing—there was no knot. There was no knot, and he didn't have claws or fangs; he was promising it was still enough, this was still real. As he ground into her, his rough hair sliding over her clit, Reyna felt herself climbing again.

"I'm gonna come," she whimpered.

"I know, beautiful," he whispered back, his teeth scraping against her jaw as his pace held steady. He had her splayed open, his to claim, and his mouth turned gentle as he nibbled at her skin. "I know you feel it too—tell me, Rey, I can take it, please..."

Reyna sobbed as he fucked her, as his cock rammed into her and his hands were tight around her thighs. As he was as honest as he knew how to be, as he begged her to echo the same truth, and as her body was pushed to the brink, it spilled out of her.

"I want it too," she cried, "fuck, Lee, it's been so good, and I want more, but I can't—"

He cut her off with a kiss, sealing their lips together as they moaned into each other's mouths. It was so good, searing, and soon it was hardly a kiss, just a desperate closeness.

Leander let go of her thigh to reach between her legs, stroke over her clit, and Reyna fell apart. She was sure he was saying something, and she was certain it was sweet, but she was lost. The kitchen was swallowed in bright light as it pressed from his fingertips, as she collapsed back against the cabinet with her orgasm. She felt Leander's hand behind her head, cradling her, keeping her from hitting her head as she sat boneless while he chased his.

"Let me feel it, Lee," she whispered, and he groaned.

"I'm so close, Rey," he gritted, his hips faltering. She opened her eyes to take him in—his sweet eyes, his flushed face, his panting mouth—and he was staring at her in open adoration. She managed a fluttering smile for him, and his hips slammed forward, his eyes closing, as he rutted into her. She saw an echo of her smile on his expression, even as his head fell back. His hands fell to her hips, clutching her to him, and he was whining with each thrust.

God, he had no right to be so pretty.

Soft and strong and blushing, coming because she smiled at him. He groaned, his hands tightening on her hips and then he thrust faster until he came. Reyna hummed, shifting slightly as warmth flooded her channel, and she reached for him.

At the slightest touch of her hands in his hair, Leander leaned forward, practically falling into her chest. He whimpered, thrusting into her, like he couldn't stop, like he had to fuck them both through it. It seemed to last forever, his orgasm wringing through him, and Reyna found herself petting his hair as he came back.

The kitchen was cold.

She realized it absently, as the morning air curled around them from the open window, and she tried to think if they'd been too loud, so close to it, if neighbors would've heard. Sweat was cooling on her skin, Leander's too, prickling as the wind wound through the kitchen. She felt him draw in a deep breath, and he pressed a kiss to her collarbone before he lifted himself off of her. He fixed his glasses and shuffled over to the sink, redoing his jeans before holding a clean dish towel under the scalding tap, and bringing it back over to her.

Reyna hopped off the counter, wincing at the tightness from the intensity and the position. The towel was warm between her thighs, a welcome cleansing, and though Leander offered, she walked it over to the bathroom herself, to rinse it in that sink.

She didn't look at him and she didn't look at her reflection.

She pulled the dress back down and hung the dish towel on the towel rack in the bathroom to air dry, and when she emerged from the bathroom, Leander was sitting on the bed.

He'd gotten his normal color back, his sweatshirt pushed up to over his elbows and he'd clearly wet a hand and run it through his hair. He was rubbing his hands across the tops of his thighs, and when she came into the room, he stood up quickly.

Reyna's eyebrows rose, but he didn't say anything.

"Okay," Reyna said, after a minute, "I assume we have to do laundry or something, before we head back? I can check the ferry schedule, see what makes sense to catch, and we can—"

"I love you."

Leander's words seemed to be suspended in the room, dangling off the dustmites dancing in the sunlight. Reyna's lips parted, and she waited for him to explain that. To quantify it, to take it back, to give some kind of explanation why he thought a weekend of sex was the same as love, and in what universe it would be okay to tell her was right after they'd both come hard enough to see stars. He licked his lips, but didn't take it back and Reyna realized she wasn't breathing.

"I'm gonna go for a walk," she said hollowly, reaching for her jacket by the door and hearing her voice echo around the room.

"Rey, wait," Leander said, suddenly springing into action, "I didn't—"

"Don't," Reyna stopped, turning to him. She knew her eyes were wide, could tell because he looked at her like she was fragile.

And maybe she was, because worse than hearing him say it, worse than knowing he was that confused from the weekend, would be hearing him say he didn't meant it.

"I'm going on a walk," she repeated, and she didn't wait to hear his response, just stepped on unsteady legs through the cottage, slipped her feet into her shoes, and walked until she reached the sea.

Twenty

As soon as Leander said it, he knew it was wrong.

He hadn't meant to say it like that, hadn't meant to lead with it, practically shout it at her as she emerged from the bathroom. He'd watched shock, then disbelief, then panic work over her face, and she'd bolted. He knew when he tried to tell her that's not how he'd meant to tell her, that she would think he was taking it back, and it'd driven her from the cottage. And he'd known the worst thing he could do was chase after her, make her feel caged, but it had hurt like hell to let her walk away.

He wasn't stupid enough to think that the sex had been good enough to change her mind. He'd just hoped that since she'd been able to admit that maybe she wanted him too, that she'd believe him when he told her.

But now it was hours later.

He'd done a couple loads of laundry, aired out the cottage, cleaned out the fridge. He'd packed his bag, packed hers because there wasn't much to pack, and thoroughly clorox-ed the kitchen counter, but Reyna still wasn't back yet.

He heard his phone go off, and felt around in his pockets for it. They came up empty, and by the time he remembered he'd left it on the porch, it'd gone to voicemail. He waited for the recording to finish, then listened to the message.

"Yeah, I guess that's fair," Reyna sighed into the recording, almost to herself, as she realized he wasn't answering. It sounded like wind was whipping around for, and Leander looked around the yard confusedly; the wind wasn't that high. "Sorry for leaving like that I just...I needed a minute. I actually, um—I'm on the ferry back. My jacket had my phone and wallet and car keys, and it just made sense. I need some space, but text Chesa, she's going to pick you up, whenever you get in. She says thanks for the pep talk, by the way; we're talking this weekend. So, I guess, thanks for running interference there. Okay... bye."

Leander replayed the message before jogging to the end of the road, lifting his hand to block the reflections of the afternoon sun off the ocean. Sure enough, the ferry was pulling out of the cove below. He couldn't see well enough to see the deck, but he imagined Reyna there, her jean jacket wrapped around her tightly.

He walked back to the cabin.

The ferries ran on a frequent enough loop in the summer, but this late in the fall, and it'd be another few hours before the next one came, so he finished up at the cabin. He stopped at the grocer's to buy some off-season cherries and make sure no one thought he was too unhinged after the incident yesterday, and made his way down to the dock. He sat on a bench in the sun with his bag and Reyna's, and counted down the time till when the next ferry came.

The ferry did come, inevitably, and he took a seat inside.

Four days ago, he'd been on this same ferry, barely able to keep his hands to himself, losing his mind at the thought of Reyna in his sweatshirt. Four days ago, he'd had the weekend ahead of him, brimming with potential and possibility and hope, and now he'd fucked it up. Now, he was eating off season cherries, spitting the pits in a nondescript Styrofoam cup from the galley, with no idea what he was supposed to do once he get off the boat.

Leander let out a long breath, leaning back on the bench seat and watching the sea out the window.

It'd been so good.

Not just the sex, but the *intimacy* of the weekend. It was hardly the first time they'd made dinner together, nor the first time she'd been stressed about her family, nor the first time he'd been awed to see her skin glow in the firelight. But all of it together made him realize how much he had missed. He had been, and would continue to be, grateful for every part of his life that she chose to be a part of, but the weekend had painted a perfect picture of how it could be if that was always.

And he knew it'd be different, obviously, he wouldn't be in a full-moon-induced frenzy. But the every day stuff, they knew how to handle. He and Reyna had fought before, had worked it out before, and would work it out this time. The alternative was incomprehensible.

Leander couldn't picture his life without her, genuinely couldn't imagine the grayscale existence it would be. And if this truly was one-sided, if it was just him projecting, he'd survived that before. After everything, he owed her honesty, and if she wasn't there, he could accept that.

As the ferry pulled into Port Cadie, Leander knew he wasn't in the headspace to garner a ride from a friend, even Chesa, so called a cab to the hospital instead. He arrived at Port Cadie Medical Center as the shift changed, the lobby clogging with medical workers in laymen's clothes, exiting the hospital.

"Després!" Whit's voice cracked across the lobby, and Leander looked over to see the doctor shouldering his way through the crowd. Whit's stride didn't break as he reached Leander, gripping his arm above the elbow and steering them both to the side of the lobby before pulling Leander to a stop in front of him.

"Are you even cleared to be here right now?" Whit asked under his breath, and Leander noticed his eyes were flecked with gold.

"I didn't come back to the hospital while still in a rut," Leander said, crossing his arms. "It broke this morning; it's fine."

Whit scoffed, but the gold in his eyes faded. "You don't look fine."

"Thanks," Leander muttered. "Have you seen Esther?"

"Who?"

That tracked. Leander shook his head, running a hand through his hair. "Never mind."

"Hey, hold on," Whit sidestepped to stay in front of Leander. "I mean it, you're lookin' rough. I know this weekend was your first time, but—"

"I'm fine," Leander repeated.

Whit didn't seem to believe it any more than he did, but he reached over and clapped him on the back.

"Ah, you'll figure it out," Whit said, easily. "That girl waited by your bed and practically growled at anyone who came to check you out before you woke up. Whatever you did, it couldn't scare her more that that."

Leander wasn't too sure about that, but he appreciated the vote of confidence.

A small crowd gathered at the door and drew their attention; Leander knew from looking that the only thing that got healthcare workers to cluster like that was free sugar. Sure enough, a gap in the crowd revealed a smiling Chesa Mendler, wearing a Jade Vine baseball cap and teeshirt, handing out day-old pastries to the staff, while doing some not-too-subtle promo for her cafe. She was handing brown boxes off to anyone who would take them and when she saw Leander across the lobby she did a double take.

For a second, Leander considered hiding, but he decided against it and gave an inane wave. Chesa handed off another few boxes as she was walking, then beelined towards Leander, who shifted on his feet nervously.

"I thought you were still on the island," Chesa said as she got closer.

"I thought you were at the shop," Leander rejoined.

Chesa's eyes narrowed. "You were supposed to text me so I could give you a ride."

Leander had nothing to say to that; she had even told him she was coming by PCMC, he'd just forgotten in the debacle of the morning.

"Sorry," he offered, and Chesa fixed him with a look.

"Don't do that, now I feel bad," she said. "Are you okay? Is Reyna? She called me to say to get you a ride, which I thought was a ruse to cover for the fact that she hasn't answered my calls all weekend, but then she was all cryptic, so now I'm worried. What happened? You sounded all smitten this morning and I—"

"Breathe," Leander interrupted. "We're fine, it's just complicated. The weekend was a lot, and she needed some space, so that's why I'm here instead of there, or asking you for a ride."

Chesa didn't look like she believed his oversimplification, which was honestly pretty valid.

"Okay," she said slowly, "so what are you going to do about that?"

Leander rolled his shoulders; clearly he hadn't gotten that far.

"You're from the Jade Vine," Whit said, and Chesa and Leander both remembered he was there. The doctor was staring at Chesa with a tense expression on his face, but, ever uncowed, Chesa raised an eyebrow.

"What gave it away?" she asked, adjusting the cap on her head and not breaking eye contact from Leander, waiting on his answer.

"No," Whit chuckled, not used to being brushed off so effectively, "like, you're one of the baristas; you make a mean flat white."

"I'm the owner," Chesa said, and she finally turned to look at Whit. It was impressive how she managed to look down at Whit from almost a foot shorter than his height. "I should hope I can pull a shot of espresso. Do you know anything else about my sister or Leander, or why are you here?"

Whit grinned, a slow smile spreading over his face, till his dimples punched out of his cheeks. That look Leander recognized, and he didn't like it leveled at Chesa any more than he did at Reyna. Thankfully, Chesa seemed even less impressed, even when Whit ramped up his accent before speaking.

"Whitman Pace," he said, easily. "I'm a surgeon here."

"Good for you," she said, barely sparing a glance at Whit before looking back to Leander. "What are you going to do about Reyna?"

Leander spread his hands. "She needs a minute, and I agree, I'm not trying to—"

"Literally what did I tell you this morning," Chesa shook her head. "You guys have to have actual conversations, you can't just pine after each other and not say anything."

Leander was pretty sure saying something was exactly the problem, but he didn't really want to say that to Chesa, much less in front of Whit.

"And it's a great point," Leander appeased. "And we will talk about it, okay, just not right now."

"When?" Chesa asked.

"When he's done licking his wounds, obviously," Whit shrugged, and Chesa shot him a look, before refocusing.

"Leander," Chesa said his name slowly, like she was talking to a child, "I'm serious."

"Me too," Leander said. "Look, if I thought going after her was right, I'd do it, but she was pretty clear—"

"Stetson!" Chesa snapped.

"Stetson?" Whit grumbled.

"Can I help you?" Chesa said, exasperated, finally turning to Whit, who crossed his arms over his chest.

"I don't get why he gets to be Stetson," Whit groused, lifting his chin at Leander, "I'm the one from Texas."

The both stared at him, before Chesa tipped her head back to the ceiling, exhaling a sigh loudly.

"Be that as it may," Chesa said to the skylights, "he's the Bruce Boxleitner lookalike. Anything else you need, Doctor, or can I talk to my friend in peace?"

Whit smiled, but something ticked in his jaw as he backed away.

"Sorry to intrude, Miss Mendler," he said easily, before turning, his boots echoing on the floor of the lobby.

"So he's met Reyna?" Chesa guessed, and Leander nodded.

"It went pretty much the same as that interaction."

Chesa snorted. "It's good for him. Character growth and all. Is that accent real?"

"It is," Leander admitted. "He's old generation Texas; It's not even an act."

Chesa whistled.

The lobby was crowded, and the silence seemed all the louder for the lack of conversation between them.

Eventually, Chesa pulled a last box out from under her arm, and tipped her head towards the hospital. "I'm gonna find a nurse's station to leave this at, with a sticky note that says *Not for Surgeons*. Are you gonna find my sister and make this right?"

Leander pulled off his glasses to rub a hand over his eyes.

He really wasn't sure.

Go after her, say something stupid again, mess it up further?

Wait for her, risk whatever time did to them, mess it up further?

He slid his glasses back on, and Chesa's concerned face swam into focus in the crowded lobby.

"I'll go find her," he agreed, and Chesa nodded, pleased.

"Thank you," she said. She rooted around in the box, grabbing a popover and pulling it out with a napkin that had materialized from seemingly nowhere, and offering the pastry to Leander in a small bag. "Come bearing gifts."

Leander took the popover with a wry smile, and Chesa squeezed his shoulder before turning in the lobby, and marching with confidence to find an undisclosed nursing station. Leander watched her baseball cap disappear into the crowd, and looked down at the popover in his hands.

Reyna should be at home; she probably had a lot of work to catch up before starting the work week tomorrow. But Leander knew that wouldn't be where she was. There was one place Reyna went when she needed to think, where she'd gone in the middle of the weekend, and it would be where she'd fled when she thought it was over—Reyna was at the ocean.

Twenty-one

Tourists complained about it, but Reyna didn't mind that the sun rose, instead of set, over the Atlantic.

Sunrises were for hope, for new starts, for injecting optimism and bright opportunities, and there was nothing like a sunrise over the ocean. But sunsets weren't half as dramatic. The sun slipped behind the skyline and the beach turned blue, an all-encompassing melancholy, and Reyna would always prefer that malaise to a brilliant sunset.

Especially on a day like today.

It hadn't been sunset when she'd arrived, with a midafternoon sun burning harshly in the sky. The beach that Reyna and the girls surfed at was more for the waves than sandy shores, but it was where she drove on instinct. As a surfer's spot, it wasn't crowded past mid morning, save for a couple elderly people walking their dogs, the odd tourist taking pictures on a disposable film camera, or a weathered local with a metal detector. Reyna kept a beach blanket in the back of her car, and spread it over the empty beach, burying her feet in the sand and watching the tide go out.

By the time it changed directions, she had no greater clarity.

The world was turning blue, the tide was creeping back up the shoreline, and Reyna still didn't know what to do with herself.

She could admit she shouldn't have run.

It didn't undo what Leander had, and it made it clear that it affected her, enough to drive her from the island. In addition to being irrational, it wasn't the kindest, and though she wasn't about to apologize for reacting emotionally to something emotional, running had been cowardly at best, selfish at worst.

Reyna pulled her knees up to her chest, wrapping her arms around them, watching a peekytoe scuttle across an outcropping of slate to the side of the beach. The crab darted from a crack in the rocks, its red shell distinct over the black slate, before retreating to another crevice, and Reyna rested her cheek on her knees.

The sand wasn't firm enough to trap the sound of a footstep, but she registered that someone was walking up to her, and she knew that it was Lee. She supposed she wasn't hiding, not technically, and if he'd driven by the the dirt parking lot, he would've seen her car.

She didn't look up at him but she did scoot down the towel, and felt the sand shift as he sat beside her. She heard a rustle and in her peripheral vision, saw a popover on a brown paper bag slide across the towel. A smile pulled at the corner of her mouth, and when she looked up at Leander, he seemed just as nervous as she was.

"It's an olive branch from me and Chesa," he said, as Reyna pulled the pastry apart. Some bakeries dumped them in cinnamon sugar, or served them with heaps of jam, but she preferred just the rich bread: the perfect not-too-sweet treat. She offered part of it to Leander but he shook his head, leaning back to rest on his palms on the sand, past the blanket behind him.

"I don't know if an olive branch is needed," she said, lifting a shoulder. "*I* probably should've brought you a popover, for abandoning you on an island."

Leander huffed a laugh. "I think it's probably best if we don't keep a tally for the weekend."

Reyna didn't like the guilt on his voice any more than she did the heaviness in her chest. She finished the pastry, wiping her hands on her dress.

"It's okay, Lee," she said quietly. "We're okay."

She could feel Leander watching her, as she continued to stare out at the ocean. It was fading into the same color as the sky, gray and blue and misty, like a dream. Leander shifted, pushing off the sand and crossing his legs as he sat up.

"I'm not," Leander said, and she looked back at him sharply. He shrugged, looked down at his hands as he picked stubborn grains of sand off of them. "I know it's not what you want to hear, but it's the truth, and I owe you at least that."

Reyna closed her eyes, pulling in a deep breath. The sea air felt cool in her lungs, and this was the conversation they should've had, back at the cottage, if she hadn't run.

"You don't love me, Lee," she said, wishing her voice was steadier. It didn't sting any less, hearing it said aloud, but if he wanted honest, then she could give him that. "This weekend was a lot, and we knew that, going in. It was a pretty illusion, for sure, but the moon is only going to fade more, and then we have to deal with the fact that it was just hormones."

"Why are you so convinced that this is just the rut talking?" Leander asked, and Reyna sighed.

"I don't know, Lee," she let go of her knees, straightening her legs as she turned to face him, "maybe it's the fact that you've never, in twenty-four years, felt the need to tell me you loved me before?"

Something in Leander's jaw clenched as he looked back at her, and Reyna lifted her chin in a challenge. He rubbed at the back of his neck, clearing his throat before he spoke.

"When I got sick," Leander said, "at Christmas, two years ago. You skipped doing the big German Christmas with your dad's family, and parked yourself in my living room. You ordered every variety of pho for a week straight, and yelled at me from the other room to make sure I ate it."

Reyna remembered it, but she wasn't sure why he was bringing it up now.

"When you ignored years of failed attempts and tried to make me a congratulations cake for getting a job at PCMC," Leander continued, "but you swapped the sugar and salt and it was literally poison. You were so proud of yourself, and so crestfallen when it was bad, and you swallowed your pride and asked Chesa to make you a backup cake because celebrating me was more important than you beating your track record."

Reyna wrinkled her nose; it wasn't her finest moment, and she didn't know where Leander was going with this.

He smiled, and the edges of it softened as he shared another memory.

"When everyone was trying to be polite at my mom's funeral," Leander said, "but Aunt Jen was so ungraciously drunk, and you spilled cider on her dress so she'd yell at you in the bathroom, away from where everyone else was trying to keep it together."

Reyna wet her lips, understanding dawning as she realized Leander was answering her question. But he couldn't be, because these were years of memories, years of friendship, and this was newer, more raw than that.

Wasn't it?

"When I absolutely bombed that AP Economics test," Leander said, "and you took that test to the principal and showed her my notes and told her how hard we'd studied, and that the only reason I'd do so poorly was if Mrs. Bailey was an inept teacher."

"Lee..." Reyna shook her head, "that was in high school."

Leander ran a hand through his hair, the ends of it sticking up without product and the humidity of the sea.

"You think I don't know that?" he asked, almost laughing. "Every time you tell off a misogynist at your work, or a narcissistic surgeon at mine, every time you come into my house after a surf and you just look like the ocean and summer, and every time you shoulder someone else's responsibility because you know it's heavy for you, but you know you can take it—every time, Rey, I've thought it. So don't tell me what I've *felt the need to say*, because I think of the two of us, I'm not the only one who's feeling things they aren't saying."

Reyna gaped at him.

His words seemed to spin in the air around them, hovering, like each time she thought about them for too long, she had to push them back into orbit. Because what he was saying was so incomprehensibly much more than the weekend, and Reyna could barely process part of it before the next phrase bowled over her.

"Why..." she shook herself, "so why didn't you say anything?"

Leander smiled, a rueful thing in the encroaching twilight. "Because I knew you'd react how you did today."

Reyna bit her lip, wishing she could take it back.

The thought of a younger, softer version of Lee knowing that she would run, that she would need to be away from him more than she'd want to listen to him, was devastating.

"It's not like that," Leander said, and he didn't sound resentful. "At first, I really didn't think it'd last. My parents showed me that good things have a habit of running out, and I figured that I could get over it in college. When I realized that wasn't possible, I figured I'd rather have you in my life, as a friend, than not at all."

The wind was picking up, cooled by the fading light and the chill of the sea, but Reyna didn't feel it. She rubbed her temples, trying to process what this meant, what it could mean. She could feel Leander's eyes on her, feel the weight of his gaze like she had all weekend, with the intensity that was at once familiar and foreign, and that's what gave her next question voice.

"What changed this weekend?" she asked, needing to know.

If it was how good they'd been, how well they'd fit together, how matched and oddly escapist it'd been...while romantic, that wasn't enough. Reyna looked over to find Leander gazing out at the sea. She studied what she could of his profile, half hidden, and wondered if this was how she felt to him.

"Nothing changed," Leander admitted. "This weekend...it was nothing new, but it was confirmation that it wasn't just my imagination. That everything I was afraid of wanting was *just there*. And not just the sex part, Rey, all of it. Talking about work, or your sister, making dinner together, walking up a hill to a house and thinking *that's where Reyna and me are*. It made me confront it, made me sick with how badly I wanted it, and how the reason I finally had it was because you would wade with me through all the undefined things to meet me in the middle of it."

He looked back at her, like he'd remembered she was there, like the words were lifted off his chest, and Reyna was certain the beach was spinning. Leander's eyes were shining, ever earnestly, the blue of them nearly gray as the light faded. And she read it in his face, the conviction and entirety of what he was saying, and she was truly speechless.

So they stared at each other, so much said that they never dared. Reyna watched the wind blow across Leander's face, lift his hair off his face and gently return it.

He lifted a hand like he was going to reach for her, but then he stopped himself, crossing his arms loosely.

"If you're really not there, with me, then we'll go back to friends," Leander said, at length. "The last thing I want to do is pressure you, and, like I said, I've sat on it before. But if the reason you're running from this is because you think it's new, it isn't. You've been it, Rey, since before I had an idea of what that meant to me."

All Reyna could do was look at him mutely.

She didn't know what she was feeling, what cocktail of disbelief and hope and anxiety was warring within her ribcage, and how she was supposed to make sense of it. If Leander said that his feelings were constant, hers was an onslaught of everything she'd refused, rejected. It felt like she was suffocating with possibility, brimming with potential energy and she couldn't condense any of it to consecutive thoughts, much less words.

"Okay," Leander said quietly, and he pushed himself off the blanket. Reyna frowned at the beach where he had been, processing that he was leaving. Was this what he had felt?

Was this terror, this absolute need to not be alone in this, was this how she'd left him at the cottage this morning?

Before Reyna could respond, she was reaching for him. Her movements were jolted, but her fingers fisted in his sweatshirt as he turned away, and she meant to pull gently, but she yanked him down, and he tumbled. And it hadn't been what she had planned, but clearly her mind and her voice were a few steps behind, because when Leander fell down onto the blanket beside her, Reyna didn't hesitate for a moment, before she kissed him.

For a second, Leander was still.

Either in shock or in disbelief, but it was fleeting, and then his lips thinned as he smiled against her mouth. His hands spanned her waist, pulled her closer to him, gentle and steady and here.

He was right, *this* was right.

Leander in her arms, grinning into her kiss, his hands pulling her closer and all the things they'd been afraid of tumbling around them in the sand. His glasses brushed against her cheek and she pulled back, gasping for breath, admiring him as he still leaned into her. His soft lashes, flushed cheeks, and beautiful eyes—so close to her, and actually maybe hers.

Reyna pushed them up, knees touching as they knelt on the blanket, sand in their hair and breathless. She pulled his hands into hers, tossed her hair out of her face, and steadied herself.

"I can't promise I'll say it back," she heard herself say, her voice breathless, "but I want to hear it again."

Leander smiled, the softest purse of his lips as he looked at her in a way that only be described as fond.

"I love you," he said.

Reyna closed her eyes, testing the words in the air, on her skin.

He loved her, he said it like it was true, like it was the only and easiest thing. He loved her, he chose her and chased her, and wasn't changing with the moon. She felt Leander's fingers tighten around hers, and she squeezed him back, absorbing the words.

"I love you," Leander said again, impossibly gentle, and though her eyes were closed Reyna could see it, like a beam of sunshine unfurling around her. Weaving its way through shadows, around corners, illuminating the parts of her she kept locked away and hidden and refused. And in the light of his love, she found she didn't wither. It didn't scorch her, didn't send her shattering, it just felt like a deep breath.

She'd thought she'd cried herself out this morning, but when she looked at Leander now, it was through watery eyes.

God, he was so sweet.

Kneeling across from her, waiting for her, and Reyna's smile tipped slightly. She reached for him, brushing sand off the side of his face, and Leander recaptured her hand in his. She anticipated the stroke of his thumb over the back of her hand, but not the gentle press of his lips over the tops of her knuckles.

"Love you," he whispered, and then smiled at her sheepishly, tucking her hands together, back in his.

Reyna realized he wasn't prompting her.

He didn't want her to say it back, he just wanted her to know, and to accept that he meant it. The same way he always waited, the same way he was gentle and steady, the final burst of light on a barren beach.

"You too," Reyna managed, licking her lips before trying again. "Lee, I love you, too."

Then she saw that his eyes were swimming too, and only had a moment to marvel before he stood sharply, tugging her up with him. He lifted her hands around his neck and wrapped his around her waist, his head burrowing into her shoulder. Leander held her tightly, like he couldn't get close enough, and Reyna was holding him just as close. The sand under their feet dampened as twilight deepened, and they swayed slightly at the uneven footing.

The waning moon emerged through the clouds, her light sparkling like diamonds over the Atlantic.

It was beautiful, it was singular, but the woman who ran to the sea did not see it. She wrapped herself in the arms of her love, let him hold her, steady her, and be that same escape.

Twenty-two

Reyna woke slowly, languidly, registering the familiar texture of the armchair she was curled into. The room around her was bright, the paneled walls of the cottage coming into focus, lined with cardboard boxes. Her skin felt hot, and she was breathing quickly, and her eyes fluttered shut when she felt the pull of Leander's tongue through her pussy.

Caught between dream and waking, she reached down for him, her hands tangled in his sweaty hair. She felt Lee's tongue go lax as he grinned, realizing she was awake, before his mouth trailing up to her clit. His tongue circled her slowly, teasing, making her jump as he played with her. He hummed like her reactions amused him, his pink lips closing around her clit and sucking gently, pulling a broken moan out of her.

"Good morning," Leander teased into her pussy, and Reyna's legs jolted at the sensation.

It was hardly morning; it was near the end of their moving day, and they'd been carrying boxes up from the ferry since the actual morning. After getting the last load up the hill, she'd sunk into her old armchair, relieved to have won the battle of lugging it up to the cottage, and had only mean to rest for a moment, but had apparently fallen asleep.

Leander had decided on a hell of a way to wake her up.

He shifted slightly, lifting a hand to run his fingers through her pussy. Reyna had no idea how long he'd been between her legs while she slept, but she knew she was drenched. The sloppy sounds of his tongue teasing her and fingers coaxing through her were echoing, intoxicating, and Reyna moaned again when he pressed two fingers into her.

"Fuck, honey, you're so wet," Leander mumbled against her, his tongue moving messily around his fingers. He was drinking her arousal from around his hands, awed like he wasn't the one on his knees, making her this way.

"Feels so good, Lee," Reyna managed, and Leander grunted against her. She loved how much he responded to her, how her grip on his hair and her reactions to his ministrations encouraged him just as much as if she were touching him.

Leander pulled back, resting on his thighs as his fingers curled into her slowly. He stroked her walls carefully, feeling along her cunt until he pressed up against the spot that made Reyna cry out. "So pretty, baby," Leander murmured, looking up at her. "You worked so hard today and I wanted to let you rest...but then I thought maybe you deserved this."

His chin rested on her thigh, and Reyna whimpered when she realized his face was wet from eating her out. Her hips bucked up wantonly, and the side of Leander's glasses dug into her thigh as he watched her. Her leggings were around her ankles, and she was writhing against his hand, and he held her gaze hungrily, like she was doing anything other than just taking it.

Leander shifted his hand, lifting his thumb to brush over her clit while his fingers still stroked inside her. Reyna's head fell back and Leander chuckled darkly.

"Yeah?" he asked, his voice low, "you like me playing with your clit while you fuck my fingers?"

Reyna whined a response, her fingers tightening in his hair, enough to make Leander gasp. He groaned, and then his mouth was back between her legs again, as he stroked her higher. His tongue and his fingers and the broad pad of his thumb wound Reyna higher and higher and she came before she could warn him. Her thighs shook as she clenched around his hand, a broken moan wringing from her as he worked her through.

"Thatta girl," Leander soothed, pride thick on is voice. "So pretty when you come for me, when you let me take care of you..."

Reyna reached for him lazily, sated but hardly satisfied.

She loved that he obliged her, that his tall body was bent nearly in half as he pulled himself off his knees but stayed close enough to kiss her. She licked into his mouth, tasting the mess he'd made of her. Leander's hands tightened on her hips, and she moaned as his tongue swept into her.

Reyna reached between them, shoving Leander's boxer briefs down with his jeans. She sighed when her fingers closed around his thick length, so hard and hot for her already. She was bending forward before she registered it, and Leander's hands shot out to grab the back of the chair when her tongue pressed against the head of his cock.

"Jesus, Rey," he gritted, bracing himself above her, "you don't have to—"

She ignored him, lapping at the head of his dick, tasting the salt of his precum mixed with the sweat of the day. She loved when he was like this—overwhelmed and overcome by her, barely able to restrain his reactions.

Leander's head was thrown back, and she reached for one of his hands, placing it at the back of her head, waiting for him to start driving.

It wouldn't happen immediately, but she could be patient.

Reyna kissed the soft tip of his cock messily, trailing spit as she pressed kisses down his length. Leander's chest was heaving as he pulled in ragged breaths above her and when she sucked him into her mouth, his hand on her hair tightened.

Reyna's eyes closed as she sank as far as she could on his cock, loving the pressure of being between his thighs and his broad hand. The weight of him on her tongue was so good, and she could hear how much it was affecting him. Soft grunts and sharp inhales echoed around her as she worked her mouth around his cock, and Reyna could feel his thighs shaking as she got closer.

She pushed her gag reflex down and felt a spark of pride when she felt the coarse hair at the base of his cock scratch against her face. Reyna swirled her tongue around him as she sucked gently, holding her breath. Leander swore, his other hand joining the side of her head to hold her to him, and Reyna moaned around his cock.

She hadn't been able to convince him to fuck her face since the rut, but this was damn close.

Leander whined, a high keening sound, and Reyna held herself a moment longer before pulling off of him, panting as she caught her breath. She reached for the base of his cock, working him lazily with her hand as she smiled up at him.

"Thought you deserved something of a reward yourself," she said lightly, and Leander would've laughed, if he had the wherewithal. As it was, his eyes glowed with a flash of silver she'd come to recognize even in broad daylight, and he reached down for Reyna, pulling her to her feet. He guided her to the side of the arm chair, bracing her against it, before spreading her thighs as wide as her leggings around her ankles would let her.

Reyna braced her elbows against the arm chair and arched her back, rocking back onto her spread thighs and looking over her shoulder at Leander.

He met her eyes.

Reyna whimpered at the sight of him, admiring her like she was a feast spread out before him. He'd kicked off his jeans, and pulled off his sweatshirt, and stood behind her in just his sneakers, his large hand tugging over his cock. A familiar flush had spread down from his cheeks, to his neck to his fair chest, and Reyna adored how much she could see the affect she had on him.

Right now, though, she wanted to *feel* it.

Leander only made her wait for a moment before obliging.

His broad chest pressed against her back as he leaned over her on the chair, his arms caging her in. She felt his cock prodding between her thighs, swaying heavily, and Leander chuckled when she whined impatiently.

"This what you wanted, honey?" he whispered, as he reached between them to press his cock through her folds. He was so warm, and she was so wet, and the slide of skin against skin was intoxicating. "You got yourself all worked up gagging on my cock, and now you want it in this pussy?"

"Yes, Lee," Reyna moaned, her head falling forward against the chair. "I want to feel you."

"So ask nicely," Leander said, dragging his cock over her cunt again.

"Please," Reyna begged immediately, "please, Lee, oh my god, I—"

She broke off with a cry as Leander pressed down with his hips as he held his cock against her, grinding her clit into him.

"Not a full sentence to be found, hmm?" Leander's voice was thick with pride as Reyna moaned. She'd woken up already oversensitized, then had a fast orgasm, then choked herself on his cock—words were not her strong suit right now.

"B-baby," she managed, her voice breaking. God, she sounded pathetic, but she knew he loved it, and she didn't care; he felt so good. "Please, fuck me, Lee—"

"There ya go," Leander groaned, and then he shifted his hips and thrust into her.

Reyna sagged against the chair, her arms scrambling for purchase, and she might've actually screamed as he pushed into her. No warning but his fingers, no warm up but her earlier orgasm, but fuck, it was perfect. Leander was pressed tightly against her back, holding her to him, and she could feel his heartbeat racing. She moaned as she adjusted to him, craving the stretch and intensity of him, the way he did exactly what he asked and then more.

"Ah, Rey," Leander mumbled into her shoulder, and she realized he was absently trailing kisses over her skin. "God, you sound so pretty. How did I get so lucky; you fit me so perfect and you sound so fucking good—"

She braced herself on the armchair, twisting around to kiss him.

Their mouths met in a clash of tongues and teeth, sloppy and needy, and so perfect. He held her to him as she adjusted, coaxed her open with his lips and tongue, until she was pushing back into him, needing him to move.

His first thrust had her breaking away from him, panting against him, barely able to keep her eyes open. Maybe it was the overstimulation, or the exhaustion of the day, but Reyna felt every inch of his thick cock pressing into her. Reyna whimpered as he reached the top of his stroke, brushing against her gspot and grinding her cunt into the arm chair. It was going to be a hell of cleaning bill, but she couldn't find it in herself to care; she just needed more.

But Leander kept his measured pace.

Slowly in, slowly out, easing his way through her clenching pussy, working her open for him. It was delicious, it was inebriating, and Reyna didn't know how she would survive if he didn't start fucking her.

"Need you harder, Lee," she whimpered, her hips shifting feebly in request.

He leaned down, nudging her chin back with his nose so he could kiss her neck. Reyna cried out when he sucked on her skin, his teeth nipping at her as he kept his pace.

"I don't know, honey," he teased, his voice a low rasp, words whispered between kisses, "you feel really...fucking... good...like this."

He licked at her, his tongue roaming over the skin of her neck like he wanted to devour her, all while his hips kept up that steady, maddening rhythm. Reyna moaned, her thighs trembling, and though her cunt was full, she needed him differently.

"Please, baby," she asked, her voice embarrassingly close to breaking, and Leander groaned into his skin.

"Rey," he practically growled, "you know I can't say no to you like that."

She felt him shifting, saw him plant his foot on the seat of the chair, but didn't realize what it meant until he pulled back, gripped her hips in his hands, and yanked her back onto his cock.

"Yes, Lee," she moaned.

Leander groaned, his grasp on her hips tightening as he fucked up into her. His thrusts pushed Reyna up onto her toes, practically lying back against Leander's chest as he thrust upwards. With his leg braced on the chair, she was all but balanced on his thigh, and she leaned into him as he rutted up into her body.

"That's it, honey, exactly what you wanted, isn't it," Leander gritted, his thrusts getting somehow harsher. "What you needed—to wake up on your man's tongue, in your home together, then sit on his fat cock, letting him fuck you to christen it, huh?"

Reyna moaned, her hand coming back to curl around the back of Leander's neck, clinging to him. God, the way he talked to her was so dirty, so perfect. With his height and the precarious position, she couldn't help him at all, could barely cling to him for balance and let him take her how he wanted.

Which was exactly what she needed.

"It's so good, Lee," she panted. "I feel you everywhere; it's so good, thank you..."

Leander groaned, letting go of her hip to play with her clit. "Rey, you have me so close. Just a couple strokes into this tight pussy and I feel like I'm gonna burst; it's so fucking good."

Reyna's knees nearly gave out when Leander's thick fingers stroked over her clit. She was lost for words, moaning wantonly at each brush of his fingers, thrust of his hips, each cant of his breath over her cheek as he worked into her. He was so strong, so steady, and he took such good care of her; she was shaking with it.

"Come with me," Leander asked hoarsely, and Reyna shuddered, even as she shook her head.

"Lee, I can't just—"

"You can," he grunted, slowing his fingers over her clit, a counterpoint to how quickly his hips were pistoning up into her. Reyna felt her mouth go slack and her hips pushed weakly against him and she felt him smile into her hair.

"That's right, honey, just like that," Leander whispered. "God, you feel so good, Rey, and I know you're close. I know you want to, honey, I can feel your cunt tightening around me. You can do it, I know you can, let me fill you as you come. Come apart on my cock, let me come inside you as you milk my cock, please baby, come with me—"

Reyna didn't have a choice.

Pleasure streaked through her, pulsed from Leander's fingers and his words and as she fell apart, she felt him come. Her fingers tightened on his neck and he bent into her, curling into her as he shouted his release. She felt him pulsing inside her, filling her, and neither of them could stop moving. Their hips ground into each other as they rode it out, and Reyna couldn't tell where she stopped and Leander started. Every fiber of her being was attuned to him, curled into him, chasing and claiming him.

Leander managed to turn them, somehow, collapsing into the armchair and pulling Reyna into his lap without knocking either of them to the floor or dislodging his cock from inside her. Reyna curled up her legs, finally kicking off her shorts.

"You should've waited until we'd made the bed," she grumbled against Leander's chest, "we could've called it a night."

She felt Leander's chest shake as he chuckled. "Next time."

Reyna pushed off of him, raising her eyebrows. "Are you planning on moving any time soon?"

Leander smiled easily, and Reyna followed his gaze as he looked around the cottage.

They had so many boxes here, both of their city apartments packaged up into cardboard and ferried across the bay. Somewhere in these boxes was a satellite internet connector for Reyna to work remotely, bags of ground coffee and chamomile tea, and a ziploc bag absolutely crammed with a wall's worth of printed photographs. Moving out to the island fulltime would be a hell of an adjustment for them both, but Reyna found she didn't feel any uncertainty about the move—only excitement.

"Nah," Leander said, pressing a kiss to the top of Reyna's head. "We're toughing it out here, come hell or high water."

"Good," she smiled, leaning into his chest. The sun cast shadows through the barren winter branches outside the cottage windows, and Reyna couldn't help thinking how different today was since the last time she'd stayed here. She thought of the longing that had marked that long weekend, the abrupt end to it, and the future she'd been too scared to envision, that Leander had been too scared to let go of.

And Reyna thought back further, to when she'd been deliberating on the house or the business loan. There wasn't a garage on the cottage, but her car was parked comfortably in a lot in Port Cadie. This house might not have been purchased with her nest egg, but her ability to enjoy it stemmed from knowing that her sister was taken care of. And the last item: *have something that's mine.*

Sun shadows danced across the room of this cottage that'd seen so much of their story over so many years, and Reyna tilted her head back to look at Leander. His kind eyes were drooping, exhausted from the day and their extracurriculars, but even at rest, a small smile played across his lips. His cheeks were still flushed, his hair still mussed, and he looked to Reyna like everything she could've asked for, and never could've believed she could have.

He felt her gaze, and glanced down at her, his smile soft and his expression curious.

"Love you," Reyna said, because now that she'd gotten used to saying it, she kind of thought she might never stop.

"Love you," Leander said, because whenever she said it, however she said it, he said it back.

Reyna settled back into him and Leander's arms tightened around her, as she looked around the cottage. It wasn't just the building that checked off her list, something that was hers, but also the man who gave it to her. Beyond that, she was his.

This cottage was going to be more than hell or high water—with this man, Reyna was more than certain she could make a home.

Acknowledgements

It's not even hyperbolic to say that Port Cadie has changed my life. This has been an indulgent journey to start on, and a healing one as well, and I'm just so profoundly grateful for it. I used to think "ugh there's no way authors have that many people to thank" but now that I'm here, I understand it.

Thank you, Sanjana, for sharing your insight with empathy. Thank you for believing in my characters and my stories, thank you for helping me polish them.

Thank you, Allison, for your unwavering support, for making me smile when Feelings are a lot, and for memories that must be printed out. Every libra needs her aries, and I'm so grateful for you.

Thank you Kat, Anne, and Christy, for being so encouraging and supportive. Your intellect humbles me, and your support means so much to me.

Thank you to Matthew, who likely won't see this, but has showed me that it can be done.

Thank you Amber, whose friendship has genuinely saved me.

Thank you to Abby, Alex, Ames, Gigi, Sierra, and also to Bailey and Sara, and a slew of other online writers, who read and cheered for the first smut I published. Thank you for showing me there is beauty and heart in it.

Another thing I used to judge—when romance authors had bits about their faith. I now understand it, but I'll save a sermon for another time. Here, I will say that I am grateful for Love, and for Grace, both of which are strong enough to withstand deconstruction.

And thank you, reader, for being here. Thank you for your letting my characters into your hearts, and I hope to see you around soon! (spoilers: with chesa and whit's story this winter...)

xx, sana

* * *